FIRES OF A KELTIC MOON

DOUBLE KELTIC TRIANGLE

*LIZZIE STARR

Dokopot
Books

Grampa once asked me if I knew who would be so proud of me. He was speaking of his father, also a writer and a dreamer. But the spark in his eyes and the wide grin crossing his face let me know how proud he is as well. So Grampa, this book is for you.

And for Mom. I doubt these pages would have happened without your unfailing love and support.

And of course for Dad and Gramma.

I miss all of you more than I can say.

PROLOGUE

L ara wandered away from her family. The big people were talking and she was bored. Her twin aunties had gone to visit the Queen and her young brother slept at Momma's side. A heavy sigh lifted her thin shoulders dramatically. A patch of bright sunlight beckoned her from under the cool shade of the thick Faerie forest.

Knowing she did nothing wrong, she toddled into the open glade. Daddy had done this many, many times. She was positive she could do it, too, so she tossed her head and pushed riotous golden curls from her face. "I'm gonna go visiting."

She moved her small fingers and squinted one eye in thought. Then, with a serious set to her mouth, she spoke the strange words exactly like Daddy did. Only a slight lisp showed her indecision. When the faint portal opened she stepped through without hesitation. Only when the shimmer snicked shut behind her did she have a moment of doubt. How would she get home again?

Make another portal, of course. She shook her head and laughed. Sometimes she was as dumb as Jaysson, and he was just a baby. Pleased with her solution, she took brave steps into the new world she was visiting.

She wrinkled her nose in disgust. There had been many people here and they had not honored the land as she had been taught. These were not Faerie. She turned away and wandered through a wide area of trampled grass and litter but found nothing to interest her. Did Daddy go to places like this? She could not believe that.

Lara was about to open the portal home when she noticed a long line of strange green buildings. This might be interesting. Giggling, she ran toward them. As she got closer the smell stopped her dead in her tracks. It smelled like...no, she wasn't allowed to say that word.

Each building was hardly wider than the door and there were no windows. She cocked her head to one side. Why would anyone go in there? These buildings needed no further investigation--this was an ugly place.

A soft, mewling cry came from the closest building. Lara leaned forward on her tiptoes and listened intently. The cry stopped then started again, much quieter. It almost sounded like Jaysson when he was a very tiny baby and she hadn't been allowed to play with him.

There were no other people in sight when she glanced around, so she went to the building and peered in the half-open door. One hand flew up to cover her nose and she held her breath against the bad smells and coughed. It was like what Jayse did in his diaper.

A tiny bundle lay close to a large hole with a wooden seat. A potty? Lara shuddered and was about to turn away when a tiny fist lifted from the bundle and waved weakly. A baby?

Turning to the slightly fresher air outside, Lara took a deep breath. She wrinkled her nose, held her breath and stepped into the building. Cradling the tiny baby carefully in her arms she rushed back into the light breeze.

She carried her bundle a few steps from the line of potties and laid it on the ground. The baby began to cry, so she patted it lightly on its bare belly as she had seen Momma do. She cooed softly until bright, unfocused eyes turned toward her voice.

"I will take you home to Momma. She'll take care of you. Why did your Momma leave you in a potty?" Lara looked around. "Do you think she'll be back? I don't."

She lifted the baby and held him against her shoulder like she had practiced with her doll. He was heavier than she thought and she clasped the baby tighter. He wiggled weakly but made no further sounds. "I bet you're hungry. Momma will feed you. I'm hungry, too. Let's go."

Lara made the sign and opened a portal. Behind the shimmer the light didn't look quite right, but she stepped forward anyway. Snow seeped through the holes in her sandals and she curled her toes against the cold. The wind blew around them and whipped a loose end of the baby's blanket. Tugging a corner over the baby's face, Lara turned in a small circle. "Where are we? This isn't right."

She chewed on her lip while she made the sign. When she spoke, the words slurred together in her haste. A shaky portal formed and she rushed through.

A desert spread before her. After laying the baby at her feet she shaded her eyes against the bright sun. There was nothing but a giant sandbox as far as she could see. Her lower lip trembled. Though she was too old to cry, tears filled her eyes anyway. Maybe the baby was making the magic work wrong.

No, that wasn't it. And she couldn't leave the baby like its Momma did. She had to try again. The shimmer of a new portal was barely visible in the reflection from the hot sun. The other side looked cooler, but was it home? She crouched, lifted the baby and stroked the fine soft hair on his head in an effort to comfort herself.

After stepping hesitantly through the portal, she was in a forest, but it wasn't her forest. Huge wet drops fell from droopy, overhanging branches and splashed onto her face. She pressed her cheek against the baby's head. "Daddy?" Her voice was a tiny whisper.

She stumbled back into strong arms that wrapped around her

protectively. Startled, she clutched her bundle tightly and cried out.

"Hush, darlin'." A deep, familiar voice sounded close to her ear. "I will take ye home."

Lara nuzzled her cheek against the broad chest. "Unca Derrik. I wanna go now."

The comfort of his arms calmed her tears. He hugged her tightly while he carried her through a portal into the glade before her grandparent's home. An anxious cluster of adults rushed toward them.

Lara lifted her head and blinked, surprised at the fear and concern in their faces. Wanting to make them smile again, she lifted the bundle in her arms and uncovered the baby. A weak wail filled the clearing. Lara gave the worried adults a brilliant smile.

"Lookit what I found."

CHAPTER
ONE

Trying to release excess tension, Lara rubbed the bridge of her nose between two fingers. It had been a long day, but her cousin Bryce had finally graduated. And with honors. She felt a surge of pride, but shook her head. What was he ever going to do with a master's in Spenserian Literature? He didn't want to teach.

She sighed. Her degrees weren't much more practical. She was still amazed the university had allowed her to do fieldwork and a thesis on etymology. The study of names and their meaning fascinated her. Releasing the clip that held her wild hair back let the shoulder-length curls fall free. A quick swipe of her fingers through the mess brought her mane under some semblance of order for a few moments.

The party was great. People overflowed Uncle Tommy's backyard, but the constant need to be pleasant and act interested grated on her nerves. Wanderlust tickled at her. It had been too long since she took her studies out of the library and into the field. Field research; that's what she needed to defeat the restlessness. Never mind the fact her degrees had been long since conferred.

A tall, willowy blonde had cornered Bryce next to the house.

When Lara caught his attention his pale green eyes pleaded silently with her. Lara grinned and shook her head. Although she fought many battles for him and, if needed, would do so again, his battle with conniving females was his own.

After a quick glance around Lara slipped through the gate connecting the backyard with her parents' and wandered to the far corner of her mother's garden. A vine-covered trellis guarded the corner--only a blank fence to those who did not believe. Lara stepped under the trellis and passed through a permanently open portal leading to Faerie.

A fond smile came with the memories of the first time she had created her own portal. At four she had been so sure of herself. She'd found Bryce abandoned in a chemical toilet and then got them lost in many somewheres before Uncle Derrik found them.

Derrik and Dad spent many weeks trying to recreate the pathways opened from her initial portal to find where the tiny infant boy came from. She had been no help; the baby was her new playmate.

Her smile widened at the vivid memory of Uncle Tommy's joy-filled face when Derrik admitted failure. In the time spent looking for Bryce's time and place, Tommy had fallen in love with the child. It would have been agony for him to give up the bond he felt with his new son.

Now that she had an adult's hindsight Lara realized Derrik had many misgivings about raising a child. But he seldom denied his Tommy anything. Lara's sigh filled with the longing for a relationship like the one her uncles shared. One of true partnership, love and devotion--one with a man who would love only her.

But such a man had not presented himself in her life. Neither mortal nor Faerie caused her heart to flutter wildly in her chest or her breath to catch painfully in her throat. She chuckled and shook her head at herself; sometimes she was too romantic for her own good.

Lara passed quickly through a deeply wooded area of Faerie to her favorite quiet place. The small glen filled with tiny wildflowers gave off a fresh, spicy scent when she walked through them. The Faerie-bright colors became even more vivid when sunlight filled the glen. She'd spent a great deal of time here when she was a teenager, dreaming of knights on white chargers and Highland heroes who fought with her image before them.

And it was here she discovered she could do something even her dad couldn't. She could open a portal through time. When she'd refused to curb her adventures through time, her great-aunt, the Queen of the Faerie clan, granted her small magical gifts. Now, she was able to study any time or place she chose without fear of discovery. And the time portal had been a wonderful research tool for her thesis.

Traveling to any time to live a life different from her own was a way to satisfy her fanciful notions. Still, Lara never found the romance she denied to herself she so desperately sought.

Now, she stood in the center of the glen and wondered when to go to. Grandda told so many stories of his youth, but once the adults discovered her *talent* he would not give her the date when he had lived in the mortal world. So, she'd been experimenting. Lara fixed a random date and place in her mind and called for a portal.

She stared at a forest not unlike her Faerie world. After she whispered the first of her aunt's spells, the resulting tingle of electricity ran along her skin and her already-wild hair lifted from her scalp. It was a good thing the spell made her briefly invisible so she could determine the accuracy of her time and place. Otherwise, she'd undoubtedly scare the devil out of anyone who chanced to be near the portal when it opened.

Lara stepped onto the crest of a low hill. After the calm of Faerie, the wind pushed at her and made her stumble forward awkwardly. She grimaced, glad no one could see her flailing her arms and trying to gain her balance.

The air was damp and salty. She turned her face into the biting wind. The forest sloped away down a hill toward a rocky beach. Waves pounded against the stones, the booming of the surf a bass counterpart to the high wail of the wind. It was a wild, desolate place.

There was no sign of a settlement nearby, but a narrow path ran along the edge of the beach. Lara took a step toward the water--and froze like a small animal caught in an automobile's headlights.

Staring intently at her, a man lounged with his back against a low stone. Her eyes widened with surprise, and her mouth dropped open. No one had ever seen her before she released the Queen's spell. How did this man?

The wind whipped her curls forward across her face. Shaking her head to toss them back did no good, so she held the mass at the nape of her neck with one hand. No, he wasn't looking at her. There must be something of interest behind her.

Barely holding back a delighted chuckle, Lara turned slowly and lifted her eyebrows in amusement. She had entered this time through the widely spaced uprights of a tall dolman. Intrigued, she moved back toward the stones with her hand outstretched.

The weathering of the stone showed small imperfections and cracks. The stones were ancient even this far in the past. She reached up to touch the bottom of the capstone. The gray rock was warm in the cool breeze.

The man behind her stood and sighed. Lara held her breath and stepped cautiously to one side when he moved beside her. He touched the same spot, walked through the rocky gateway, paused and retraced his steps. A shiver coursed visibly through him, and he shook his head. After retrieving a bulky bag from near a low stone he started toward the seaward path. He paused once again at the dolman and peered straight at Lara, his light brows drawn together, confusion clouding his intense blue eyes.

Lara finally let herself breathe after he shrugged elegantly and strode off. She watched his back and the play of the tight muscles of his thighs as he walked. A very fit man, and handsome. She sat on the low stone. Something was vaguely familiar about him--a memory she knew she should be able to recall. She must have known someone who looked like him somewhere. Or some when. She really needed to return to the practice of journaling her adventures.

Ah, adventure. She leapt to her feet and hurried after the man. She would follow where he went and then decide if she wished to stay. A thoughtful smile tugged at her lips. He could make the visit interesting.

Lara blew out a frustrated breath. Here she was, still looking for that perfect romance. She should have left her white knight ideal at home. She'd never find a man like that. Or a love like her mom and dad's. Mentally slapping her forehead, Lara turned for one final look at the stones. *Maudlin, girl, maudlin. Get a grip*.

Sure of his footing on the narrow path, the man walked swiftly. A natural grace flowed in his loose-limbed gait. His features were fair, the long, straight nose and high cheekbones familiar. The almost-memory nagged at her. Perhaps there was Faerie blood running through his veins.

Her face grew warm. It had been quite some time since she had been attracted to a man. Could there be the pull of a possible shared heritage? Or maybe it had just been longer than she realized, making her susceptible to the charms of a handsome face and lean hips.

He had moved further ahead, so she hurried to catch up. Lara wanted to discover more about this intriguing man, find out what lay beneath his calm surface. And why had he been staring so intently at the dolman?

Mulling over her questions--and the view of the man's tantalizing backside--Lara took a misstep and gasped at the painful turn of her ankle. The man stopped with a jerk, turned, carefully lowered his bag to the ground and reached for the long knife at his side.

"Who follows?"

Lara bit her lip against the pain shooting through her ankle and hobbled behind a tall rock. A few short, mumbled words later, the guise of invisibility slipped from her. She took a deep breath, whispered her second spell and felt her jeans and cotton shirt change.

A grimace wrinkled her forehead when she looked down at her new clothing. A rough, homespun shift covered her to the tips of her toes, which were thankfully bare. An overmantle with bright geometric embroidery at the hem covered the shift. She took a deep breath, tried to pat her wild hair into some semblance of order and stepped from behind the rock.

"I beg pardon, sir. I did not mean to startle you." The rhythmic, long vowels of her words attested to the completeness of her aunt's spell. Lara smiled. She did so love the flowing sounds of a Gaelic language.

She took a step, lurched forward with a sharp cry and sank to her knees. Sitting cross-legged she cradled her ankle between her hands and sighed. It was already swollen and turning purple.

He released his defensive posture and frowned at the young woman. Another delay. There was a strangeness about her sudden appearance, but his thoughts had been on the ancient gateway and the longship riding the waves at the horizon. He inhaled deeply, but the faint scent of magic dissipated in the wind before he could detect the source.

Simple folk feared the stone gateway, and he had been assured this path to the next holding was seldom used. He snorted--fearing a pile of rock when there was much more to fear in this world.

The woman looked up at him. He held back a smile as he recognized tears of pain glistening on her lashes. A jolt of the familiar surged through him and followed the magic into the wind. He sank into the depths of those wide eyes. A step closer. Those violet eyes.

He halted with a sharp intake of breath and narrowed his eyes suspiciously. "Who are you?"

She cringed at the harsh tones but kept her compelling gaze steady on his. He approved. Golden-brown flecks danced with deep purple swirls within her eyes. Such a myriad of color, of emotion, of passion. Drawn, he took another step.

"I am Lara."

"What?"

"My name is Lara. Who are you?"

The wind blew her hair wildly about her face and brought a

flash of desire such as he had not felt in many years. What harm could there be in giving her a name? He chose a favorite and smiled. "Aubrian."

The reaction to his smile was expected but still satisfying. Her eyes swirled an interest that edged toward sultry. He accepted his effect on women. Lifting his bag to one shoulder he held the other hand out to her. "Do you require assistance?"

Her golden eyebrows drew together and she shook her head as if to clear it. "No, I..." She tried to stand but collapsed with another gulp of pain.

Concentrated low and heavy, heat suffused Aubrian's body. Lovers he'd had, but none affected him as swiftly or as strongly. He grinned in anticipation of the hunt.

"I guess a hand up would be helpful." Her voice was hesitant.

The smile frozen on his lips and he stared at her. There was a strange quality to her speech, a lilting difference to her words. A memory tickled the far reaches of his mind of a voice he had thought buried deeply away. It brought another aspect to the hunt--another discovery to be made.

"May I assist you to your home?"

She flushed a bright pink. "I'm...not from around here."

Aubrian sighed dramatically. "Then there is nothing for you to do but come with me." He paused and watched fleeting emotions cross her fine features. This would be a swift, intense and satis-fying hunt.

"I, too, am a traveler and far from home. There is a holding near. The lord is a fair man and welcomes strangers to his board. I will pay for our lodging with entertainments."

"I am perfectly able to--"

"I am sure you are, my dear, yet I feel somehow responsible for your injury. I insist you allow me to aid you in this small manner."

Anticipating her answer, Aubrian held his breath. A halo of light blond hair curled around her face. His body grew tighter with the yearning. Had he somehow become the prey in this game? Ruthlessly he tamped down the uncomfortable feelings.

Lara stared at the ground at Aubrian's feet. "I guess that would be okay. But you owe me nothing." Her gaze lifted to his, and the blood boiled through his veins. "You did not make me trip."

"Ah, but you were following me, were you not?" The blush that rose instantly to color her cheeks brought renewed anticipation and the smile to his lips. "Come, now. You may lean against me. Or, if the pain is too great, I will carry you."

Lara couldn't believe Aubrian's matter-of-fact statement. A man offered to carry her? At five-eight she was no frail, tiny woman. She gazed at him and let her skepticism show. "I hardly think that will be necessary."

The smile he flashed at her vowed to prove her wrong. Aubrian held a long-fingered hand out to her and lifted one eyebrow. Still, she hesitated before taking his help. Would he pull her into his arms when she stood? The vow in his smile turned to promise.

What the heck. Why shouldn't she follow her attraction and see what happened? With her hand encompassed by his, Lara let herself be pulled easily to her feet. She stumbled forward on her injured ankle but Aubrian caught her arm to steady her. Then he stepped away.

Strangely disappointed, Lara tried to stay upright by balancing with the toe of her injured foot. Aubrian returned to her side with a thick branch. He held it up, peered seriously at it and back at Lara then knelt to break a short length over his knee.

Aubrian held the altered branch out to her. "Perhaps this will be of assistance as well." He eased a split in the branch under her arm and brushed her side with his fingers. A tingle of fear caught her breath and chased after the brief pleasure from his touch. Aubrian stood back as if to survey his handiwork and nodded with satisfaction filling his expression.

The makeshift crutch fit her perfectly. Lara took a few careful steps forward before Aubrian joined her on the path. "When you are weary, we will rest. I do not believe the holding is far." He slung his bag over one shoulder and sauntered away.

Lara's anger faded as quickly as it rose. She wouldn't be in this time very long anyway, so why worry about a man's strange behaviors or her reactions to him. Applying only light pressure on the toe of her injured foot, she hobbled after Aubrian as quickly as she was able.

The wind carried the faint musical sound of his voice to her. "The game begins." Between watching her footing and the path before her carefully, she barely registered the meaning of the mumbled words.

TWO

Iain crumpled against the garden wall; the large hand pressed to his chest holding him in place. His cousin's boisterous laughter quieted suddenly, and he became contrite and apologetic. He lifted Iain by his shirtfront.

"I am sorry, coz. I dinna mean to startle ye." Laughter rumbled deep in his chest before escaping through his thickly bearded lips. "Ye shouldna study so much."

Iain used the wall to brace himself as he stood and rubbed one shoulder. Thankfully, the small packet of parchments he'd been reading had missed the mud puddle beneath the ancient apple tree. After brushing damp earth from the thick pages he smoothed the handwritten parchment and the irritated wrinkles in his brow before turning to Castantin.

Iain used the parchments to point at Castantin. "Da sent me to the monastery to learn languages to assist in the governing of the holdin'. 'Tis ye who have decreed I devote m' life to study, no' to yer holdin'. I dinna deny ye yer inheritance. The choice of destiny was taken from me at Athair's death."

Iain stared at Castantin and tensed. The blows would fall swiftly and he would willingly accept the punishment. His unthinking tongue... Even family would not speak so to the MacDhuibh.

"Eh? Ye would defy me right, coz?"

Iain lowered his head. "Ye ken I waudna. But, I dinna relish the life of the monastery. No matter how much ye wish to be rid of me."

Thick brows were drawn together with Castantin's genuine confusion. "But ye enjoy the learnin'?"

"Aye. But I would prefer to use the knowledge here as an asset to the family and our...yer lands," he amended at his cousin's fierce, possessive scowl.

Iain held back a sigh. His enjoyment of reading rankled the nearly illiterate, overbearing Castantin. But to be sent away to the far south under the excuse of further learning...

The death of Iain's mother had brought unwelcome changes to his life. There was no longer a buffer between the more physical Castantin and Iain's own interests, even though both strove toward the same goal of a peace-filled, prosperous holding. Castantin desired no challenge to his leadership, so Iain would be effectively banished from the holding after the harvest.

Castantin tapped his foot impatiently. One fist clenched and relaxed before he clasped Iain's already-tender shoulder. "So, scholar, think ye can best me in the practice yard this day?"

Iain took a deep breath--the moment of retribution had passed. "Ye ken I canna. But mayhap I can give ye a challenge to think about."

The deep sound of Castantin's laughter rumbled through the small garden. "Me? Think? That's what I have ye fer, coz."

Iain ducked his head to hide a smile and tucked the parchments inside his tunic. Aye, there lay much of the problem. He followed Castantin's stocky form and left his mother's pleasaunce, hating to leave the peace of the enclosed garden for the noisy yard before the large stone house. Iain glanced up; the thatched roof covering the stables needed patching. He grimaced and added the work to his already lengthy mental list. The repairs would be done before he was forced to leave.

As much as Castantin cared for leading men, he knew nothing of managing them. or the holding. Sword drills and tactical practices took men away from their farmsteads. and even the servants had been taught simple defensive techniques. Iain admitted Castantin was a master at his art. At least his cousin was wise enough to take care whom he armed.

If the Vikings attacked their shore, as they had the western lands, and the area erupted in battle there would be none left at the manor but the very young or very old; and Castantin would certainly lose the holding. If not as the spoils of war, then to marauding raiders who took advantage of the weak and desperate. It was a common enough tale throughout history.

Castantin gestured impatiently from the center of the yard. Iain took a deep breath and crossed to the training area, looked over the wooden practice swords and tested the grip and weight of a few before selecting one. Taking a wide, two-handed swing he smiled at the sharp whistle of the blade through the air. He might not have his cousin's brute strength, but Latin was not the only thing he'd studied with the friars.

Sword lifted in salute, Iain advanced on Castantin.

F ollowing the harsh sounds of effort and the hollow thunk of wood against wood, Aubrian stopped at the edge of a small crowd of cheering men. Lara sank gratefully to a log obviously placed so one could observe mock battles in the wide, open area. Carefully keeping as much of her legs covered as possible, she lifted her injured ankle across her knee and probed it carefully. Although it was swollen and deeply bruised, she didn't think it was broken. Maybe she could find some cloth to bind it. That should help.

A coarse man dressed in browns and reds turned his head toward Aubrian, paused as if sizing up the newcomer and then gave a brief nod. An elbow jab to his neighbor opened a path so Lara could see part of what was obviously a training session. A thick, red-bearded man shifted his stance and slashed a long wooden sword forward. Unable to see the opponent, Lara smiled at the soft chuckle that followed the warrior's failed attempt.

As swiftly as he could lift the two-handed sword he attacked; rapid thuds followed each swish of wood through the air. Angled so his broad back hid her view of the other combatant, the large warrior danced lightly from foot to foot.

Lara watched with a critical eye. The long hours of watching her brother, Jayse, practice for historical reenactments gave her some understanding of sparring techniques. The warrior bent slightly to one side, escaping a swift sword thrust. Delighted, Lara clapped as the crowd cheered again.

The fighters circled. The warrior's face flushed a ruddy color to match his beard. He lifted his weapon high above his head with one hand and grinned. Lara gasped as the wooden sword began a rapid descent. The man slipped his grip to the end of the pommel to extend the reach of the long sword a few more inches. Lara chewed on her lip. The extra force of the blow could easily disarm any adversary.

But as the sword's edge flew downward the opponent's foot lifted in a swift sideways kick to the man's stomach. A harsh grunt followed by a whoosh of air was the only sound in the suddenly silent practice yard. Doubled over, the red-haired warrior dropped his long sword and wrapped both arms across his belly.

The voices of the gathering rose in a united cheer that echoed off the stone walls of the surrounding buildings. An observer stepped into Lara's line of vision and partially obscured her view. Frowning, she started to rise, wanting to see the one who had bested the warrior with a simple trick. The crowd surged to one side, giving her an unobstructed view, and she settled gratefully back onto the log.

Bowing his shaggy red head, the man bent to retrieve the practice sword. When he straightened he held his empty hand up before him. "Hold, coz. 'Tis enough for this day." A broad smile split his face and he lifted his hand to his forehead in salute. "Well done, Iain."

Lara's curiosity jolted to full force. She leaned from one side to the other trying to see through the throng to the man's opponent. To have defeated the large warrior so handily he must also be an impressive man.

Finally, the crowd moved away to pound the loser on his wide shoulders and Lara got her first glimpse of the back of the man called Iain. Slender and wiry, he appeared small next to the bearded warrior, although they were of the same height. The big man called him "cousin" but there was little family resemblance. Lara gave a mental shrug. Although they shared no blood ties, she and her cousin Bryce looked more alike than she and her brother.

Iain turned toward her. The small, triumphant smile told her he did not often best his cousin in battle. Her gaze locked with his and made his dark eyes narrow. After a long, breathless moment his eyes grew wide and narrowed again. He opened his mouth as if to speak but his lips moved soundlessly.

Aubrian moved closer and rested his hand casually on her shoulder. One of his fingers moved softly against her collarbone. "It appears we have been noticed."

The bearded man strode forward. When he held out his hand in greeting, the long practice sword dipped threateningly. Red infused his face as he hastily turned and handed the weapon to a dirty man next to him. "Yer pardon, friends. I am Castantin MacDhuibh, laird of this holdin'. Ye be welcome."

Aubrian's finger touched the bare skin just below Lara's ear. A soft tremor ran through her and she turned her head to look past Castantin's shoulder. Iain's dark eyes glinted with an indecipherable emotion. Aubrian's hand tightened on her shoulder and squeezed until she was forced to look up at him.

"We are Aubrian and Lara." There was a minute pause before he added, "My lord."

Lara tensed at the subtle slight in his voice. It rankled him to call another *lord*. Who was this man? A glance from the corner of her eye confirmed Iain had also noticed the insult--a muscle ticked rapidly along his jaw. Would they challenge Aubrian?

The red-haired giant chuckled. "Well met, friends. How is it ye travel this far from the more oft-used roadways?"

Lara drew a deep breath as Iain's tightly strained shoulders relaxed. The intensity of his gaze held her motionless. Aubrian's fingers tightened painfully when she tried to shrug his hand away. Angling her gaze from Iain's, she set her expression to her most scathing glare and looked up at Aubrian. Something...dangerous twinkled in his eyes. A deep fear traveled down her spine.

Then that something was gone replaced, by a fond smile. Had she really seen the brief flash of evil intent? Aubrian ran the back of his finger down her cheek before he turned his smile to Castantin. "I am a traveler offering tales and entertainments. I discovered this injured girl along the seaward path."

Concern drew Castantin's thick red brows together and he knelt before Lara. "She is injured?" Exposing the ankle, Lara lifted her skirt to the middle of her calf. Castantin drew a sharp breath at the sight of the deep purple bruises. "Ye should have made this known sooner." He looked over his shoulder toward Iain.

Iain had turned from the visitors when the woman's eyes lifted to the man beside her. The loss of eye-contact with the wild-haired woman ripped the soul from his body and he was shaken to the very depths of that sudden emptiness. His movements were jerky as he returned the practice sword to its place in the rack.

To accept his caress so openly, she must be the traveler's woman. A tiny surge of anger found no reason, no outlet. Iain repressed a shudder of sudden desire. Why did one glance, one meeting of their eyes affect him so greatly? Although some of the friars discouraged liaisons, his time with the religious men had not been entirely lonely. Nor had he lacked offers of companionship upon his return to the holding. This urge was not mere need.

Although he kept his back to the visitors while the man introduced them, the woman's face and form hovered in his mind's eye. Lara. Somehow the name fit her.

His shoulder muscles froze painfully at Aubrian's next words. They had only just met? The anger grew righteous. How could a man take such liberties with a woman he barely knew? Iain refused to believe Lara was a woman who gave herself freely. Telling himself it was none of his concern he turned toward the house.

"Iain, hold." Iain froze and turned reluctantly toward Castantin. At the meaningfully raised red eyebrows, he returned across the yard to stand at his cousin's side. Castantin's heavy hand came down on his shoulder.

"Me cousin, Iain." Castantin looked around helplessly. "The old woman who cares fer our injuries attends a birthin'. But we canna let our visitor suffer from the absence, can we, coz?"

Iain shook his head. He looked over Aubrian's shoulder, to the stable and then just off into the distance. Anywhere but at the woman, Lara. Castantin jostled his shoulder.

"Ye'll care fer the girl. Ye did learn some healin' in the monastery, dinna ye?"

"Aye, some." He was forced to look down at her. "How're ye hurt?"

Lara lifted her skirt again and pointed to her ankle. Castantin folded his arms across his chest, waiting. Iain drew a deep breath and knelt, cradled her foot in one palm and prodded the bruised ankle carefully. She jerked and trembled under his touch but did not pull away or cry out when he probed the tender spots.

"Aye, 'tis badly bruised but I dinna believe 'tis broken. Ye have walked too far on it today." The need to accuse the traveler of not caring for this precious woman rose like a red anger he didn't try to hide when his gaze rose.

Aubrian returned the look coldly and patted Lara's shoulder before he turned toward Castantin. "Is there a place here for Lara to rest? I, too, am weary and would welcome the opportunity to pause in my journey." He assumed a pathetic, wistful expression that made the bile rise in Iain's throat.

"Yer both welcome, friend." Iain rolled his eyes at Castantin's fawning. "If ye have tales we havena heard, yer presence be doubly welcomed. Come, I will show ye the manor and Iain will tend to yer woman." The thinning crowd parted as Castantin led Aubrian toward the large stone house.

Iain tensed. His lips formed a thin line. That man had no right to this woman. Forcing a self-deprecating smile, he tried to relax. Come to that, neither did he.

THREE

"I am not his woman," Lara called after the retreating men. Aubrian's white teeth flashed with a knowing smile over his shoulder before he turned his attention back to Castantin.

Trying to force calm into his churning belly, Iain chuckled at Lara's indignant response. When Lara touched his arm to capture his attention his gaze lifted slowly to meet her concern.

"Is everything okay? My ankle isn't that bad, is it?" A brown swirl of fear clouded her wide violet eyes.

Iain rushed to reassure her. "'Tis no' so bad, merely overused since the injury occurred. Ye were hurt on the seaward path?"

Lara nodded. Iain gave a shake of his head, stood and held out a hand to her. "The path is dangerous in places." A smile replaced the serious slant of his mouth. "Even those who ken their way oft visit the old woman with scrapes and bruises from falls. I shall ask ye to travel only a short distance more. Then ye shall rest until ye're healed."

Lara bit her lip against the anticipated pain and used the makeshift crutch to lever herself to her feet. She took a tentative step, dropped the crutch and lurched forward with a cry. Strong arms caught her and held her against the firm planes of a purely male body. A musky scent filled her with a longing that brought tears to her eyes. Great. She hadn't done much that day but fall into the arms of handsome men. Wiping at the tears, she grinned. Not such a bad way to spend a day.

Unspoken questions filled his dark-as-midnight eyes when Iain lifted her chin gently with a callused finger. "I beg yer forgiveness, Lara. I shouldna make ye walk with such pain."

"I...I mean...that's...Oh." Her heart fluttered at his words and the tenderness in his eyes.

One arm under her knees and the other around her shoulders, Iain lifted her easily. Her arm wound around his neck and brushed the shaggy ends of his coal-black hair. A shudder passed through him and his hands clutched in tiny spasms against her. The shudder became Lara's, shaking her to the depths of the sigh that she couldn't disguise.

"My pardon, lady." Iain moved toward the house, taking care not to jar her ankle.

Lara felt...cherished. Her head tipped toward his shoulder and she relaxed against his body, eyes drifting closed. Not a bad day at all.

A proud, booming voice filled her ears. "And this be me great hall." Lara opened her eyes when Iain paused to signal a servant with a jerk of his head. Aubrian stood next to Castantin, seeming to listen closely to the big man. Except his eyes were fastened on Lara. And Iain. A flash of raw hatred twisted his lips for a moment so brief Lara wasn't sure she had seen it. Why would he hate Iain?

She dared a glance at the man who cradled her with no obvious effort. Relief eased her tense muscles. Busy directing the servant to bring supplies to a small room off the pleasaunce, he had not noticed the powerful look.

With a brief nod to his cousin, Iain carried Lara swiftly through the hall. Prickling heat on the back of her neck told her Aubrian's intense gaze followed every step of their passage.

The soft tickle of Iain's fingers as he gently bathed her foot with herb-scented water made Lara giggle. Her feet had always been particularly ticklish--her brother could send her into hysterics simply by pretending to run his fingers along the sole of her shoe. Trying not to jerk from his touch, she bit her lip until tears trickled down her cheeks.

Iain looked up to speak and noticed her tears. His smile froze and his hands trembled, tickling her even more. "Is something amiss? The pain too great? I could-"

Although the sharp pains shooting from one side of the ankle to the other made her gasp, Lara jerked her foot from his hand. The gasp quickly turned to a fit of giggles. Iain stared at her blankly, his dark eyes unreadable, the damp cloth dangling from his fingers.

"No," she was finally able to gasp, "nothing's wrong." Wiping the tears from her eyes, Lara took a few calming breaths. When she focused on Iain, he had not moved, but confusion and concern were etched deeply across the angles of his face.

It was a nice face. The nose was long and straight, centered perfectly between high cheekbones. Firm lips below it curved into a tentative, worried smile to create waves of heat flashing through her. But it was his eyes--the intense, dark gaze that drew and held her rapt attention. Dark enough to nearly hide the even darker centers. Frozen in time...Lara shook her head.

"I'm sorry. I didn't mean to worry you. I'm just ticklish." She leaned forward to whisper, "Really ticklish."

The worried smile vanished to be replaced by a mischievous grin. "'Tis guid to ken."

The leaping of the heart in her chest was almost painful. She restrained the urge to giggle again, this time nervously. It would be better if she didn't give him reason to question her or her presence. And it was very important he didn't think her a fool.

She had played the fool many times before as a convenient way to cover any mistakes she made when traveling through time. Not wanting to analyze why this time was any different, Lara stared down at her tightly entwined fingers.

Iain touched her knee. His fingers inched upward to cover her clasped hands. "I must bind the ankle. The binding will give support and prevent further swelling."

"Yes, I know."

Dark eyebrows lifted in surprise but she paid no attention. "Is it too late in the year for ice? That would really help bring the swelling down." Lara bit her lip. Had she unwittingly said too much?

The eyebrows rose higher. "Ice? I dinna think so, 'tis been a mild winter. I canna see what good ice will do."

Lara had a quick debate with herself, until the throbbing of her ankle prompted her decision. In for a penny, in for a pound. Her forehead wrinkled. Where had that old saying come from?

"We have no ice, but the water from the seaward well is said to be as cold. Do ye wish fer that instead?"

"Maybe if we soak a rag in the water then put it on my ankle. I don't think I want to soak my foot in ice water." Raising goose bumps, a shiver ran down her arms. She rubbed her skin, refusing to accept the true reason for her trembling. "When the swelling has gone down you can bind it." Iain gave her a dubious look. "Really, it'll work great. You'll see."

Rising in one fluid movement, Iain spoke to the servant hovering in the doorway. The young woman gave Lara a look bordering on fear and backed away. Iain clutched the servant's arm and leaned close to her ear, whispering earnestly. After a less strained glance at Lara she nodded and rushed away.

Iain spread his hands when he turned back. "Some of the folk are superstitious of change and new ideas."

"You aren't."

"Nay." The shaggy head lowered. Lara thought irreverently that he really could use a haircut and ached to smooth back the stray hairs. A wry grin lit Iain's features when his gaze lifted to hers. "I try no' to be, although childhood fears are no' easy to forget."

Iain sat at her feet and pulled a long strip of cloth from the basket left by the servant. Gauging the length against her exposed ankle, he nodded once before crumpling the material in a fist. His voice was soft, as if he were afraid of being overheard. Lara bent her head to listen to the earnest words. "What the people fear is magic. There is no such thing. Charlatans and tricksters, perhaps, those who prey upon the uneducated and already fearful." Serious, he leaned closer and his arm brushed against her knee.

Suddenly, there was no breath in her lungs. Just as suddenly she was able to breathe. One of his finely arched eyebrows lowered minutely before he continued. "I think perhaps yer friend," he paused before grinding out the name, "Aubrian, is one of those tricksters."

"He's not really my friend. I only met him today. He helped me here after I fell."

A bright twinkle lit Iain's eyes. The intensity of his gaze-- or her reaction to it--tugged at her, drawing her infinitesimally closer. Her lips parted.

Iain blinked and the moment was gone, leaving Lara filled with vague disappointment. After clearing his throat, Iain spoke words as hesitant as the taut expression on his face. "He seems very possessive of you."

"I'm sure he only wants to make sure I'm okay."

"Okay? What is this word?"

Lara made another tic mark in her long mental tally of mistakes. "Oh, umm, it means fine." She nodded as she spoke. "Aubrian just wanted to make sure I was fine."

"Still, I dinna trust him, whatever his purpose." Iain cocked his head to one side. "If he tries to trick ye, remember, Lara, there is no such thing as magic."

Ah, if he only knew. "I will remember, Iain." Lara tasted his name, liking the way it felt to her tongue. "And I thank you for your concern."

Iain rose to his knees and leaned toward her, eyes intent upon her lips. "Is there any man who claims ye?"

"Claims? Claims me? What do you think this is, the thirteenth century?" Lara drew back. No man would *claim* her, ever.

Confusion fought with lingering interest in Iain's eyes. "'Tis, as the friars say, the year of Our Lord 839.

The stone wall was a solid comfort behind her. The ninth century? She'd not planned to travel to this distant a past. How had she miscalculated? She should have been in the twelve hundreds. In all her journeys through time, she had never traveled so far before. Amazing. And whatever the cause of her appearance in this time, it called for a lengthy stay.

The soft touch of a large hand upon her arm brought her back to the small room and the dark man who gazed so avidly at her. "Lara? Are ye faint? I dinna mean to..."

Squaring her shoulders and leaning forward, she took his hand. "I'm fine, Iain, just a little surprised at the date. I, umm, have lost track of time in my travels." The wide palm was warm under her own. Touching his work-roughened fingers brought fresh longing tingling in her breasts. Heaven help her-- she wanted to kiss the tip of each callused finger.

"Ye have traveled much?"

Quickly recovering from her start at his words, Lara dropped his hand. Blatant interest evident in his features, Iain sat back on his heels. "Oh, yes, since I was young. It is a great way to learn about other peoples, other places." Barely able to speak with him watching, Lara tried a change of subject. "Do you have a short stool?" She glanced around and pointed to a squat chest. "That would work. I really need to elevate my foot."

Iain followed the direction of her point and slid the chest carefully across the stone floor. Glancing at her from under lowered lids, he pulled a cushion from the bench and padded the top. Lara wrapped her hands under her calf and lifted her foot. Iain repositioned the cushion before she lowered her ankle.

"Tell me about Scotland." Chewing on the inside of her cheek, Lara hoped at least her destination had been correct. If she'd misjudged that as well...

The soft question gave Iain a chance to take another deep breath that did little to calm the fierce pounding of his heart. Clearing his throat would ease the raw huskiness of his voice. He hoped she would not recognize his distress at the loss of her touch.

"I know nothing of the Scotland. Though Scotti have invaded the land to the south."

"Oh."

Iain reached out to sooth confused wrinkles from her forehead, but jerked his hand back. He had no right. Golden lashes caressed her cheeks as she closed her eyes in thought. In that short time he already missed the odd mixture of violet and brown.

"Oh," she said again, "839? Have you had Viking attacks, since you're this close to the sea?

Curiosity warred with caution. How did she know of the Lochlannaich? Attacks had come to the south and far on the western shore, but no longships had been sighted along the coast for nearly a year.

Before he could form an answer, Lara spoke again. "Do you know of Kenneth MacAlpin?"

Concern for his land tightened Iain's jaw. She knew of the MacAlpin as well? Kenneth had only just begun his campaign to unite Scotti and Pict. A woman would normally have no knowledge of such things, unless her companion was a spy. But for whom? Iain pondered the possibilities for a few moments and then shrugged. He could no more believe evil of this fair, golden woman than he could deny the memory of his mother. The questions remained in her intriguing eyes.

Iain smiled to himself. Lara was no ordinary woman. Seeing no possible harm if she already knew of the existence of the MacAlpin, he made a rapid decision to continue the conversation.

"Aye. He tries to unite many holdings, many diverse people. He wishes to hold a large area of land."

"Do you agree with him?"

"I havena made a decision. My people were here long before the Saxons or Scotti, long before the Romans who built the wall named us Pictii." Iain spat the word and turned his face from her.

"Picts? I understand."

"We accept the name as common usage, but in our hearts," Iain touched his chest, "we alone know the true name of our people." Rising without looking at Lara, he paced the room, angry with himself for letting pride and politics ruin the pleasant conversation.

"You are tall for a Pict. I had heard you were a smaller people."

Iain turned toward her slowly and tried to maintain a bland expression. If her comment was a slur on his heritage he would stomp from the room and never look back upon his growing desire for the wild-haired woman. He had borne taunting enough for many lifetimes.

But her expression was sweetly curious. Iain fought to relax his muscles and sank onto the bench next to her. Leaning forward, he clasped his hands between his knees and stared at the tender flowers his mother had long ago brought inside against the harsh northern winters.

A sad smile lingered on his lips as he thought of the tall, exotic woman who had borne him. He cast his gaze sideways at Lara. "My blood does no run pure." A slight hitch of Lara's shoulder told him the mix of blood in his veins was unimportant. "My father, a true Caledonian laird, had a passion fer foreign women. My mother came from far across the sea, carried from Gaul as a slave. She was tall and dark. This was her room, her sanctuary." Iain fell silent, his head bowed.

When Lara made a soft sound of sympathy and touched his arm, Iain sighed. "My life has been turned upside down since her death."

Shocked by her reaction to the simple statement, Lara longed to pull Iain into her arms to offer comfort. The delightful twinkle had faded from his eyes and she wanted to return the smile to his firm lips.

A soft scratching at the door drew their attention. Lara jerked her hand from Iain's arm and rubbed the palm against her thigh. At Iain's summons the young servant entered carrying a heavy bucket of water and a handful of soft cloths.

Iain rose, took the proffered items and dismissed the servant.

Dropping the cloths into the bucket, he knelt beside Lara. His fingers reddened as he wrung most of the water from a cloth.

Lara closed her eyes and gasped when he laid the icy cloth over her ankle. The water was nearly as cold as ice, but after the initial shock the cold eased the pulsing pain. Opening her eyes slowly, she found Iain's coal-black gaze focused on her face. When their eyes met she felt the same jolt she had in the court-yard. The intensity pulled another gasp from her lips.

Iain looked at her ankle but kept one hand lightly over the wet cloth. "'Tis too cold?"

"N--no. It needs to be that cold. I was just surprised." *By you.*

Rubbing his palm against his stomach, Iain wiped the damp-ness from his hand. "How long should the wrap remain?"

"Until the swelling goes down." Missing his touch, Lara reached out to him to replace the warmth herself. She took his dry hand between her own to prevent him from rising. "Will you stay and talk with me?" The flash of eager reluctance on Iain's face when he nodded thrilled Lara to the tips of her toes. She didn't want him to leave. Ever.

A ubrian paused in the shadows just beyond the edge of the doorway. The serving woman had left the door slightly ajar; and he leaned closer, listening intently to the rise and fall of voices. Cold anger settled like sodden bread in the pit of his stomach. The thrill of the hunt had heightened his senses to razor sharpness and he did not like the tones underlying the man's voice. Nor the responsive trill in Lara's.

Lara. Aubrian leaned against the wall and folded his arms across his chest. What was it about her that intrigued him? Called to some long-buried passion? Now, as her delighted giggle filtered through the doorway, he was convinced she carried some measure of fey blood. That would account for part of the attrac-tion, but there was more. Something primal drew him to her.

Her eyes. Violet. He had always been tempted by the rare woman with deep purple eyes. The swirls of brown marring their perfection troubled him, provoking a memory to poke at thoughts he had long kept hidden. Aubrian shook his head. He would discover that thing, that memory, in the course of the hunt and turn it to his advantage. And bring Lara to his arms.

Lara would be his. And if the dark man got in his way-- Aubrian shrugged slightly--so be it.

CHAPTER
FOUR

Iain let his hand rest within Lara's grasp but could not lift his eyes to her face. An uncomfortable shyness such as he had not felt since his first time with a woman filled him with anticipation and trepidation. He tugged his hand away and put his full attention to drying, then wrapping her ankle with a clean length of cloth. When he was done he could only stare down at his handiwork. Lara wiggled her toes. He had to force himself to swallow the sound of desire that rose from his chest.

The tiny toes waved at him a second time. "Oh, that feels so much better."

Somehow, Iain found his voice. "The binding is no' too tight?"

Lara's slender hand entered his vision to press gently on her ankle and one of her fingers slipped under the bandage. Heavy breath caught painfully in his throat.

"Nope, feels just right." Her hand lifted to pat his shoulder. "You did an excellent job, Doctor."

Puzzled, he was finally able to meet her clear gaze. "Doctor?"

"One who heals?"

Iain nodded in understanding. "I have no' studied that discipline and only followed yer instructions."

Lara's eyes closed briefly and a wary look passed over her

features as if she berated herself for some unknown slight. Hoping to offer consolation, he reached for her hand.

"Ah, there ye be. Have ye no' finished yet?" Castantin's deep voice preceded him into the workroom. Iain's hand jerked back to his side and he stood, reluctantly turning toward the doorway.

"We have only just finished, Castan. Lara insisted we wait to bind the ankle until the swelling reduced." He shrugged negligently. "I saw no harm in conceding to her wishes."

Aubrian's expression was tightly closed as he followed on Castantin's heels. One eyebrow dropped minutely at Iain's familiarity, but then returned to level neutrality. The tiny hairs on the back of Iain's neck rose in response. A deep breath did nothing to calm his unusual response to the man.

"So, lady." Castantin leaned toward Lara. "Will ye join us at a feast this day? To honor yer visit?"

Lara's eyes twinkled brightly but dimmed with pain and regret when she sat forward and jarred her ankle. She looked at the three men towering over her and shook her head.

"Not tonight, I'm afraid. Could we have the feast tomorrow when I am able to move about more easily?"

Concern filled Castantin's stance and he bowed slightly at the waist. "I had no' thought, my lady, that ye would be incapacitated. I will break fast with these two only." He swept his hand between Iain and Aubrian. "And celebrate yer visit on the morrow." His thick eyebrows lifted in question.

Lara smiled, and Iain's knees threatened to give way at the brilliance that filled the dimly lit room. "I'm sure that will be fine."

A broad grin split Castantin's face and erased his concern. "Guid, 'tis settled then." He turned to clasp Aubrian's shoulder.

Iain winced as the heavy hand landed with a loud thump, but Aubrian barely acknowledged the overly friendly gesture. "Perhaps, Seanachai, ye will regale us with a tale unfit fer a fair one's ears."

Aubrian inclined his head in assent. "It would be my...pleasure." When his gaze lifted, he focused on Lara. A faint pink infused her face.

The bristly tingles covering the back of Iain's neck intensified until he had to clench his fists to prevent himself from stepping in front of Lara to smash the smug, knowing look from Aubrian's face.

Castantin chuckled. "Well, then, m'lady, we will show ye to the room prepared fer ye."

Lara held up one hand and shook her head. "Please, do not call me lady. I have never been a lady." Her mutter continued under her breath, "and never plan to be one." Iain turned his face away and bit back a smile. "Please, just call me Lara."

Castantin held out a hand. "Well said, sweet Lara. We shall all be family, then." The hand landed again on Aubrian's shoulder. A slight frown wrinkled Aubrian's high forehead and his eyes narrowed slightly. Castantin lifted his other hand to clasp Iain's arm. "Brothers all, eh? Ye shall all call me Castan."

Iain let a long, slow breath escape past his taut lips. "Of course, Castan." Castan's exuberance in welcoming any stranger that passed the manor threshold would be his downfall. Especially in these perilous times. Iain added speaking with him again to a mental list. And soon, before Kenneth fielded his armies this far north or the Viking raiders landed on their shores.

"Iain." Castan slapped his arm. "Return from yer thoughts. We must show our guests to their chambers."

Lara reached for the branch she had used for a crutch, moved her foot from the low chest and tried to stand. A soft cry of pain filled the waiting silence and forced her to lean back against the wall.

Silently, Iain cursed himself. He should never have let her put weight on the sprain. Her closed eyes met his apologetic glance. Lara held her lower lip between her teeth as if to bite back the pain. Another silent curse crossed his mind before he spoke. "She should no' walk fer at least the rest of the day."

Aubrian stepped between Iain and the bench where Lara rested and he bent until his face was close to hers. "Then she shall not." In one quick, graceful movement she was in his arms and he straightened, pulling her close to his chest. Propping one foot on the chest that had lately cradled Lara's ankle, he settled her on his thigh and reached to curl a strand of hair behind her ear. "Castan?"

Iain froze at Lara's startled gasp. His hands clenched around the thick leather of his belt and his mind filled with additional curses. But he was not sure if they were directed at the other man or at his own slowness.

"Bring yer woman, then, storyteller." Castan turned and strode from the room.

Lara drew a breath, her eyes wide. "I am not..."

Two of Aubrian's long fingers touched her lips, gently stopping her speech. Her eyes grew even wider when Aubrian gave her a smile that made Iain's stomach churn in tight knots. The belt folded in his fists. How could he watch? But he could not tear his eyes from Lara and the one who held her so possessively.

A slight hitch in Aubrian's eyebrow made Iain wonder if the man knew his thoughts. Aubrian cocked his head to one side and gave Lara a long, slow wink.

Iain forced his muscles to action, moving forward to rush from the room, only to skid to a stop before plowing into the waiting Castan. Aubrian's low chuckle grated against his raw nerves as their guest carried Lara into the hallway.

T he few bites of roasted mutton she was able to swallow were delicious, but Lara didn't feel like eating. Unconcerned with her unusual lack of appetite, she pushed the dry bread trencher to one side of the small table. Wrapping her hands around a heavy mug, she took a wary sip. In order to savor the flavor of the dark ale, she let the liquid swirl slowly in her mouth and sorted through the many essences. No microbrewery could ever duplicate this original flavor.

She held the mug between her hands and looked around the large room she'd been given. A low platform held a thick pallet covered with furs and tightly woven wool blankets. Heavy russet drapes hung around the bed, open now to gather the warmth of the fire. A chill trembled along her spine; even with the heat from the fire the room was cool. She would need the extra warmth during the night and be thankful to cocoon herself with the thick hangings.

A small chest and the low table and chair placed near the crackling fire were the only other bleak furnishings. Two narrow slits in the thick stone wall served as windows. More heavy wool weavings in a mixture of brown and red had been pulled back from the opening to let in the cooling night air and the sounds of feasting in the great hall.

Sighing, Lara almost regretted her decision to avoid the festivities. A twinge in her ankle when she fidgeted in the hard chair told her she had made the correct decision. For once. A night of rest could do wonders for restoring her ability to walk.

A grin twitched her lips. Dad would have healed the sprain immediately. But Mom could only ease the pain. Lara would have accepted her mother's help this time, using the sprain as an excuse to stay longer in this past. The thought of her aspirin bottle safely stored away at home brought another sigh. The herbed tea an elderly servant brought her had worn off and her ankle throbbed painfully.

The grin turned to a lazy smile as she relived the pleasant tingles Iain's touch created when he'd wrapped her ankle. They had spoken of many things while waiting for the swelling to reduce and she liked the man she had gotten to know. Intelligent and caring, his ideas were well beyond what she thought would be the common thoughts of these times.

A loud burst of laughter drew her attention to her small windows. Castan's boisterous chuckle rose above the rest. Aubrian must have told an enjoyable tale. She would have enjoyed a bawdy song or story.

Lara had no doubt of Aubrian's skill as a bard; he easily charmed everyone he met. Including her.

Never before had Lara felt the need to analyze her feelings for a man. Her few past relationships had been simple and basically unsatisfying. Oh, they filled the hours and her lonely need for a short while. Still, she'd easily realized there was something missing.

But now, ages into the past, she found herself attracted to two completely different men. Lara shook her head and took a long sip of ale. Definitely attracted to Iain, for she found it difficult to replace his image in her mind. How she felt about Aubrian-- it was so different, strange and compelling.

Laughter bounced again off the stone walls, drawing her gaze back to the windows. With a grimace of determination she set the mug aside and struggled to her feet. Grabbing the crutch from its place against the wall she hopped, hobbled and stumbled across the cold floor.

Breathless, she leaned against the wide sill and looked out into the dark night. Light flickered from the window slits lining the side of the manor that contained the great hall, but the laughter had faded away.

Made awkward by the need to care for her throbbing ankle, she stretched to ease herself onto the high sill and leaned back against the rough-cut stone. The breeze refreshed her and dried the light sheen of sweat caused by her exertions. Stars twinkled overhead, brighter than any she had seen in the mortal world, the absence of pollution and electrified cities evident in the clear night sky.

The moon rose over a nearby hill, the barest sliver of silver shining in the velvety sky. Lara tried to clear her mind to relax into her thoughts. She put the two men side by side and chuckled at the image of a police lineup.

Aubrian was light and fair; his fine, aristocratic features shone with the Faerie blood she suspected ran through his veins. Did he know his heritage? Then she nodded to herself. He knew. And used his gifted, glib tongue to gain an advantage. Unlike any Faerie clan she had met, Aubrian was kind and considerate one moment, cold and aloof the next. Most fey behaved either one way or the other.

And so possessive. Baby-fine hairs on the back of her neck lifted in irritation. He had no right to treat her like she belonged to him. *Until you do*, a deep, resonant voice spoke from the depths of her mind. Lara tried to shake away the comments. The flash of fear faded as quickly as the voice, leaving no presence in her memory.

Aubrian hid much from others, of that she was sure. There was a strange glint in his eyes when he looked at her, a glint that sent shivers coursing through her, tremors of an exciting-- fear? But what did she have to fear from a Faerie storyteller? Goose-bumps rose on her arms and she tried to rub them away.

Lara massaged her forehead wearily before a smile pulled her lips. Warmth flooded through her to replace the icy chill. Iain made her tingle as well. Dark and brooding, he also hid much from others. But his dark, expressive eyes and angular face were open, with his thoughts exposed for anyone to see. Not believing many took the time to look, Lara vowed to learn the meaning of each expression.

And take the time to know Aubrian as well, if only to understand her strange compulsions whenever he was near. There was no need for her to make a choice between the two. She would not be in this time that long and would leave them both behind in any case. Sudden sadness filled her, bringing sharp, stinging tears to her eyes.

Lara dashed the tears away impatiently. She had never cried over a man and she wasn't about to start now. She would use the time she had in this age and enjoy the attentions of both men.

The moon had risen higher, the crescent angled so the evening star shone to one side like the point of an arrow notched in a celestial bow. The Huntress moon.

Castan's laughter burned Iain's back when he rose and stalked from the great hall. He'd had enough of the Seanachai's tales and thinly veiled insults. And more than enough of his cousin's thick head. He'd wanted to shake sense into the man, but instead clenched his fists under the table until he could contain his frustration no longer.

After the heat of the fire, cool night air slapped his face with welcome freshness. The wind blew salty damp from the sea and Iain shook his head in pleasure. Moving to the center of the yard, he stood full in the breeze and yanked the strip of leather from his hair to let the shaggy mass blow free.

Eyes lifted to the dark sky, he strained to understand the turmoil roiling in his belly. He accepted Castan's decree as leader of the clan. He would return to the monastery, although he would never be able to take the vows. Castan hoped his acceptance of the church would remove him from contention for ownership of the holding.

Releasing tension from his shoulders, Iain shrugged. He really did not want his father's lands for himself, understanding the importance of the laws of succession to the people. But he willed the land prosperous for the people's sake. Castan would not listen, and now the stranger fed the big man's insecurities. Iain watched the rise of the moon over the stable roof. There was only one reason to stay within the holding now. When that reason no longer existed perhaps he would simply travel wherever his feet led him.

There was a slight movement high to one side. He canted his head to look without looking. The beautiful reason for his discomfort sat in the narrow window, highlighted by the firelight behind her. Starlight glistened on her golden hair, making it shine like a halo about her head. None of the friars' angels could surpass her loveliness at this moment.

Iain tried not to stare, forcing his eyes to follow her lifted gaze back to the sliver of the newest moon. What did she see there in the heavens that held her attention? Unable to resist, he turned his head and watched Lara for the brief span of an eternity. One long, deep breath filled his chest with increased longing.

She would not remain at the holding, but travel on with the storyteller. He would never see her again. Longing he did not understand pounded painfully with each beat of his heart. When

Lara lifted one hand to brush the glorious mane of her hair back from her face he could stifle his groan no longer. The sound of aching need escaped between his clenched teeth.

Lara's head turned slowly as she scanned the yard. Rooted to the spot, he could not have moved had his life depended on it. Although her face was hidden in shadows, a shudder ran along his spine the instant her searching eyes touched him.

Lara's hand lifted in greeting. Iain sketched a sharp bow in return and forced himself into movement, walking swiftly from the yard and onto the seaward path.

The crescent moon guided his feet, sure upon the well- known path. Iain began to run and tried to force thoughts of Lara away with the pounding of his feet. At the edge of the sea the roaring surf stopped his headlong rush for only a moment. Fully clothed, he stepped into the frigid water and hoped to ease his fevered body.

Waves lapped at his chest and the spray shot around him, soaking his hair. The cold pressed on him until he could no longer draw breath. Iain returned reluctantly to the rocky shore and sat on a slippery boulder. He shivered and stared into the dark sky. How long would she stay? Would she still be here when the moon became full? Would the planting be blessed by her presence?

Iain searched the sky for answer, but the moon mocked him with silence.

A ubrian watched Castantin stumble from the great hall before he lifted his head from the table. Brushing crumbs from the front of his loose tunic, he peered with disgust at a stain spreading on one sleeve. He took a deep breath and stood, the lithe movement stretching his cramped muscles.

He disliked playing the fool when others around him were so much more foolish. Like so many other *lords*, Castan had forced drink on him and refused to end the feast until barely able to crawl off to bed. Aubrian learned long ago to hide the fact he did not drink and often resorted to feigning drunkenness. With the storyteller's head on the board, others at the feast soon slept or crept away to other entertainment.

However, Castan had a huge capacity for drink. Aubrian's face had lain uncomfortably close to a puddle of ale, and he'd watched his host secretly through barely slitted eyes.

Now, with the occupants of the manor asleep or otherwise occupied, Aubrian smiled wickedly to himself. He would wander unaccompanied and learn what he could. Crossing to the wide doors leading to the yard, he stepped through and pulled the heavy wood closed behind him.

The moon was a mere sliver high overhead and the near-darkness suited him. Moving through the deeper shadows, he stayed close to the building.

He sensed her presence. Lara. Aubrian's head swiveled like a hound in search of the scent of its prey. Surprise lifted his brows; she sat in a window high above the yard. Then his brows lowered, his teeth clenched painfully. She displayed herself like a common whore. He would teach her the humility of woman, a woman's proper place.

Aubrian knew when she recognized his presence. Sure of the bond he'd initiated, he nodded in satisfaction. Lara's head turned as if searching. Aubrian pressed further into the shadows. Her shoulders lifted in confusion before she scooted from the window ledge and moved from his sight.

A slight dip of his head was the only acknowledgement Aubrian allowed himself. Once sure she would not return to the window he stood in the center of the yard and peered up at the moon. With his head cocked to one side in assessment he smiled with sensual anticipation.

When the moon reached her pregnant fullness, Lara would be his.

CHAPTER
FIVE

Shivering uncontrollably, Iain paced slowly along the beach. By taking the longer path back to the manor he would not pass under Lara's window. Confused by his shivering, he rubbed at his arms. It was not the cold. The sea had always called to him and he swam the wild waters even in the depths of winter.

Unfortunately, he knew what affected him so strongly, who affected him. The immediate attraction, the strange connection he felt with Lara. Her name tasted sweet, like the first honey of summer. He stopped to savor the taste, the feel of her name on his lips.

A blast of early spring wind blew the thoughts from his mind. The smell of rain-dampened earth mixed with the sea, a good sign. Iain trotted the last distance to the large wood-and-stone house, thoughts of the golden-haired woman fading as his plans for spring planting took precedence.

Until he entered the kitchen. In search of the herbs his mother taught him would chase chill and fever from an overly cold body, he discovered the dregs of the tea made to ease Lara's pain. The cup, centered on the smooth workbench, had been left there by the servant in her rush for bed. He lifted the mug and held it between his palms before placing it with the few pots in the tub for morning cleansing. There was no need for the woman to be punished for the small lapse of her duties.

Iain ladled water into a small pot and hung it on the metal hook over the fire. Three steps brought him to the last of the dried herbs stored in a tiny alcove set in the outer wall. The supply was much depleted, and Iain added replanting the herb garden to his list of springtime duties.

The tea steeped in the deep cup as he walked through the hall to his rooms. A fire in the large open fireplace crackled merrily, chasing the chill from the air. Pulling a hard wooden chair closer, he sat before its welcomed heat. The large mug of tea remained cradled in his hands while he searched for answers to his sudden desire for an unknown woman.

The bright flames mimicked her golden hair, the crackling of the resin-filled wood and rising sparks were indicative of her spirit and the temper he guessed lay beneath her calm exterior.

His gaze drifted to the blackened stone edging the fireplace. Mathair had often told him his hair was as dark as the soot of a winter fire. If only she were still alive. She would know the answers he searched for. Answers to questions he dared not ask. A harsh chuckle passed his tense lips. If he were a man who believed in signs he would ask her spirit to send him one.

A long finger of flame exploded from the fireplace and curved sensuously along the rough stone edging the dark opening. Heat caressed the black stones and a corresponding heat rose in Iain. Disbelief widened his eyes and he gasped, leaning forward to stare at the errant flame.

Blinking owlishly, Iain shook his head. That was no sign. It meant nothing. Even as he denied the possibility, his heart sang with hope and promise. A cool breath of air swirled from the fireplace to caress his face. The faint scent of much-loved summer flowers flowed over him.

"Mathair?" The whisper met with a flare of firelight. The

flower scent surrounded him. A single word echoed through his mind. *Believe.*

Frustrated and tempted to toss his mug into the fire, Iain clenched the thick vessel in one hand and scrubbed his fingers through his hair. What should he believe? That his tired mind created images to taunt him? The fire died back to a tiny blaze along one charred log. That spirits did send signs to the living? The long finger of flame rose to tickle the blackened stone. That his mother was with him despite the long year since her death? *Believe.*

Hesitant, he formed the question that had haunted him since the moment he first looked into Lara's eyes. Did his destiny lay entwined with the golden beauty sleeping on the other side of the thick wall? The faint hope within him grew as the fire blossomed to a barely contained inferno. His mother's scent faded away, but the word remained burned eternally in his mind. *Believe.*

No. This could not be. He was muddled by the cold and lack of sleep. Flames burned behind his closed eyelids when he gulped a mouthful of the cold tea. Grimacing at the bitter taste, he downed the rest of the drink in one long swallow. When he dared to open his eyes the logs had crumbled to bright red embers. No flames flared to touch the stones. Or his confusion.

Iain set the mug on the floor and rose, turning from the fireplace. There was no message there. Quickly stripping, he tossed the salt-stiffened clothing to a pile at the foot of his bed. After diving under the thick blankets and furs he lay on his back and stared at the ceiling. Sleep was what he needed to clear his befuddled mind.

But when he forced his eyelids closed the dark inner vision was filled with Lara and bright fire. Flames fueled the desire he tried to ignore but could not deny. Pressing his knuckles to his eyes he rubbed fiercely to wipe away the tantalizing vision. Iain turned to his side, curled into a tight ball and willed himself to relax. The burning faded slowly, but one word remained to haunt his dreams.

Believe.

L ara woke with early morning sunlight warming her face.
She smiled happily as she stretched the kinks of an unfamiliar bed from her back. Large wet drops had splashed
against the roof most of the night and she was anxious to see this
time in the fresh newness of a rain-washed morning. And rid
herself of the strange dreams plaguing her through the night.

She slid to the edge of the bed and swung her legs carefully
over the side. Flexing her ankle, she chewed at her lip, waiting for
pain. But other than a dull ache there was no discomfort. The
crutch lay beside the bed. She glared at the branch, but picked it
up with a sigh, knowing one night would not have repaired the
damage.

The struggle to stand was painfully difficult, since she did not
want to fully test the ankle until she was steady on her feet.
Finally, she touched her foot to the floor and held her breath as
she put a small amount of weight on it. There was a twinge, but
no sharp pains.

Determination set her lips while she crossed the room, each
step carefully placed to avoid further injury. Halfway to her chair
before the fireplace a strange sound filtered through her concentration. Scratching? Someone was scratching at the door.

"Yeah?"

Only silence answered her. She remembered protocols of the
past and sighed. "Enter."

The heavy wooden door opened inward, scraping against a
high spot in the floor. An elderly serving woman balanced a tray
against one ample hip. She gave Lara a shy smile before entering.
Iain followed close on her heels. Lara's breath caught, binding her
chest with a delicious tightness.

"What're ye doin'?

Lara blinked at his harsh tone. Hackles rising, she struggled to
keep her voice calm. "I'm trying to get to that chair. As if you can't
see that for yourself."

Iain stepped around the servant and crossed to Lara in three long strides. Standing before her with fists planted firmly on his hips, he glared down at her.

Strangely pleased that for once she had to tilt her head up, Lara looked into his face. She bit her tongue against another sharp retort. He looked like death warmed over. Red accented his dark eyes, the shadows surrounding them hinted at a long, troubled night. Surprised, Lara lifted her hand to the dark stubble covering his tense jaw.

Iain jerked back before she could touch him. "Ye should no'..." His voice softened. "Be walkin'. Do ye wish to further injure yerself?"

"I'm much better this morning."

A slow, doubtful smile touched his lips. "Aye? We shall see."

Lara grasped at Iain's shoulders in surprise when he lifted her off the floor. At the first delightful tingle from the movement of his firm muscles, she caressed the tense knots along his upper arms. She could definitely get used to this.

Iain deposited her in the chair and knelt at her feet. He pushed at the hem of the long linen shift she had worn for sleep and touched her foot. Lifted eyebrows signaled the servant to set the tray on the low table. After a short bow, she backed from the room.

Returning his attention to Lara's ankle, he spoke. "Since I am yer doc--doctor." He glanced up at her from under long, sooty lashes and waited for her nod before he continued. "Ye will wait fer my opinion."

"Yes, doctor." Lara giggled. "But, really, it doesn't hurt near as bad this morning."

"Aye, but I dinna think ye need to be walkin' unassisted, at least until the bandages are tightened."

"Then I can look around? Will you show me around the house and the holding? I want to see everything."

"Ye canna see all in one day. Ye overused the ankle yestern. Castan will be displeased if ye are no' able to attend his feast this night."

Emotions played across his face. Her analysis was right. Everything he felt was there for anyone to see. All she had to do now was decipher those quick, flickering emotions.

"There, Lara. What d'ye think?"

Reluctantly pulling her gaze from his face, she glanced down at her ankle and gasped. Deep purple covered the outside of her foot rising up past the point of her ankle. There, the bruises wrapped completely around the ankle. But there was very little swelling. Disappointment lifted her shoulders with a heavy sigh. Even with a tight wrapping she had no business walking.

"I think you were right, Iain. But can I at least get out of this room?"

"I think that would be a fine idea." Aubrian's lilting voice sounded from the doorway.

Iain jerked at the voice and sat back on his heels. The vein along the side of his neck throbbed. "She will no' go anywhere until the ankle is bound."

"Of course, of course. Finish, then, and I will take Lara to the great hall. Together, we shall break our fast."

The vein pulsed rapidly and Iain's jaws tensed. Lara wanted to smooth the tight lines of his face with her fingers. Would he come to the great hall as well? She fervently hoped so.

His gentle hands made quick work of the rebinding. After testing the tightness he stood. "Dinna use the foot more than ye must." He inclined his head to her then turned and repeated the gesture to Aubrian. "The servants will attend to yer needs."

Lara drew a quick breath and lifted one hand to call him back when he strode from the room, but Aubrian stepped into the place Iain vacated, blocking her vision. He took her hand and lifted it to his mouth to place a cool kiss on the back of her fingers.

"Shall we go then, my dear? I find I am in need of-- sustenance." Although she tried to ease her hand from his, Aubrian held tightly as she rose. "Shall I carry you as I offered at our first meeting?"

The sensual promise underlying his words dripped cold terror down her spine. Unable to place the reason for her fear of the enigmatic man, Lara shrugged and decided she was probably just disappointed because Iain did not join them. "First, I must dress. Then, I would like to try to walk, if I could lean upon your arm?"

"Certainly, Lara."

There it was again. That way he said her name, like she was a possession. Aubrian stroked his fingers over the rust- colored kirtle draped across the end of the bed. He handed the garment to her and waited until she pulled it over her head. Lara turned her back on Aubrian and shook the possessive thoughts away. Dreading what she must look like, she ran her fingers through her mass of curls. She'd give just about anything for a comb and a mirror.

"Your beauty outshines the sun, my dear. Shall we?" Aubrian held his crooked arm out to her with a gracious smile.

Lara linked her arm through his and he pressed it close to his side.

Panic rose in Lara's chest, chasing away the soft pleasure of his compliment. She was captured and couldn't get away. Blinking at the fanciful thoughts, she gave herself a mental nudge. Hadn't she vowed to get to know both men? And enjoy her stay? She smiled up at Aubrian. "Let's go. I'm hungry."

The walk to the great hall took more energy than Lara thought possible. Unwillingly, she conceded Iain had been right. She really should not be on her feet. Breakfast revived her somewhat, although she found herself wishing for raisins and brown sugar for the large bowl of coarse-cut oatmeal the servant set before her. And it had been a long time since she had tasted anything but low-fat milk. Sure the milk had been 'squeezed' that morning, she tried scraping the slick, creamy feeling from her tongue with the soft rasp of her teeth. Now, she needed a toothbrush.

Aubrian was attentive and conciliatory during the meal. He offered her bits of salted meats and breads, to the point she bit her lip to keep from screaming at him to leave her alone.

"Aubrian, where do you come from?" Lara smiled sweetly at

him. She had asked many questions, but each had been effectively evaded. One of his fair eyebrows arched higher as if he contemplated his answer.

"I have traveled for so long, I no longer remember."

Another dead-end. Lara frowned. Maybe... "I don't think your name comes from this area. Does it have a meaning? Mine means 'mare' in this land. Not very pretty, huh. In another place it means cheerful. I like that meaning better."

Aubrian chuckled softly. "Do you take great stock in the meaning of a name?"

Lara nodded. "Sometimes it is an important clue to how a person thinks or feels. Perhaps it might even have something to do with how their life turns out."

"And which Lara do you choose?"

"Horses are fine animals, but I prefer cheerful."

"But is not the mare a symbol of honor, a deity once worshipped?"

"Oh, I suppose." Lara paused and swirled a cup of water in her hands before setting it aside. She stared into her lap. "I've not received much honor for my name."

"Then you must let me worship you." Aubrian took her hand, turned it palm up and traced the lines with a long, square- tipped finger. Thrills ran from her hand, up her arm and down into her full belly.

"But--but you have not answered my question." It was difficult to get those simple words out and she was barely able to catch her breath. Aubrian was a master of sensual torment. His finger's attention moved to her wrist and forearm.

"My name," he paused considering, "my name comes from a land far across the sea." Some private joke amused him and he chuckled.

His finger traced a pattern to the inside of her elbow. Aubrian followed, leaning toward her. Lara discovered the movements of his lips fascinating. Warm breath caressed her cheek. "My name means 'rules the elves'."

Aubrian's lips were cool when they touched the heat rising in her cheek. He sat back slowly and laid her arm on the table, patting her hand. "A clever name, do you not think? What future would you see for me with such a name?"

Twisting her hands together in her lap, Lara stuttered and stammered. What had he done to her? Why was she so affected? Why didn't it feel--good?

Castan stumbled into the room, one hand rubbing his temple. "Gads, man, I dinna mean the drink to keep me abed this long." He slapped at Aubrian's shoulder, drawing a deep frown from his guest. Castan grabbed a pitcher and drank from the spout, milk dribbling through his beard onto the front of his shirt.

"Ah, 'tis better. Aubrian, Lara." He bowed carefully to each. "Would ye care to see me holdin' now?"

Lara patted the crutch propped at her side. "I think I need to continue to rest. I would not care to miss the feast you promised me."

Preening like a peacock, Castan puffed out his chest. "Aye. A wise woman."

Lara hid a smile behind her hand. "Is there a garden where I could enjoy the sunshine? It looks like a beautiful day."

Castan frowned. Then his expression brightened. "Iain's mathair kept a small garden near the kitchens. But I fear there is little to see this early in the year."

"It doesn't matter. Just to be outside will be pleasure enough."

"I will send a servant to lead the way."

"'Tis no need, Castan. I shall take Lara to the garden. There is work to be done there this day." The voice she'd been hoping to hear was flat and emotionless. But the tones still chased the tremors of Aubrian's touch from her body, replacing them with warmth. No, not warmth--heat.

"Aye, Iain. 'Tis guid, then. Will ye make sure of the feastin' meal as well? We ride the holdin' this day." Castan turned his attention to Aubrian, easily forgetting the others. "D'ye ride, Seanachai?"

Iain stood in the arched doorway until Castan and Aubrian left the great hall. Castan's voice echoed through the manor yards as he called for the best horses to be readied. The storyteller had hesitated, casting a strange look at Lara before he followed his host. Iain tried to slow his breathing. What should it matter to him if the man's eyes dripped lust?

Fearful of what his own eyes might reveal about his feelings, Iain lowered his lids briefly. His mother often told him his heart was in his eyes. This was one time he hoped she was wrong.

Lara smiled at him as he crossed the room. "I'm ready to go--I really do need some fresh air."

"Aye. 'Twill do you good. Come, 'tis not far."

Patiently waiting while Lara stood, Iain ached to assist her, to feel her warmth beside him. But he dare not. She took a few tentative steps and lurched forward with a moan.

The distance to her side was short, but he could not cross it fast enough to catch her before she sank to her knees. On his knees next to her, Iain lifted her lowered chin with a cupped palm. "Lara?"

"Oh, I'm okay. I should have listened to you and not walked today. I'm sorry to cause so much trouble." Tears filled the violet-and-brown swirls of her eyes.

Iain brushed an escaping tear away with his thumb. "Then ye shall no' walk. I am at yer command, m'lady."

Lara captured his hand under hers and pressed her cheek into his palm. Unable to find release, a sharp inhalation of air burned in his chest. When she spoke, her breath seared the side of his hand. "Thank you. Can we still go to the garden?"

Swallowing past the lump in his throat proved more difficult than breathing. "Aye. I dinna wish to miss this fine day. There is much to be done to prepare the earth."

How much would he be able to do with her there? Just the thought of her was a distraction; her presence would be torture. But a torture he found himself willing to bear as long as she would stay by his side.

He gathered her in his arms and rose slowly. A tall woman, she was still light, a welcomed burden. She wiggled a bit, settled against him and let out a long sigh. The release of his breath matched hers.

"This becomes a habit, m'lady."

"You are supposed to call me Lara." The grin was infectious and he was glad the crystal tears had dried from her eyes. His lips pulled into an answering smile before he nodded.

CHAPTER
SIX

Aubrian glared at Castan while trying to settle more comfortably on the wide back of the docile mount provided for him. He had been closing quickly on his prey. Given a bit more time, the hunt might have been successful this day.

No matter. Prolonging the hunt increased the pleasure, and he was determined to find his pleasure with this one. And discover if there were more than just her violet eyes that drew him to her. Perhaps after the feast...

"Aubrian, there is much I wish to show you. Do not dally, Seanachai."

When his heels pressed into the horse's sides, Aubrian's mount plodded forward and drew next to Castan's prancing courser. "I beg pardon, my lord. I was lost in admiration of your lands."

Castan's chest lifted and he tugged at his beard in pleasure. A wide smile split his drooping moustache from the full beard. "From the rise of this hill ye will see all the lands within me holdin'. Spring plantin' will begin soon, me lands shall prosper this season."

They crested the hill and reined in the horses. Castan's tall stallion danced to the side and tossed his noble head. Nostrils flared to the wind, he snorted and reared slightly, throwing Castan off-balance.

"Ho, Aonghus. What ails ye? Hold, horse." The roan pulled the reins from Castan's fist and jumped to one side. Castan wrapped a fistfull of mane around his hand. "Hold, ye mange-ridden beastie."

Castan slid to the ground and grabbed for the reins. Hooves carving deep grooves in the damp earth, Aonghus pulled fiercely against the man straining to hold him. Curses, increasing in loudness and tempo, flowed from Castan.

Aubrian let his eyes roll to the sky, looped one leg in front of him across the horse and leaned forward. His mount stood quietly after he touched her lightly on the arched neck, though her ears twitched as her wide, soft eyes watched the stallion warily. A sharp whinny from the bottom of the hill made Aubrian smile. He was not the only being who enjoyed a hunt this day.

"It would appear, my lord, there is a mare in season nearby." Aubrian chuckled at Castan's ruddy face. Castan froze, shoulder muscles bunched with the effort of controlling the raging animal, and turned his head toward Aubrian.

"What say ye?"

The bugle of the stallion covered any reply Aubrian would have made. Realization dawned on Castan as the ringing cry faded and was answered with a softer welcoming call. His head swiveled toward the bottom of the hill and back to Aonghus.

"Oh, ho, me boy." Fighting to slip the halter from the tossing head, Castan smiled broadly. He jumped back and slapped the wide rump as it flashed by him. The grin turned wicked when it turned to Aubrian and his eyebrows lifted. "Soon me lands will blossom with new life, eh?"

Equine cries of welcome and demand echoed up the hill.

Aubrian's mare tossed her head once and flicked her ears before she eyed the lush grasses blowing around her knees. Aubrian patted her neck and slid lightly to the ground to join Castan in looking down the hill. It was not the powerful horses he envisioned enjoying the fierceness of mating, but a golden- haired girl bowing to his demands, violet eyes shining with desire--and pain. His body grew pleasantly heavy, filling with tension to fuel his increasing anticipation. Ah, the hunt.

Aubrian sensed Castan staring at him so turned a lazy smile to his host. "So it would seem, Castan. So it would seem."

Iain called for a wrap as he carried Lara swiftly through the manor. Lara had not realized the size or extent of the building; the turnings and twisting hallways were reminiscent of the oldest castles she haunted while on vacations. During her explorations of the past she tried to discover the time when the ancient buildings were new and life flowed through them. On occasion, she had been successful.

But none of the castles or manor houses held the attraction of this remote holding. Was it the architecture that drew her--or the occupants?

Sunlight filled the garden and warmed the cool, winter-rested earth. Even though now only seeing the death brought by winter, Lara imagined lush plantings grown large in the heat of summer. The vision of beauty filled her so completely she hardly noticed when Iain set her gently on her feet.

He held her to his side while he draped a length of pale wool over a strange stone bench. Lara was only able to glimpse the highly wrought carved animals supporting the seat, but guessed they were griffins. She wanted a closer look, but Iain turned her too soon and eased her onto the bench. A thick slice of a log elevated her foot before he wrapped the ends of the woolen shawl around her shoulders.

Lara tugged the ends tighter and felt infinitely cared for and cherished. She liked the feelings and her growing attraction for the man whose presence created them.

But what had she felt with Aubrian? Before Castan interrupted that morning she had been ready to fall into his arms and...and what? The danger lurking in the depths of his eyes confused her. She didn't want danger. She wanted security and comfort. The differences in her reactions to the two men added a frightening element to her confusion. Perhaps she should be like a character in one of her favorite books and think about it tomorrow.

After settling her, Iain turned his back, knelt beside a plot of dark, rocky earth and began to pull tiny sprouts and toss them in a pile on the path.

"Are you pulling weeds?"

"Aye."

"How do you know which are the weeds?"

"The herbs were harvested in the fall. The plants were old and had been ill-cared-for after Mathair's death. They have been removed. I shall replant with winter-grown cuttings when the plot is cleared."

Lara sighed at his back. Iain didn't seem to want to talk to her. Well, he could not want to talk, but it wouldn't stop her from trying. Although watching the muscles play across his back and shoulders as he worked was a pleasant way to spend the morning, she wished he would turn around. "Wouldn't it be easier to use a shovel and just turn the earth over?"

"Aye, but after the rain, digging would compact the earth so any seeds I plant would fail to grow. The heavy earth would crush the tender roots of the seedlings"

"Oh. Don't you have a servant to do this?"

A long breath lifted his shoulders. Lara sensed his hesitation and willed him to face her. The short moments his features were hidden from her dragged by. Iain swung his head toward her, eyes closed as if in resignation, and moved to her side. Folding his length to a cross-legged sitting position at her feet, he picked at the small pile of weeds before him.

"This was m' Mathair's garden. None but she tended the plants. Here she raised herbs for healin' and cookin'. And the flowers that brought her joy. Athair searched far for the plants she begged for." A soft smile touched his lips and he looked up at Lara, deep shadows darkening his expressive eyes.

"Since she is gone, I tolerate no other gardener but m'self. No other has learned her secrets, or the ways of plants." He paused to give her a mischievous grin. "I pestered her until she taught me. My time with the monks taught me more that I shall incorporate into the gardens. And in the plantin' of all the holdin'."

A proud glint filled his eyes as he looked into the distance. His face lit with an inner fire that made her breath catch low in her throat. "You love this land, don't you?" Reverence filled her whispered words.

"Aye. If only Castan would listen to me."

"He does not take well to interference by others, does he?"

"Nay. I fear his methods will ruin the land so 'twill be no' good for crops. Where will his holdin' be then?"

Lara cast an appraising glance his way. Farmers and ecologists in her time faced the same worries. She took a deep breath and hesitated before asking the question burning on her tongue. "Do you want to be the lord of this holding?"

Iain jerked back, eyes wide with denial. "I do no' wish it. Nor have I ever desired lordin' over others." Wry laughter filled the small, enclosed garden. "As Castan often tells me, I have no' the temperament for it."

"Your cousin can be a cruel man."

Iain's shaggy head swung back and forth. "Nay, merely unthinkin'."

"How is he the lord here? Did your father have another wife?"

"Athair loved but one woman. He is not athair to Castan, but uncle. Since my own mathair was foreign, there could be no right of succession. Castan's mathair is my aunt, and the line flows from her."

"But--" The resigned expression on his face stopped her speech.

"'Tis m' life. I dinna care to rule over the land, but wish Castan took more responsibility. All he cares for is the power, and the honor he believes comes with that power."

After he ripped a tiny weed into tinier pieces, Iain watched them flutter away on the light breeze. "'Tis because of that lust for power that he sends me to the monastery after harvest."

Lara stared at his profile while his unfocused gaze followed the flight of a small bird. A priest? Denial rose and exploded from her before she could think. "No. You can't do that."

His face turned slowly to hers. "I am no' given a choice. If a choice were given me, perhaps I would become a traveler such as yerself and explore the lands far across the sea."

"You can't. A priest, Iain?"

Dark brows lowered over equally dark eyes, and with head cocked to one side he studied her. Then the eyebrows rose high into his forehead. He chuckled. "I shall no' be a priest. I dinna believe in a way to make that vow. But Castan fears I shall somehow take his power from him so sends me away. He is the MacDhuibh, I do as I am bidden."

"That's not fair." Anger toward the jovial red-haired man filled her with righteous indignation and she trembled with the force of it. Iain lay a hand on her arm, instantly dampening the anger.

"Perhaps 'tis no'. 'Tis the way of things."

Lara took a deep calming breath. It didn't work, so she took another and covered his hand with hers. "Aren't there any other options for you? You could get married."

Another laugh, dripping with sarcasm, surrounded her. "Aye? And what family would have me? M' mathair was foreign; there are no lands, no succession to bring a bride. If I marry it must be to a foreign woman who cares no' for possessions I canna bring."

Although for a moment she tried to deny her thoughts Lara's heart beat the truth. She wouldn't care.

Iain turned his hand until long fingers captured her hand. Lara bit her lip against the sudden flare of heat centering in her palm and spreading swiftly to her breasts and belly. He stared at their joined hands. Beneath his wind-roughened skin a deep red colored the tips of his ears. He feels it, too. Whatever it is.

The heat flared in Iain's face as though he had been outside too long after a dim, sunless winter. He could not lift his eyes past the hand that looked so small, yet fit so perfectly in his. Was it possible she trembled at his touch?

The need to feel his lips against her honey-gold skin drew his head lower. At the same time his hand lifted until her fingers were a mere inch from his mouth. He tasted her name before touching her skin. "Lara."

The back of her hand was warm, the gentle kiss the barest brush of lips against her. Reluctance pushed her whispered name past his lips again before he pulled back. "I beg pardon, m'lady."

Soft and breathless, she asked, "For what?"

"I took liberty 'twas no' mine to take."

Lara eased her hand from his and rested it against his cheek. He barely felt the touch of her fingers as she guided his face toward her. The violet swirl of her eyes swallowed him. "What liberty?"

"To kiss ye so." *To desire ye so.* "Ye belong to another."

"Another? I belong to no one but myself. Who would I belong to?" Lara's hands swirled through the air to point through the kitchen doorway. "Aubrian? I only met him yesterday."

And came to this holdin' but yestern as well. Already my heart belongs to ye. Iain jerked with surprise. Had he spoken the words or only thought them? *I have no right.*

"I chose who I will. No man makes decisions for me." Lara reached for Iain and clasped her hands at the back of his neck. "I give you permission to take such liberties."

Her fingers tangled in his hair, caressed the back of his head and exerted a gentle pressure. Iain rose to his knees before her, unwilling to lift his eyes to hers, afraid of what she might see. Weakness assailed his muscles and she closed the distance between them. His hands found Lara's waist and rested there.

Iain held back, letting Lara touch her lips to his. The lightning jolt of her kiss brought a low moan from the depths of his chest. At the sound, Lara's lips parted beneath his, inviting, teasing. Splaying his hands on her back, he leaned into her and deepened the kiss. His tongue stroked her lower lip, begging entrance, and met the silky-smooth, sweet dance of her own against it.

Time was lost in her embrace. There was no garden, no sun, no spring song from nesting birds. There was only Lara and the desire surrounding him with her touch, each soft sound of her pleasure.

Noise from men gathering in front of the house filtered through a haze of growing passion. Iain's soul was ripped away when his lips lifted from hers. His hands, wrapped in the bright mass of her hair, tilted her head so he could look into wide, luminous eyes. The dark brown swirling through the violet deepened to black. Her lips were red, moist and slightly swollen. She tugged on his shoulders, but by holding himself stiffly he maintained the slight distance between them.

"Nay, lady. We must no'..."

"Yes, Iain. We must." Lara scooted forward until she could trail kisses along his jaw. Determined to resist the insistent touch, he pulled his lower lip between his teeth. He desired her. His body overflowed with an aching need he feared only her touch, her kiss would satisfy.

He could not allow that satisfaction and jerked away. Catching herself on the log footrest, Lara fell forward. The log slipped sideways and her foot fell heavily to the ground. Her cry of pain shattered the remnants of Iain's passion.

"Lara?" He bent to her foot and cradled it in his palms.

"That sure was dumb. I'll be fine, Iain. Guess we got carried away."

"Aye." Aye, ready to carry her to his rooms. A deep breath did little to calm his body, but the dangerous moment had passed. He cast a tentative smile at Lara. "I must attend to the gatherin' of men while Castan is away."

Lara nodded. "May I stay here for awhile?"

"Aye. I shall return when the matter is settled. Is there anythin' ye need?"

A headshake tossed her wild curls and nearly drew him back into her arms. Instead, Iain rose and executed a short bow before escaping into the cool shadows of the hallway.

A small cluster of ragged men circled around a pale, knock-kneed horse. Heavy callusing on the quivering flanks showed she was a frequently overused draft animal. Iain's eyes narrowed; and he folded his arms across his chest, spread his legs and waited for the farmers to notice his presence.

"Master Iain." A man tugged on the animal's lead rope and stepped forward. He executed a poor bow before pointing back at the horse. "Master, I demand satisfaction. Me poor mare's been ill-used."

Eyebrows lifted, Iain glanced at an old, weeping sore on the animal's side. "Aye, she has."

The farmer covered the wound with his dirty hand and stammered, head lowered. "A branch, Master Iain."

"Aye? This is no' why ye come to the MacDhuibh."

"Nay, 'tis another matter. This day a stallion broke into me home, me sheep pen and mounted me mare. I demand satisfaction, sir."

"None control the wild ones ranging the highlands, Edwin."

A shrewd glimmer touched the man's normally dull eyes. "No wild one, sir. 'Twas that demon horse of Castantin MacDhuibh."

"The laird rode the beast this morn. He waudna loose Aonghus while away from the manor."

"He waud an' did. Noise frightened me woman but I be too late to save me mare. The beast destroyed me steading. I demand-"

"Aye." Exasperation flowed through Iain. Surely, Castan would not be so stupid as to let Aonghus free. He closed his eyes. Aye, Castan would. "What do ye wish of the MacDhuibh?"

"Payment for the damage done to my animal."

Iain did not repress a low chuckle. "Damage? Ye should welcome a foal from so great a steed."

"What use be there fer a war beast? 'Twill no' pull stones from the ground. 'Twill no' carry me loads. 'Twould be taken from me with no thought for me losses."

Edwin rambled on, looking to the gathered farmers for support while Iain stared into the distance over the man's shoulder. Would Castan ever care for his holding or the people who looked to him and supported him with tithes of the land's meager bounty? *How different would life be if I were laird?* He gave a mental shrug. 'Twas of no matter. He would be away soon enough and, as Castan willed, forbidden to return.

The man droned on until Iain thought his head would burst. "Hold, Edwin." Edwin's speech sputtered into silence. The gathered men shuffled closer to hear Iain's judgment. Iain lifted one hand, palm up. "If the horse quickens bring her to me. I shall give ye fair price or choice of a suitable replacement. If she dinna quicken there be no loss."

A broad, self-satisfied smile filled Edwin's face and a calculating glint flared in his eye but faded quickly. "'Tis fair, as Master Iain is always fair." He turned to his companions and led them from the yard. "Honor the wisdom of Master Iain, me boys."

Iain took a long breath, relaxed and let his hands fall loosely to his sides. Edwin's final comment did nothing to lessen his dislike of the man. Ambitious and scheming, Edwin would bear watching.

Commotion at the gates drew his attention. Castan's long stride carried him into the yard. He called greeting to the retreating farmers and grinned at Iain. Aubrian waited by the gate and spoke quietly to the farmers before following Castan. He led one horse.

So, 'twas true. Iain met Castan at the center of the yard. "Where is Aonghus?"

"Och, he be off havin' a bit o' fun." Castan chuckled and gave Iain a long, slow wink.

Iain struggled to form words through his clenched teeth and pointed at the backs of the farmers. "Edwin claims Aonghus destroyed part of his home in the frenzy to mate with a draft horse. Is this true?"

"Oh, aye, probably. I dinna see which way the lad went."

"There is little humor in this, Castan. The man demanded retribution."

Castan only smiled and shrugged. Hands clenched into tight

fists, Iain leaned toward him. Catching a glimpse of Aubrian's interested smile, he swallowed his anger and eased back.

"Ye took care of the matter, dinna ye, coz?"

"Aye. Remember, m'lord." Iain paused after his unusual use of Castan's preferred title. "I willna be here after the harvest. Ye'll deal with yer problems yerself." Spinning on his heels, Iain retreated to the coolness of the manor and his rooms.

Plopping onto a hard chair, Iain leaned forward with head in hands to rub his temples. He cared too much for the land and the people who lived under the family's holding. Then he threw his hands in the air. Why should he care? If only he could convince himself it was not important. Once he was gone, any influence he might have would also disappear.

Lara. The unbidden memory of her brought him from his dour thoughts. He leaned back in dismay--he had left her alone in the garden. One of his windows looked out over the area, so he bounded across the room. The garden was empty. He hoped she took care with her ankle.

It was well she was not in sight. The mere memory of her basking in the sunlight brought his body to aching life. Leaning over the wide sill he clasped his hands and peered into the brilliant blue of the cloudless sky. Had the sky always been so blue, or was it because she was here?

Iain scrubbed his hands over his face and back through his hair. *Stop, fool.* She'd returned his kiss, but that didn't mean she wished for more. But he did, and feared those desires. Strong, focused, undeniable desires.

Deciding hard work would strike her from his mind, he turned from the window. Unable to face the now-lonely garden, Iain left the manor for the small plot of land where he planned to experiment with a few precious seeds given him by the friars. Aye, working in the warm earth would remove the memory of his hands in her soft hair.

Perhaps.

CHAPTER
SEVEN

T he pleasaunce was dismal and lonely without the warmth of Iain's presence. Lara took a long, aching breath to try to still the trembling deep within her breast. The heat of his kisses centered there and remained, the force holding her thoughtless for a long moment.

Chilled as if a cloud passed overhead to block the sun, Lara shuddered. No longer enjoying the peaceful garden, she rose carefully. If she went slowly, the distance back to her rooms should not re-injure her ankle. She held her breath and took a first step.

There was no pain. Good. Now, if she correctly remembered the way. As an adult she'd never lost herself in time, but had a hard time finding her car in a parking lot. Pausing in the doorway she gave a small snort of self-derision. Consumed by the feeling of Iain's strong arms holding her, entranced by the scent of him and the feel of hard muscles against her, she had paid little attention to her surroundings.

Low-pitched voices and the smell of fresh-baked bread floated to her, and she turned. The kitchens lay in that direction. Which meant her rooms were the opposite way. Planting the crutch firmly, she turned to face a masculine chest. Startled, she jumped back and cringed at the injudicious movement of her ankle.

Aubrian clasped her upper arms to steady her. Goosebumps rose under his fingers and moved down her arms. His head cocked toward her, eyes filled with a predatory glint. It was like looking into the eyes of a great cat lying in wait for an unsuspecting meal. A dark chill replaced the lingering warmth in her chest. A slow, sultry smile pulled Aubrian's lips but didn't reach his eyes. "Dare I hope you are as pleased to see me as I am you?"

The silky words slid across her consciousness, leaving a strange, bitter taste filling her mouth. How had she ever imagined being attracted to this man? Fey heritage or not, she was suddenly sure Aubrian was one slimy character.

Gentle hands moved down her arms to her elbows, paused, and then caressed their way back to her shoulders. The goosebumps tingled unpleasantly. Half-lidded, his eyes held hers as he slid his hands down to her wrists and up under the loose sleeves of her smocked chemise. It was sensually hypnotic, alluring and yet uncomfortable.

"Don't..."

His smile broadened and Aubrian continued moving his smooth hands in a slow, sensuous trip up and down her bare arms. She had to look away, had to stop him. Mesmerized, she was unable to move. A tiny, unfamiliar voice whispered through her mind. *'Tis Faerie glamour. Realize and resist.*

Faerie glamour? Her dazed mind rebelled against the notion. Not the nonsense in tales of mortals lost for lifetimes in the Otherworld? Lara wanted to laugh at the absurdity, but Aubrian's caressing hands and intense gaze gave her second thoughts. Perhaps the glamour was true. What other explanation could there be for this strange attraction? She held her breath until her lungs burned, willing herself to look away, to step back, anything to somehow break the enticing contact.

Aubrian closed the short distance between them and gathered her just close enough so the tips of her breasts brushed against him. A slow, deep breath lifted his chest and Lara's world exploded in a gasp of sensation.

Trying to form words to deny the feelings, to stop the torture and unwanted pleasure, Lara bit her lower lip until she tasted the sharp coppery tang of her blood.

There was a slight hitch in one of Aubrian's eyebrows and his face loomed before her, wicked intent glowing in his eyes. Hot breath caressed her cheek. She could not turn away. *Faerie glamour. Help me.*

The tip of Aubrian's tongue darted out to lick a droplet of blood from her mouth and traced the fullness of her lower lip until she trembled uncontrollably. *Please, help me. I can't fight him. I don't know what to do.* The far-off baying of hounds jerked Aubrian away from her.

Pushing her back and planting his hands on the wall at each side of her head, Aubrian leaned to exhale softly, seductively into her ear. Cold chills ran down her spine. He dropped one of his hands to her breast. Lara bit at her lip again to contain the moan that rumbled at the back of her throat.

Aubrian touched her earlobe with his tongue. "Do not attempt to call the hounds. I do not acknowledge Faerie rule, dear Lara." With one finger he tipped her unresisting head toward him and closed his lips over hers.

A scream built within her, raging to escape through her clenched teeth. Lara squeezed her eyes shut--she would not open her mouth to him. She would not.

Aubrian lifted his head. "You have a stronger will than I anticipated. Good. I shall enjoy breaking your spirit. Now, my dear, shall we continue?" He pressed the length of his body against her, pinning her to the wall, the rise of his desire throbbing against her hip.

The high-pitched, excited voice of a young boy preceded the speaker around a corner. Aubrian stepped back. The contact and glamour were gone, leaving her weak and confused. Eyes wide, Lara turned toward her unwitting savior as a typically dirty boy appeared, dragging an elderly serving woman by one hand.

"Gran, come on. Ye must see this."

The servant stopped short when she noticed Lara huddled against the wall. Somehow, Lara found her wavering voice. "Help me, please."

The servant stepped forward. "Are ye lost, mistress?"

"Make him leave me alone." Lara wrapped her arms about herself and shuddered, refusing to turn toward Aubrian.

"Who?" Concern filled the old woman's eyes. The boy peeked from behind her skirts, brows lowered over bright brown eyes.

Lara focused on those eyes, finding some elusive familiarity there. She loosened her hold on herself and gestured behind her. "That man."

"There be no one there, mistress." After glancing around, the servant hesitated before touching Lara on the arm. Startled, Lara sank back against the wall with a soft cry of denial. "Beg pardon, mistress. I should no' be familiar with ye." The grayed head lowered in shame.

"No, that's okay." Lara inched closer to the comfort and concern radiating from the woman. "He was here. I know he was."

"There be many dark corners where one may hide, mistress," the boy's voice squeaked from behind the old woman.

The servant's warm concern and one final shudder chased away the last of the glamour. The baying hounds faded into the distance and into Lara's memory. A tentative smile touched her lips. "I think I'm okay now." She paused at the woman's confused expression. "I'm fine. Please, call me Lara."

A bright glint of pleasure lit the woman's eyes, but she shook her head. "'Tis not seemly."

"When we're alone? I'm not used to such formality. It makes me uncomfortable." Lara lowered her gaze. She needed a friend in this time.

"I will try. Lara."

"Thank you." Lara peered closely at the woman. "Now, what is your name?"

"I am called Beitris." She reached behind and pulled the boy in front of her by one ragged sleeve. "This be my grandbairn, Stephen."

Lara inclined her head to the boy. "Well met, Stephen." He blushed fiercely before stammering a reply.

"Beitris, I could use some help to my rooms. I'm a little confused."

"Aye, an' ye must no' be walkin' so much."

"You sound just like Iain." A happy chuckle surprised Lara. The constant flux of her emotions was alarming. Somehow, she had to get a tight grip on her feelings.

"Master Iain be a wise man. Much different than m'lord Castantin. Come. Be there anythin' else I may do fer ye?" Beitris took Lara's hand and led her carefully through the hallways. Openmouthed, Stephen trailed behind. Beitris leaned toward Lara. "Ye have impressed the boy. Never have I seen him so quiet." She winked.

Lara laughed again and glanced back at Stephen. "Come now, young sir. Perhaps when you have no chores you could tell me about the holding."

The boy brightened and moved ahead of the women. Turning to face them he skipped backwards. "'Twill be fun, mistress."

Progress through the manor was slow, allowing plenty of conversation. Lara learned the rumors of the manor and holding and more of the private life of the MacDhuibh than she cared to know. It was true--servants did know everything that went on, right down to the number of pigeons in the dovecote. But, to Lara's disappointment, Beitris was closemouthed about Iain.

The elderly woman settled Lara in a chair by the fire and stood back, appraising her. "Guid. Ye need rest before the feastin'."

Lara stretched, using one hand to pull her cramped arm and shoulder muscles toward the ceiling. "Ah, what I'd really love is a bath."

"M'lady, Fronia, Iain's mathair, followed the Roman custom as well." Beitris shuddered. "Ne'er did see the enjoyment of it. The tub be stored away. I shall direct the cooks to bring it to yer room an' start fillin' it." She cast another appraising look over Lara.

"Aye, ye be close to the size o' the lady. Mayhaps I can find ye a new dress fer the feast."

Lara leaned forward, interested in new clothing despite her denial. "Oh, no, don't bother."

"'Tis a pleasure to serve ye, Mistress Lara. Stephen, come, ye can help fill the buckets."

The boy's lower lip pouted, a sullen dullness dampened his earlier enthusiasm. Lara's heart dropped. Someone so young should not be forced to work so hard. She took a deep breath, and a chance.

"Beitris? After Stephen finishes his chores could he sit beside me at the feast?" Wary interest brightened the young countenance.

Beitris shook her head. "'Twould no' be... ."

Before Stephen's face could fall into despair, Lara amended her offer. "Could he then serve me and stay at my side in case I need anything?"

The old woman's eyes sparkled when her gaze moved between Lara and her grandson's rising hope. Beitris closed her eyes in thought. "Aye." She grinned and opened her eyes to Stephen's shining happiness. "Aye, 'twould be acceptable. So, ye must hurry, boy. I willna have ye servin' the lady with a dirty face."

Stephen's whoop echoed off the high ceiling as he ran from the room. Beitris turned her smile to Lara. "Thank ye," she whispered before she followed the boy into the hall.

Aubrian waited until the soft echoes of footsteps faded from the hallway before he slipped from a dark alcove. Contemplation pulled his features into a slight frown when he stared down the dim passage.

Pleased by Lara's fear, one corner of his lips twitched upward but fell again as he narrowed his eyes. The lingering scent of her desire teased his nostrils. Not the desire he created with his touch, this essence preceded her down the hall. She had felt passion not long before their fortuitous meeting.

Even the last vestiges of that desire were intense, the strong bouquet tantalizing his tongue. Aubrian rolled the piquancy around his mouth, testing it, although he already knew the cause, the source of her passions.

The threat he felt from the first moment Lara looked upon Iain exploded through him. The pleasure in his mouth grew bitter as angry bile rose in his throat. He spat and strode quickly past the wet spot. The anger could be used to his advantage and turn Lara's affections from the human. It complicated the hunt, but with a smile he realized the intensified joy of pursuit and antici-pation of capture.

Thoughts of Lara and her submission faded to a pleasant tingle at the back of his mind. Tonight he would earn his keep. What tale would he tell? Random thoughts sped through his mind chasing each other like hounds after a rabbit.

Chill touched the base of his neck. The response of Faerie hounds to Lara's fear had been strong. Earlier, he'd sensed some connection to Faerie, some drop of fey blood in her veins, but had not considered the bond to be strong, or direct. Somehow, she held the favor of some Otherworldly folk. Aubrian's eyebrows lifted quickly and then lowered. Perhaps, at long last, he would be able to return.

Anticipation blossomed until he was forced to stop and take a few long, calming breaths. Possession of Lara and a way to return to Faerie...the day improved immeasurably.

A leather-bound book with thick parchment pages lay on the table in front of Iain. Handmade by his mother, it was a prized and carefully guarded possession. The illuminated manuscript was a rare compilation of poetry and tales his mother collected from the many lands where she had been forced to serve. Normally, the calming effects of reading her hand worked quickly. But today nothing would chase visions of

Lara from him. Every passage he tried to read became a love saga, even tales of war and deceit.

Disgusted, he shoved the heavy book away, crossed his arms on the table and lay his head against his arms. What was he to do? Possible actions, centered around Lara, flitted wickedly through his mind. How could she have taken residence in his mind, his soul so rapidly? *And your heart, my son? Did she find her way there as well?*

The soft remembrance of his mother's voice lulled him to exhausted sleep, the final word echoing long into his dreams.

Believe.

The insistent scrabbling of rats infested his dream and brought Iain fully awake. Confused, he stared blankly around his room. His gaze rested on the book; he'd fallen asleep at the table. Shaking his head did little to clear it.

The scratching continued, so he turned his head toward the door. "Aye, What'd ye want?" The door opened slowly, and Beitris peeked around the thick wood. Iain eased back in the chair and looped one leg over the armrest. "Well?"

"Master Iain, I be thinkin'." She paused and nervously adjusted the cloth burden in her arms. Iain waited patiently. Beitris had been his mother's friend and a second mother to him. Seldom had he seen her at such a loss for words. He smiled.

A hint of relief touched her wizened face. "Mistress Lara has only one dress."

"Aye?"

"It canna be washed and let to dry before this even's gatherin'." Iain shrugged one shoulder and motioned for her to continue.

"She canna go naked to the feast." Iain felt his smile broaden at the tantalizing thought. Beitris chuckled softly. Burying the response deeply beneath a cool exterior, Iain hoped Beitris did not understand the blazing rise of his feelings.

"She is near the same size as yer mathair. "

"Aye."

"Ye make this difficult, young master."

"Do I, Beitris?" The easy love he felt toward the old woman was evident in his teasing. He grinned, enjoying the faint blush of color covering her wrinkled cheeks.

Dropping the bundle on the table in front of him, Beitris wedged her hands against wide hips, the smile on her lips in contrast to her stern gaze. "I dinna have time to take these to mistress Lara, sir. Will ye see she gets them soon enough to dress fer the feast?" Without waiting for an answer, Beitris whirled about and left Iain staring after her. She closed the door softly.

Iain touched the pile of cloth, lifted an edge to his face and inhaled deeply. The fragrances of unnamed flowers blended with heather eased the cords of tension from his neck and shoulders. The word he had come to dread in a short time whirled through him. *Believe.*

Believe? What should he believe? What could he believe? The ancient ways, the old gods of his people interested him, called to him, but he did not believe in the magic of the old religion. The newer way of the Christ? Neither did that fill the empty need within him. In the first months of his study with the friars he tried to find a way to combine the two beliefs. Instead, the so-called holy men merely adapted the ancient celebrations, corrupting them to fit their dictates.

Iain dropped the cloth back onto the pile and glanced at the embers glowing red in the fireplace. Scrubbing his hands roughly over his face, he contemplated the dance of the flames the night before and tried to make sense of his dreams. The only thing he could believe in was a lonely destiny, forcefully cut off from the land and those he loved.

Again the tender words, in his mother's voice, twined through him. *Your heart. Believe your heart.* Iain shook his head. He would listen to common sense and use the intelligence he cultivated with the myriad of his studies. His heart always led him to trouble.

Now, his heart was leading him to Lara.

Beitris had joined in forging the golden threads binding him to the remarkable woman. And the old servant was pulling the chain of those knotted threads taut. Should he fight? He did not know.

Fanciful thoughts, he mused, more suited to the visiting storyteller. The man made his hackles rise, and Iain's hand clenched as if around the hilt of a sword. Given any provocation, Aubrian would not hesitate to visit Lara. Iain shook his hand to relax the curled fingers. So, why was he hesitant just to take a rumpled pile of clothing to her room?

Iain gave a soft snort of disgust and slammed his palms against the tabletop. Rubbing his stinging hands together, he stood and snatched at the clothing. His long strides carried him to the doorway and into the dim hall.

He caressed the material, glanced down and wondered if the violet of her eyes would darken when she wore the soft, deep-blue gown. There was, at the moment, nothing more he wished to discover.

Pausing at the door to her room gave Iain the chance to take a deep breath and plan his action. He would hand her the clothing and leave immediately. Before he could change his mind, he scratched at the door, and then rapped lightly on the wood with the back of his knuckles.

Her dulcet voice bidding him enter was muffled through the thick wood. It took him two deep breaths before he could push the door open and step into the room. He froze at an indescribable sight.

EIGHT

L ara's back was to him, her bare back. She was curled in
the old bathing tub and wet, dark-golden hair straggled
between her shoulder blades.

Iain could not breathe, would not be able to move to save his
life. Until she shivered.

"Ooh, close the door, Beitris, you're letting in cold air." Iain
sank against the door and stumbled back as it slid closed. The
latch fell with a finality that made Iain jump away from the warm
wood. A tremor ran along his skin. He should leave, should look
away at the very least. But, he could not.

Lara lifted one arm over her shoulder, dangling a rag. "I'm
almost done, but could you do me one more favor? Would you
wash my back?"

Forgotten, the pile of clothing dropped with a soft swoosh to
the floor. Iain moved in a trance, one hand lifting to take the rag
from her fingers. Lara hunched forward exposing the narrow
width of her back. He knelt behind her and dipped the rag in the
warm water. Lara's other hand lifted holding a lump of soap.
When his palm touched the tips of her extended fingers, the soap
plopped into his hand.

A pleased sigh expanded Lara's shoulders. "Thank you. This is wonderful. And the soap is wonderful, too. The fragrance is much like what my grandmother makes for me."

Iain soaped the rag but hesitated with it nearly touching her golden skin. Strange thin stripes of pale, creamy skin stood out in stark contrast to the darker tan. He ached to touch those stripes and taste them with his tongue. The breath burned tight in his chest.

Lara gasped when Iain rubbed the cloth softly over her back. Then she rotated her shoulders. "Ah, yes. That's what I needed. You have been a great help to me today. Don't stop, please."

If he only could. Intense concentration kept him breathing, for the swirl of suds over her back was a potent aphrodisiac. When she swiped her hair forward over one shoulder, he could see a tiny red mark at the base of her neck, a birthing mark that begged for his kisses.

The growing tightness of his loins became unbearable. He shifted position. And dropped the rag. Unable to allow the torture of reaching beneath the water to search for it, he cleared his throat.

"Oh, my God. Iain? What are you doing here?" Lara sank as far into the water as she could and tried to cover herself with her hands. Accusation glared from her eyes. "Where's Beitris?"

Iain willed himself to look away from her nakedness, to offer her the honor she deserved. All he could do was lower his gaze to the lump of soap still clutched between his fingers. Lara turned sideways in the narrow tub, arms wrapped over her breasts, and cocked her head to one side. Her eyes were wide while she waited for his answer. The sudden hard lump in his throat mimicked the firm ache of his groin. Somehow, he swallowed and found his strained voice.

"I brought you fresh clothing." He winced and glanced at her. Did he truly sound so dull-witted?

"Oh. Beitris hasn't been here?"

Iain shook his head. A shy grin gently stretched Lara's lips. He could not draw his gaze from the rosy fullness. At least it was more honorable than looking at the pink skin below the waterline.

"You will have to finish rinsing my back, then." She turned and leaned forward. After fishing through the water, she lifted the sopping rag to him. Iain held his palms out to her in denial and shook his head. "Please, I will itch terribly if you don't wash off the soap."

The thought of causing her discomfort centered painfully in his chest. He sighed the feeling away and took the offered rag. Using long, careful strokes, he rinsed the drying suds from her bent back. Even when there was no soapy residue remaining, Iain continued to swipe the rag across her skin. Her breathing changed subtly, matching his.

She straightened, lifting her chest from the water. The rag slipped from his fingers, but he continued to rub his palm lightly over her back. Her damp skin glistened. Unable to draw moisture to his mouth, Iain licked suddenly dry lips.

There was only one relief. He lifted the dripping mass of her hair and touched his lips to the birthing mark.

Lara relaxed into the glide of Iain's hand up and down her back. Abstract thoughts flitted across the heated haze in her mind. Was the fire burning through her veins able to reheat the cooling bath water?

The touch stopped, and Iain lifted his hand from her skin. Lara bit back a cry of despair. The damp ends of her hair tickled across her back and warm breath touched her neck.

Motionless with anticipation, she waited until firm, masculine lips pressed softly against the base of her neck. A jolt of startling electricity arched her back and drew a soft moan of pleasure from her lips.

Iain moved his lips slowly, gently along the top of her shoulder and paused to make intricate patterns on her skin with sharp teeth and soothing tongue. Trying to control the surges of feeling and desire, Lara gripped the edges of the tub until her knuckles turned white.

The kisses stopped, but Iain's lips remained close to her

shoulder. "What causes these pale stripes on yer skin?" The damp trail from his tongue traveled to the point of her shoulder blade and back again. "So sweet."

Stripes? She didn't have striped skin. Iain traced a slow line from her other shoulder and across her back with a finger. Her nervous giggle sounded loud in the quiet room. "Those are my tan lines. From my bathing suit."

Iain lay his cheek against her shoulder and spoke into her neck. "But ye wear no clothing now."

"No." She swallowed thickly. "For swimming."

"Oh, aye."

He stroked the tips of his fingers across her back as if fascinated by the paler skin. Lara forced herself to loosen her death grip on the tub but immediately regretted the freedom. It would be much too easy to turn slightly and capture his lips with hers. Too easy to beg him to trace the tan lines left by the front of her suit.

And much too easy to crawl from the cold water and make love to him then and there, consequences be damned. He had pulled away when she returned his earlier kisses. Did he think her a loose woman? The thought sobered her desire. What would he call her in this time? Searching through the haze in her mind Lara discovered the ancient word. Bizzem. Would he laugh behind her back and call her bizzem, a promiscuous woman? Lara bit at her lip. What should she do now? She really wanted this man, needed his glorious bare skin next to hers.

She closed her eyes and leaned back into Iain's support. With one of his hands splayed across her back he held her in place, while his kisses moved to the hollow at the base of her throat. Tiny sounds of pleasure moaned from her. She didn't care what he thought--what anyone thought.

Turning minutely, Lara ducked her head and kissed his cheek. Slight spasms of pressure from Iain's hand gave her the response she desired and she lifted her hands to cradle his face. Meeting his lips she tasted a hunger to match her own. Their tongues danced together, stroking, caressing and then retreating and chasing. She grew breathless and drew back.

Iain tasted of the salt of the sea, of wind and rain and the damp earth. Lara licked the flavor from her lips and smiled. He could become an addiction, a taste of which she would never grow tired. She reached for him again.

But Iain shook his head and stood, offering his hand to her. Taking his support, Lara struggled to rise, but the slippery bottom of the tub and her weak ankle made her pull heavily on his arm until she stood. Iain wrapped an arm under her knees and lifted her, dripping, from the tub.

Standing her carefully on the cool stone floor, Iain held her tight against him. The rough weave of his clothing drew the moisture from her skin. Lara snuggled against him, accepting the warmth of his arms. His shoulder lifted against her cheek.

"Lara, I dinna mean--"

Lara gasped at the feel of his lips moving against her fingertips when she covered his mouth to stop his speech. "It doesn't matter. Just kiss me, Iain. Please."

He wanted only to look at her, to learn each curve, to touch each inch of her. But her invitation burned through him, the feel of her fingers on his lips broke his tenuous hold on sanity.

Crushing her against him, he wound his fingers through her damp hair and tipped her head back. He wanted to be gentle, to slowly entice her to the heady level of passion he fought to control, but then her hands were angling his face down, her lips searching frantically for his.

He cupped her bare bottom to fit her to him. The breath caught in his throat when she pressed closer, trapping the length of his arousal. Her urgent movements and soft sounds of pleasure increased the pressure in his loins until he could not think--only react.

He took a careful step backward and then another. Lara followed his movements, not allowing an inch of space to cool the air between their bodies. When Iain felt the edge of the bed press against his calves he fell to his back and cradled her safely on top of him.

Sprawled against his chest, Lara rained kisses over his face while tugging at his shirt. The material wouldn't budge, so she moved reluctantly from his body and slid her hand under the loose tunic. The taut muscles of his stomach quivered at her touch and she smiled. A light smattering of hair cushioned her hand as it rose to stroke his chest. He felt as good as he tasted. Would she ever get her fill of him?

Lara glanced at the bulge straining the front of his trews. That would go a long way in filling her. Her eyes drifted closed. Yes. She'd waited a long time to feel this way. "Iain?"

After gently removing her hand from under his shirt, Iain stroked her shoulders until she relaxed onto her back. He scooted close, the firm muscles of his leg pressed against her thigh. Propping his head on one hand, he smiled down at her.

His eyes were dark, glistening and full of wonderful promises.

The flat of one palm covered her breast to stroke and knead gently. "Aye, my sweet one?" She had no words and only drew her bottom lip between her teeth. His palm rested on the tender underside of her breast and he circled the nipple with his thumb.

Pressure grew in her nipple and swirled through her. How could she be so aroused with just this touch? Her breathing grew rapid, and she fought to contain the wild sounds of pleasure he drew from her. Iain's thumb was relentless while he played soft rhythms with his fingers across her sensitive skin. She opened her eyes to meet the dark smoke of his gaze. A tiny smile graced his lips. He dipped his head and captured the other nipple in the heat of his mouth and drew firmly on the pebbled peak.

"I--oh!" Lara cried out as she exploded. The world twirled around her, centered on the pull of sensation at her nipples. Never had she...

Iain claimed her lips even before the soft echo of her joy faded and draped one leg possessively over her hip. Lara arched to him, eager for more.

A loud, insistent voice rose from the yard. Aching to deny the interruption, Lara tried to shake her head against Iain's kisses. The deep voice intruded again.

"Iain, where be ye? I need ye. Now."

Iain lifted his head. Silence greeted him, so he returned to nibble at Lara's neck.

Castan called again. "Iain!"

"Bluidy hell." Regret warred with passion in his face when Iain slid from Lara's side. His chest heaved with repressed desire. "He willna leave be until he finds me. He must no' find me here." After a deep breath, Iain leaned on one hand and hovered over Lara. He kissed her, a deep kiss that shook her to the tips of her toes.

Lara bit her lip to hold back her cry of denial when Iain slipped from the bed. He faced away from her, watching the door. "I dinna mean for this to happen. Now I dinna wish to leave ye."

"Iain, where the hell be ye?" The rising voice was closer; Castan had entered the house and was prowling the halls.

Iain turned back to Lara. She shivered with delight as his eyes roamed hungrily over her. "I must go, sweet one. I shall be with ye at the feast?" A pleading tone filled his voice, and Lara hurried to reassure him.

"Yes." She lowered her eyes as he spread a coverlet and tucked it securely around her. "And perhaps after?"

Hope lit Iain's face. "If ye so wish."

"Aye. How could you think otherwise?"

Iain only shook his head and backed away. "Until later, sweet one."

Tears of frustrated loneliness filled Lara's eyes when Iain shut the door behind him. There was such a feeling of finality. She shook away the morbid thought and curled under the coverlet. She licked her lips to taste the lingering essence of his kisses. A sigh filled her. It would be a long time until the feast.

•　•　•

"Ah, there ye be, coz." Iain rolled his eyes at Castantin's imperious tone. "I have been callin' fer ye."

"So I heard, Castan. The entire household has as well. What'd ye wish of me this time?"

Castan leaned back slightly, folded his arms across his wide chest and gave Iain an appraising look. Heavy brows drew together in confusion, but he shrugged and slapped Iain on the shoulder before turning to stride away.

Motioning over his shoulder, he urged Iain forward. "Come, then. First, I need yer help wi' the cooks. Then ye must tell me yer plans fer the plantin' again. Where were ye? Yer a fine mess, coz."

Iain jerked to a halt. Had he been unsuccessful in fully tamping down the evidence of his recent desire? Cautiously, he looked down and blew out a breath of relief. His hand met cool dampness when he pulled at the hem of his tunic. Dark splotches covered his chest and the front of his thighs.

When he touched one of the spots in confusion, his body responded quickly to the memory of Lara's body, wet and glistening from her bath, pressed against him.

Trying to focus on what the man was saying, Iain continued after Castan. Thankfully, Castan was too caught up in his own concerns to be overly curious. Iain knew his clothing would dry quickly and Castan would not remember to ask again. No harm was done.

No harm? His body ached, crying for release. Nay, no harm. But it couldn't happen again.

Aubrian stepped from a shadowed doorway and glared after Iain. Outside his door, servants had grumbled about carrying heavy buckets of hot water to the lady's chamber. The enjoyment of imagining Lara at her bath shattered. He had no doubt how Iain's clothing became wet. The press of Lara's body was evident upon the material.

A frown turned his lips down. The direct pursuit had failed, chasing his prey into another's arms. Aubrian stared into the empty hallway as an alternative plan coalesced. Appearing to lose interest, he would treat Lara with only cool respect, yet find a way to keep the usurper from her.

The celebration of Bealtaine drew near, the culmination on the night of the full moon. His hunt would end in consummation. The human stood no chance against his power.

Aubrian turned back to his room and smiled as he prepared for the evening's feast and the tale he would tell.

T rembling with unspent desire, Lara lay on the bed for long, lonely moments as she tried to will the need from her body. Then she stretched languorously and cuddled under the blanket Iain had so chivalrously tucked around her.

Turning to curl on one side, she grinned at the puddles glistening on the stone floor. Large splotches near the tub led to small, nearly dried spots next to the bed. The floral essence of soap lingered, mixing sensuously with the smell of earth Iain brought to her. Lara lifted her fingers to her face, imagined them tangled through Iain's hair and inhaled deeply, letting the essence of the man fill the last empty spaces in her being.

Why hadn't she met someone like him in her own time? How could he affect her so strongly and entice her with such a tantalizing combination of peace and immediacy? Her breast tingled and the nipple peaked against the soft wool blanket. How did he bring her to such an orgasm with just that one touch? How could she ever leave him now?

Lara sat and clutched the blanket to her chest. She needed to talk to her mother. A chill ran down her spine and back up to tingle at the back of her neck. It would be foolhardy to create a portal within the castle. Aubrian would know--and that would surely be a dangerous knowledge.

So, she would have to leave the castle and find a safe place for her to travel between time and worlds. The feeling of danger dissipated. A short visit with her mother would help her sort through her feelings. And what she needed to do about them. Maybe tomorrow her ankle would be better.

Lara held her foot into the air and slowly rotated the ankle. There was only a slight twinge, so she smiled and scooted to sit at the edge of the bed. Realizing her sprain would not heal if she continued to use it, she silently berated herself and slid back to rest against a thick bolster and snuggle under the cover.

After the previous night's disturbed sleep, it was not long before her eyelids drifted closed. Desire and need still tickled through her, so she held the feeling close and pictured Iain's strong features--his sharp nose, the sensuous fullness of his lips ripe from kissing her. And eyes, eyes that bared every emotion in his soul. A soft smile touched Lara's lips.

Beitris opened the door and peeked into the room. Wrapped in a woolen blanket, Lara slept crossways on the wide bed. The smile on the young woman's face brought an answering grin to stretch the old one's lips.

But, Lara was alone. Beitris' gaze flittered from the bed to look quickly around the room. A heavy sigh lifted her chest and she frowned in disappointment. However, when her gaze landed on the clothing lying in a rumpled heap on the floor the frown turned back into a tiny grin.

Beitris gave a soft "Tsk," moved into the room and bent painfully to pick up the dress and shake it out. She arranged the gown carefully on the end of the bed and smoothed the deep-blue material with practiced ease.

Stepping back from the bed, she cleared her throat. Lara rolled over but did not wake, so she called softly. "Mistress, 'tis time to wake."

"No, Mom. I don' wanna. Wanna stay with him."

Beitris chuckled. Lara's eyes popped open. She sat and looked around wildly.

"Oh, Beitris." Lara slumped against the pillows. "What a dream I was having." She took a deep breath, started to speak then paused, heat covering her cheeks.

Beitris thankfully ignored Lara's discomfort and pointed out the window. "The afternoon, 'tis far gone, m'lady Lara. Ye must prepare fer the feast. M'lord Castantin will be sore displeased if ye are no' there on time. He has little patience."

The heat rose to fill her face once again when she thought of how Castan's impatience had interrupted her earlier pleasure. She slid across the bed, wrapped the blanket around her and stood. "Will you help me?"

Suddenly self-conscious, she was sure the tingles from Iain's caresses were visible on her skin. The knowing glint in Beitris's eyes confirmed the fanciful notion. Blazing heat covered her chest as well as her face. The old woman turned away, but not before Lara caught the smile deepening the wrinkles of her cheeks. The servant straightened the bed coverings.

"I dinna doubt but Master Iain will be pleased to see ye as well."

Lara stole a quick glance around the room. The evidence of her sudden departure from the tub and damp trail to the bed were long dried. Did Beitris know Iain had already seen her? Touched her? Lara's lips trembled at the thought of his kisses. Her fingers lifted, but she caught herself before touching her mouth and glanced at Beitris.

"Sit ye by the fire and I shall dress yer hair." Lara sat obediently while Beitris tried to pull a thick-toothed wooden comb through the dried tangle of her curls. "Ye shouldna let yer hair dry before ye comb it out, dearie. I beg pardon fer the pullin'."

"That's okay, I'm used to it," Lara said absently and stared into the tiny fire Beitris had stirred from the embers. Some compulsion drew her to watch the flicker of the flames. There was a message there. She frowned. Why did she think there was a meaning to the flare of flames? And why couldn't she shake away that notion? This time, this journey to the past confused her, and she didn't like the feeling. If only she were able to understand.

Beitris smoothed Lara's hair to the top of her head and fastened it securely with combs she removed from a deep pocket. "Aye." She patted a curl into place. "Yer hair be the color of the golden flame. 'Tis a glory, m'lady Lara."

Startling Lara from the memory of Iain's desire-darkened eyes, a single long finger of flame burst through the smoky haze. When the flame curled around the edge of the fireplace to caress the soot-darkened stones, Lara shivered violently.

"Are ye chilled, Lara?"

"No, no. I'm fine." Lara hitched the blanket over her shoulders.

"Hmm, perhaps ye are, perhaps no'." Beitris hugged Lara's shoulders, lifted slightly and encouraged her to stand. "'Tis time to dress.

NINE

L ara took a deep breath, stretching the already tight material across her chest. She glanced down at the low neckline and high swell of her breasts and paused in the entryway to the great hall. Push-up bras had nothing on this dress. Iain's mother must have been an exceptional woman; just slipping on this gown made Lara feel beautiful.

A timid touch on her hand brought her attention to the boy at her side. The excitement filling Stephen's young face brought a broad smile to Lara's lips. "Are you ready, Stephen?"

"Aye, Lara, I mean, m'lady." His small body bounced, the energy recharging her. He took a better grip on her crutch and offered her his shoulder.

It was important to make her entrance without the use of the makeshift crutch, so Lara lay her hand on his shoulder and they stepped into the hall. Conversations ebbed while she made her awkward way across the room, stepping carefully to protect her ankle. She tried not to lean heavily on Stephen's shoulder, although the boy told her earlier he barely felt her weight.

Castantin lounged in a large chair set a step above the rest of the hall. Aubrian sat at his right, the place of an honored guest. Castantin rose, and the entire gathering followed his example.

Heat flushed across Lara's face as all eyes turned toward her in frank speculation. The hall was crowded with long trestle tables running the length of the room.

Wondering where all the people came from, she scanned the assemblage. Castan must have required the attendance of most of the tiny hamlet beyond the manor gates. Lara looked at the clothing, the foods, or the early medieval setting, but she knew she lied to herself. There was only one thing, one person she wanted to see in the crowded room. Her heart fell to the pit of her stomach. He wasn't there.

"Och, m'lady Lara. Ye have finally arrived." Castantin gestured toward her. "We have waited impatiently fer ye."

Lara was sure he was impatient, although his ruddy face told her he had been waiting with a mug in his hand. A smile she hoped was gracious flashed toward her host.

"I am sorry, my lord." Lara dropped a brief curtsey. Pleased at how she carried off the unaccustomed gesture with a tender ankle, she straightened and rested her hand on Stephen's shoulder.

"'Tis no matter." Castantin focused blurry eyes on Stephen. "Lad, bring the lady to sit at me side." Castantin relaxed back into his seat and turned his attention to Aubrian.

Stephen's gaze spoke the question as he cocked his head toward the dais. Lara gave him an answering smile and they stepped forward. As soon as Castantin no longer spoke to her, the rest of the gathering returned to their own conversations and quiet games of chance.

Lara sighed. Where was Iain? He said he would be with her at the feast. Had she misread another man's interest? Did he regret her easy acceptance of his touch and had moved on to another conquest? No, he didn't seem that kind of man, not with his innate honesty and honor. She glanced around the edges of the room. Where was Iain?

Tiny prickles covered the back of her neck and shoulders. Although he appeared focused on their host, Aubrian's glittering eyes followed her progress across the floor. Lara lifted her head regally and glared at him. Now that she knew what he was, she could fight whatever Faerie trick he attempted. A slight hitch in his eyebrow acknowledged her determination, and then he turned his gaze to the pattern Castantin was sketching with one finger on the tabletop.

"Mind the step, m'lady." Stephen's soft whisper intruded on Lara's thoughts. The boy held her hand while she stepped onto the dais, then indicated a bench next to Castantin's broad, heavy chair. The long folds of her skirt made it difficult to position herself so she could sink gratefully onto the bench. Stephen lay the crutch on the floor underneath and took two long steps back to stand with his hands clasped behind his back.

Castantin slapped his palms against the table. Lara jumped along with the pitchers and heavy mugs scattered along the tabletop. His loud voice boomed. "Now, we feast."

Firelight did not reach the shadow-filled recessed doorway. Shrouded in darkness, Iain ran his fingers through hair still damp from an icy swim. The long, dull afternoon with Castan had done nothing to quench the desire burning through him, so he had taken to the sea for the second time in as many days.

Iain eyed the empty space on the bench next to Lara. How would he make it through the meal at her side, sharing a trencher, making conversation--and not touching her? He did not dare even let his hand brush against hers as they ate. If only his resolve was as stiff as his body's traitorous reaction to the mere thought of her.

Castantin glanced toward the doorway. His brows drew together and lowered over his eyes. Impatient anger simmered in the gaze, and Iain could delay joining the feast no longer. Facing Castan's wrath was more than he cared to deal with at the end of this trying day.

He gave a slight tug to the hem of his jerkin, took a deep breath and stepped into the great hall. Only slightly more at ease, he wondered if he should have adopted Castan's more formal dress, wearing an overtunic that fell to his knees.

Arranging his face into lines reflecting a calm he did not feel,

Iain crossed to the dais and bowed formally to Castantin. The laird's eyes glittered happily before he waved one bejeweled hand toward the seat next to Lara and returned to his conversation with Aubrian.

The smile Lara welcomed him with as he carefully lowered himself to the bench burned through Iain. But it was nothing when compared to the fire from the gentle touch of her hand on his arm in greeting. Sitting next to Lara through the elaborate meal would not be as torturous as he imagined. It would be worse.

Stephen hovered behind Lara, serving her when the platters were offered, refreshing her mug of water before she asked. Iain flashed a grateful smile at the boy when he turned to serve him as well.

The boisterous talk around the room covered the fact they sat in silence. Iain often felt Lara's questioning gaze on him, but refused to return the look.

Finally the meal was nearly over. Enthusiastic applause broke out when the cooks presented an elaborate subtlety shaped like the manor house. The servings of thick slices of pastry dripping with honey lacked any appeal to Iain. There was another dessert he craved, but he forced himself to deny the desire.

Lara turned to him, took a deep breath and spoke. "You spent the afternoon with Castantin?"

"Aye. He had many duties fer me."

"What did you do?"

"Nothin' important."

Lara frowned at him and picked at her pastry. Guessing from the bright pink covering Lara's cheeks, he hoped she also craved a different sustenance. His heart leapt and thick desire pulsed through his veins. Ruthless, he squelched the feeling.

Lara's soft voice lingered between them as she asked question after question, speaking quickly in the silences left when he did not answer. Her lips turned down and hurt filled the violet depths of her eyes, the brown swirls darkened to the color of damp earth.

The realization he caused her pain lanced through him and

brought a short gasp to his lips. Concern covered the hurt in her expression, and she lay her trembling hand on his arm.

"Iain?"

Intelligent conversation was impossible, and he could not grit his teeth hard enough to force the rampant desire from his veins. All he wanted was to pull the magnificent woman into his arms and rain kisses over her face until she begged him to...

"My lord Castantin," Aubrian's voice carried easily to the far corners of the hall, "I feel a tale within me that must needs be told."

Iain glanced at the storyteller. To others it would appear he waited for Castantin's response, but his concentrated gaze flickered between Lara and Iain. The soft hairs at the back of Iain's neck bristled.

Castan put his hand on Aubrian's shoulder. "No' yet, Seanachai Aubrian. I feel generous this night. I would bestow a gift."

Low murmurs of speculation raced around the hall. Castantin stood and let his gaze travel the room slowly, lingering here and there on a hopeful face. Finally, he turned to where Stephen stood sleepily behind Lara.

"Come here, lad."

Iain's breath caught as Stephen moved next to the wide chair and bowed low from the waist. He held the breath a moment longer until Castan ruffled the boy's hair and smiled broadly.

"Ye have served our guest, the lady Lara well."

Stephen nodded, cast a quick glance back at Lara and bit his lower lip before dropping his gaze to the floor. Castan lifted the boy's chin with one finger and then pointed to a corner of the hall where his favorite hunting dog lay surrounded by her recent litter.

"Ye like the dogs, boy?"

Stephen's eyes sparkled. "Aye, m'lord Castantin."

"Guid. Chose the one ye wish, lad. Train it well."

Castan gave the open-mouthed boy a shove toward the puppies and lifted one hand to the gathering. "Let it be known, the lad Stephen has me favor this night." He waved a grandiose signal to waiting servants. "Now, refill the vessels of all with the best of me brew before the tellin' of tales begins."

Intent on Stephen, the touch of Lara's soft body against his arm startled Iain. Her hand on his shoulder kept him rooted next to her. Hesitant, he turned his head toward her and followed her gaze. Stephen lifted the smallest puppy in his arms and sank to the floor, surrounded by squirming black animals.

Lara leaned closer to whisper in his ear. "That was nice of Castan." The imprint of her breast against his back heated his skin through the heavy fabric of the jerkin.

"Aye. He should acknowledge the boy."

"I don't understand."

"The lad is Castan's by-blow."

Lara folded her hands in her lap and glanced at her fingers. "Do you mean Castan is his father?"

"Aye."

"Does Stephen know?"

"I dinna think so." The excited rise of conversation ebbed so Iain lowered his voice and angled his body to lean his head toward Lara. "Beitris keeps the fact from him."

Castantin slapped his hand twice against the tabletop. "Och, the lad has chosen." He turned toward Aubrian and stretching his legs under the table, leaned back in his chair. He lifted a large mug in salute. "Now, teller of tales. Entertain us."

Aubrian arranged his tunic and stood. "Aye." His eyes narrowed as he bowed. "My lord." Then he straightened, adjusted his clothing once again and turned to face the people waiting anxiously for a new tale. Pausing as if in contemplation, he glanced sideways at Castantin.

"I had thought to tell a tale of daring deeds and heroic battles." A slight, self-satisfied smile formed on his lips. "But the telling of no tale could match the strength and bravery of m'lord Castantin."

A roar of laughter erupted from Castan and he puffed out his chest. "Well said, friend storyteller. Perhaps ye'll be tellin' me story in another, less magnificent holdin'."

Aubrian canted his head in thought. "Perhaps. It would be a tale interesting for any lesser man." The gathered people added their laughter to Castan's. Aubrian's smile grew broad.

"I will not tell a tale of great deeds in battle." Aubrian walked slowly to the center of the hall, turning as he spoke to hold the gaze of each avid listener. "I shall tell you a tale of the deeds of love."

A soft sigh followed the dying laughter around the room. Aubrian sat cross-legged on the floor. "Aye, a tale of true love and of love mistaken. A tale of love enough to last through a night of interference by the fey of the fairy otherworld."

Only part of Lara's mind listened to the beginning of Aubrian's tale, dimly measuring the rapt silence filling the room at each dramatic pause. In that silence, she listened to the rapid pounding of her heart and the heavy rasp of her breath. Iain's knee brushed against her leg, sending a jolt of lightning coursing through her veins.

A glance sideways confirmed Iain's shared discomfort. His eyes were tightly squeezed shut and a deep red flush filled his face. The color spread down his neck to fill the wide circular neckline of his jerkin. Lara licked her lips, eyeing the firm planes of Iain's pectoral muscles. So, she wasn't the only one affected. Lara both wished they were alone and blessed the presence of those gathered for the feast. She longed, ached desperately for a repeat of the powerful desires of that afternoon.

Stephen sat on the floor behind her, a black, wiggling burden securely in his lap. Lara turned her head to smile at the boy and searched his face for evidence of Castan. She found none, but paused at the happy sparkle in his young eyes. The sense of the familiar filled her again.

"Fetch me that flower, the herb I showed ye once. The juice of it on sleeping eyelid laid will make man or woman madly dote upon the next living creature..."

Lara glanced around the hall as Aubrian's words registered.

She knew this tale--it was one of her father's favorites. She lowered her head and grinned at the memory of her family gathered around the television or trooping to the theater each time there was a production of *A Midsummer Night's Dream.*

Her eyes narrowed. Years after memorizing the play to surprise her father, she still remembered every speech, every nuance of Shakespeare's creation. Aubrian's words were slightly different, but the cadence and meaning were exact.

How would Aubrian know this tale, practically word for word, a play that wouldn't be written for centuries yet? Of course, Shakespeare could have simply retold an older tale. But the rhythm of the words and the Elizabethan language puzzled her.

Iain's arm brushed against hers as he reached for a pitcher. Biting her lip kept her from sighing at the pleasure that surged through her. Somehow, she resisted leaning into his arms. The tale of Shakespeare's lovers was lost as her own desire swept her into a haze of fantasy.

"Tomorrow, good listeners, I shall tell you another song of love. A very fine piece I assure you, the most lamentable comedy and most cruel death of Thisby and Pyramus."

Silence hung in the hall a few moments as Aubrian sat quietly. He rose in one fluid motion and bowed to Castantin, to the assembly and to Castantin once more. After Castantin's pleased nod, excited shouts of congratulations echoed through the room. Bits of Aubrian's tale were repeated as servants refilled mugs.

"Well told, Seanachai Aubrian. Ye be honored in me holdin'. If yer next tale be as fine..." Castan left the words hanging.

Aubrian inclined his head in gracious acceptance. "If you will excuse me, m'lord. I am fatigued. The telling of tales is tiring work."

A flash of regret passed over Castantin's face, but a hearty belch brought the return of his jovial nature. "I waudna wish to spoil yer next tale with yer exhaustion. Off wi' ye, then, Seanachai." Castan waved his arms broadly. "To the gamin', me friends."

A quick glance from under her lashes showed Aubrian's back

as he left the hall. Lara took a deep breath; relief at the fey story-teller's exit filled her. Now, she could focus on Iain without feeling the intensity of Aubrian's gaze. Lara cared little for games of skill and chance and hoped they held little interest for Iain as well. Heat filled her cheeks as she turned toward him.

"I'm ready to leave." Interest flared in Iain's dark eyes but was soon gone, leaving his face blank. Concerned at his lack of expression, Lara angled closer and touched his hand. Iain jerked away as if burned.

"I canna leave yet."

"Why?"

"'Tis my duty to stay until dismissed by the MacDhuibh."

"That's silly." Lara sat back. "Do I have to stay?"

"Ah, ye dinna need stay. 'Tis time fer the men." Iain flushed slightly. "An' a few women. Ye waudna find it..." Bright red infused his tanned face.

Lara felt her eyes grow wide and she giggled. "Oh, is there someone special you wait for?" Keeping a teasing note in her voice was difficult, fear of an affirmative answer gnawed at her belly.

The flare returned to his eyes, desire haunting the depths. "No one."

"Oh."

Iain's gaze traveled over her before angling to a far corner of the room. "Ye should retire. Yer ankle needs restin'."

"Oh." Despite the heat of his gaze, the words settled like a frigid breath between them. Lara bit her lip. Had she made a mistake? Did her actions earlier brand her the kind of woman who hung around after the feast? Although words of invitation hovered on her lips she would not speak them. She was in no mood to humiliate herself.

"I'll go to bed then." Lara glanced at Castan who hovered over the toss of large dice. "Will you give my regrets to Castantin, if he notices I'm gone?"

"Aye. Rest well, m'lady."

I doubt it. Lara tapped Stephen's shoulder to draw his attention from the black ball of fur in his lap. "I'm ready to go, Stephen. Will you help me to my room?"

The boy nodded, rose and carried his puppy back to its mother. After rubbing behind the short ears, he returned and bowed. "As ye wish, m'lady." A wide yawn split his face.

Iain ruffled the boy's hair. "Get yerself to bed, boy. Ye'll need energy to keep up with that hound on the morrow. G'even to ye as well, m'lady Lara." He turned to gaze into the mug clenched between his hands.

Awkward because her ankle had stiffened during the feast, Lara lurched to her feet. Grateful for the support of both the crutch and Stephen's bony shoulder, she hobbled from the hall. Each step brought the sting of fresh tears to her eyes. Iain didn't want her; she'd made a total fool of herself. She sniffed back the tears and entered her room. After bidding Stephen good night she fell into the bed, clutched a rough blanket to her chest and let one tear escape.

Blotting the wetness with the blanket, Lara took a deep breath. *No tears, girl, it's not worth it.* Her mother's helpful concern filled her thoughts and she knew she would return to her time in the morning.

CHAPTER

TEN

Watching the gentle swirl of the dregs, Iain stared into his mug. Although filled with the rousing cries of gaming and song, the hall felt cold and empty. He closed his eyes against Castan's attempts at ribald humor, and then simply grinned at his cousin in the expectant silence. Tonight the tall tales and bragging grated on his ears.

He wished for the calm, low tones of Lara's voice and a repeat of the soft cries of pleasure that had filled his ears that afternoon. It was not to be, it could not be. Not with his uncertain future.

Did he even have a future?

Lack of true birthright burned through him like never before. He'd spent an idyllic childhood, free of the added responsibilities of learning to govern. He realized now how many of the games his father taught him honed skills usable should he ever lead men.

But such leadership would never happen. Castan had firmly ensconced himself in the manor and relished lording over the land and its people. Sending Iain away further solidified his rule. Iain understood the reasoning and had accepted it. Until now.

Now, he wished for land of his own. Not a wide holding such as under Castan's heavy hand, but a place of his own. Land he could be proud of. A home where he could raise a family, secure in the love of a wife and children.

Iain sighed deeply and set the mug on the table with a heavy thud. The painful lurch in his chest and the tightness of his breathing as he thought of Lara as that wife and the mother of his children added to his misery. Soft golden hair filled his vision when he closed his eyes in defeat.

Lara. As a younger man, he'd a fair sampling of women, but none filled him as she did, encompassing his very being with light and hope.

The thoughts circled back to his reality. He could not have Lara or offer her a place at his side. Better to avoid the woman and hurt her now before he was forced to leave her.

But at what cost to himself? After only two days, precious memories were stored away, enough, he hoped, to last his lifetime. Memories of the touch of her hand, her smile, the burn of her kisses, the feel of her taut nipple pressed against the palm of his hand.

Taut. The thought brought his body to rigid life to strain against his clothing. He shifted uncomfortably. How could he imagine two days of brief encounters and shattered opportunities to be enough? As desire pooled low in his body he knew those memories would never be enough. If a mortal blow pierced him at this moment it would never be enough.

Slamming his hands against the table, Iain jerked to his feet. Conversations and laughter fell silent as the heat of every drunken gaze in the hall turned toward him. Facing his cousin and schooling his expression to neutrality, Iain jerked in a short bow. Castan's bulk lolled in his chair, leaning drunkenly toward the storyteller. Iain frowned. When had the Seanachai returned? The man's smug smile chilled Iain's overheated body.

"M'lord, I would retire."

Castan leaned to the other side of his chair. His head wobbled on his thick neck as he tried to focus on Iain. "Eh?"

"I am retiring, M'lord Castantin." Iain used solemn formality to cover his disgust.

"Och, so early, coz? Ah, well." Castantin waved one hand in a failed regal gesture and turned back to the dice on the table. Finding no interest in the activities of the old laird's son, the gathering returned to songs and gaming, leaving Iain's departure unnoted.

The hairs on his arms lifted and a rare tingling caressed the back of Iain's neck. After he reached the small doorway leading to the family chambers he angled his upper body to look behind him. The intense gaze of the storyteller met his.

Aubrian stared at him over Castan's shoulder. A speculative glint in the frosty blue eyes disappeared when Iain turned to fully face him. Aubrian lifted an eyebrow and tilted one side of his mouth into a smile that sent cold shivers skittering down Iain's spine.

With the barest dip of his head, Iain accepted the unspoken challenge.

Dark halls stretched before Iain as he prowled the manor. He paused at each open window to gauge the slow movement of the stars across the deep night sky. One hallway he studiously avoided, knowing even rushing past her door would shatter his foolish decision to avoid Lara. There could be no repeat of the afternoon. He would not compromise her.

But Lara's essence floated through the halls, a siren's call luring him to forgetfulness. With her he could forget the destiny others had forged for him. Forget his questioning. Forget everything--but her.

Heavy footsteps took him to the gardens and past the thorn-covered archway leading to his mother's sanctuary. Cocooned in the safety of her private world, he sank to his knees on the damp, night-cooled earth and lifted his face to the night sky.

The spiritual force of the moon pulled at him nearly as strongly as the remembered passion of Lara's body. Rising from the earth like the shimmer of midsummer heat, the low voices of the ancient gods thrummed around him. But intense concentration brought him no closer to understanding the faint whispers.

The slow filling of the moon brought a sigh to his lips. The swift passage of a few days would bring Bealtaine, one of his mother's favorite festivals. Her deep-rooted beliefs in the old gods had come with her from her home across the sea. These beliefs sustained her through long years of slavery, until she captured the heart of his father. Iain had grown to manhood under those beliefs, the Christian god hiding in far-flung monasteries and the hovels of the anchorites.

An elderly woman had guarded his mother and their beliefs from zealous priests. That same woman had approached him before the feast to seek his participation in this year's rites.

In past years Iain had considered acting the role of the horned one, providing planting magic with one of the willing young women presented for his, and the god's, pleasure. Dark eyebrows lowered and a tiny frown touched his lips at the memory. In his younger years he did not feel the strength of belief he considered important to performing the rite. Evidently, the ones chosen held those beliefs, for the planting and harvests over the past years had been bountiful. The chosen maid often gave birth to a lusty bairn as well. And each year, Iain gave thanks he did not father a by-blow whose standing within the family and holding would be even less than his own.

He had gently refused the honor again this year. The lack of belief ripped at his belly, churning like the twist of an opponent's knife. Why could he not act, simply live without belief? Why could he not take the moment's pleasure and ensure continued abundant harvests? One thing he knew with all his heart was that he would be unable to lay with any woman but the beautiful golden-haired visitor. The crone had given him a strange look before a sly a smile lit her dark, rheumy eyes and she turned away.

Fighting the temptation of the renewed thoughts of Lara, Iain wondered briefly who would be chosen to portray the horned one. He shrugged that thought away as well.

The emptiness of his life burned like a lump in the pit of his being. How could his mother have believed so strongly when he could find nothing to believe in?

A vision of golden fire formed behind his closed eyes. Long, bright flames curved and undulated sensuously against a night sky. From the center of the hot swirl rose a mist. The fingers of flame molded the mist to an achingly familiar female form. Arms lifted, beckoning him, drawing him into the vision, calling him into Lara's arms.

A violent shake of his head shattered the vision into a shower of golden sparks. He would not think of her, would not allow the savory dream of her body wrapped around his. If only he could...

Iain stood, movements stiff and jerky. Deep, unheard voices whispered after him when he turned toward the house. Pausing with one hand resting against a thick wooden doorframe, he stared toward the eastern horizon. Pale tints of color touched the shadowed edge of the dark sea.

Resolution firmed Iain's jaw. It was better to believe in nothing at all.

ELEVEN

F inding her way out of the large house the next morning
alone proved more difficult than Lara imagined.
Stephen slept curled under a thick blanket in front of
her door. Stepping over the softly snoring boy was easy enough,
but she forgot the length of dress trailing at her feet. The small
dog clutched in Stephen's arms gave a startled yelp when the
material flowed over its head. As she knelt to quiet the animal,
Stephen's eyes eased open.

"M'lady?"

"Hush, Stephen," Lara touched her finger to her lips, "I'm just
off for a short walk. You go back to sleep."

Struggling to sit, he rubbed sleep from his eyes while still
holding onto the wriggling puppy. Stephen frowned. "Ye must no'
go by yerself, Lara. I shall go wi' ye."

Lara pushed gently on his shoulder and then rubbed behind
the puppy's ears. "No, I'll be fine. You stay here. No arguments,
now," she added when Stephen opened his mouth to speak.

"But, m'lady, 'tis me duty."

"And one you carry out very well. I merely need a little time
alone. I won't be long. Promise me you'll be here when I return."

"Oh, aye, m'lady." A relieved grin showed the gap from a half-grown front tooth. His eyes closed as he lay back and cuddled the dog to his chest.

"Sleep well, Stephen. Watch over him, little dog." Lara patted the puppy's dark, furry head.

Hobbling as quickly as she could through the halls, Lara held her breath at every sound and imagined footstep. Loud snores rang from the rooms she remembered were Castan's. She doubted he would stir until well into the morning. Silence echoed from Aubrian's chambers. She fervently wished he slept soundly as well.

Deciding to head away from the sea, Lara inched her way past the early morning noise of the kitchen to exit through a small rear entryway. She froze when Beitris's disgruntled mumbles echoed down the hall. A quick search led her to a narrow alcove. She had barely squeezed into the dark recess when Beitris rushed by, arms laden with piles of pale cloth.

When she was finally able to slip from the building Lara was exhausted. She struggled on, placing the crutch carefully before each step. The wooded area was farther than it appeared from her window, and her breath came in ragged bursts long before she reached the shelter of the trees.

Limping into a small glade she glanced behind her with a sigh of relief. No one had followed from the manor. She canted her eyes toward the sky; the sun barely peeked over the tops of the low-growing trees. If she decided to return to this confusing time... Of course, she would return, if only to satisfy her curiosity about the fey storyteller. She shook her head back and forth, nearly unbalancing herself. The real reason she'd return was the dark, enigmatic Iain. A deep breath pressed her breasts against the tight bodice of her dress, bringing physical memories of his touch. Yes, that would be why she'd return.

Lara wondered briefly if she should leave the borrowed clothing. Unsure if her aunt's disguise spell would work if she had no clothing to start with, Lara thought returning home nude might not be such a good idea. A tiny smile touched her lips as she imagined the outrage of the men in her family. Better not to temp fate.

A soft scrabbling sounded in the brush beside her, jerking her attention to the dim undergrowth. Had she been followed after all? The noises were not repeated; and after a few, long seconds, she slowly released her breath. Just a small animal, she hoped.

After a few more deep breaths Lara felt ready to call for a portal. Her hands lifted while she spoke softly, the words barely passing her lips in soft puffs of air. Shimmering grew from a tiny pinpoint until it was large enough for her to step through. With one final look around the glade she passed into the Otherworld.

The portal snicked closed with a shuddering finality. Aubrian waited a few moments before he stood and brushed leaves and small sticks from his clothing. Eyes narrowed, he stared at the spot where Lara disappeared. Anger simmered, heating his chest until it burst forth in a primal scream of rage.

He'd been so close. The bitch closed the portal too quickly, there had been no time for him to follow. Had he not snapped a twig with a misstep, he could have moved closer.

Panting, he spun in a circle, hands grasping, trying to capture the last vestiges of power lingering in the cool morning air. His shoulders slumped in defeat, his fists clenched and anger surged through him again. She would pay for denying him the chance to return. Aubrian stumbled to the edge of the clearing and sat with his back against the rough bark of a gnarled tree.

A smile burst across his face. She would return; he felt it deep within his bones. Her human lusts would bring her back to the dark human's side. Then he, Aubrian, would have her. And he would use her, tame her wildness, bind her to his will. Faerie hounds be damned.

Aubrian glanced at the slow movement of the sun. Lara had marked the placement of the sun as well--she would return soon. A sharp nod accompanied his thoughts. He would wait, hidden in the brush, until she returned. Sultry contemplation quickened his breath; perhaps he would not demand a portal immediately.

Heat swirled low in his abdomen and his body grew tight. Pleasure first. Many years had passed since his banishment; so a few days of earthly satisfaction before he returned to his rightful place would be of no consequence. The violet-eyed wench would serve him well.

Aubrian crawled through the underbrush to settle comfortably in a darkened hollow. No matter the length of the wait, he would be patient.

L ara stumbled into the clearing before her grandfather's cottage. The air was still and quiet; only a tiny puff of air lifted the curls away from her face. Glad the entire family appeared to be elsewhere, she sat on the low bench by the door, propped her foot on a thick slab of wood and shoved her crutch to one side. Eyes closed, she leaned back against the rough wall. She needed to feel the reality of her home, her world. But the present already seemed empty.

How could she possibly feel so strongly for a man she'd barely met? How could the mere brush of his hand against her bring her to such joy? Could she imagine never feeling that again? Did she even want to imagine it? Why couldn't she stop these questions?

A whuff of hot air filled her face shortly before a large slobbery tongue swiped a path across her cheek.

"Noid." Lara grabbed the large dog and pulled him into a fierce hug. Burying her face in his thick fur, she let her questions fade.

The dog stepped back and sniffed at the hem of her dress then gave intense attention to her fingers. He sat, head cocked quizzically to one side, and stared at her. Then the shaggy head tipped to the other side. What questions would the animal ask if he could speak? Lara was saved from further introspection by the arrival of her grandparents.

"Grandaughter." Stephen lifted Lara to her feet and engulfed her in a hug every bit as tight at the one she had given Noid. He released her and stepped back a pace, still holding her shoulders. "You have been long ago, have you not?"

Lara nodded, then turned to her grandmother's embrace. "Very long ago, Granda. Back to the ninth century." She returned to her seat on the bench and looked out past the edge of the clearing. "Will Mom be here today?"

"Aye. And your da, too."

Lara turned to the sound of her father's deep voice. Kelene tugged on Stephen's arm and led him into their home. Jaye glanced after them with a slight frown, then smiled at Lara.

"Lara, darlin', I'm glad you're here." Jaye dropped a quick kiss on her cheek. "I need to talk business with you. Walk with me to the Queen's pavilion?"

"Love to, Dad, but I've twisted my ankle and walked too far on it already." Lara gasped as Jaye quickly knelt in front of her and gently lifted her foot. After unwrapping the tight linen binding he prodded the ankle, then closed his eyes in concentration.

"Nice dress," he commented when he opened his eyes and lowered her foot. "Been traveling?"

Flexing her ankle, Lara nodded. A quick glance down confirmed Dad had completely healed her. Secretly she would miss the special care Iain gave her injury. "I wanted to talk to you, too."

Jaye sat beside her and gazed toward the edge of the clearing where Noid romped, chasing butterflies. "Shoot."

Not knowing how to start, Lara took a deep breath and the words rushed from her mouth. "Dad, I need to take some time off."

Complete silence met her statement, so she looked sideways at Jaye. He stared at her, mouth agape. "You? Want time off? Darlin', you're more of a workaholic than I ever was."

"I know, Dad. But I found an interesting time and I'd like to study it further."

Speculation filled Jaye's dark eyes. "Research, huh?" Lara felt heat rise to her face, becoming more intense, and she knew a bright pink blush followed.

Jaye leaned back against the wall and stacked his hands behind his head. Lara glanced at his strong profile, so much like her grandfather's. Another resemblance hovered at the edges of her memory, and then was gone.

"Well, Lara, business is uneventful." With one lifted eyebrow, he looked sideways at her. "Calm right now, nothing Tommy and I can't handle. Take as much time as you'd like." He held up one hand. "Just let me know when you are."

Rebellion rose in her chest, replacing the heat of her blush. She wasn't a child any longer and was fully in control of the portal when she traveled. Nodding meekly she hid her thoughts and knew she'd slip away without telling her parents how long ago she traveled.

Confusion touched her briefly. She'd never been reluctant to share details of her travels. Why did she feel this strange need, this compulsion to keep silent about this past?

Allyn entered the clearing, and Lara smiled at her mother. Jaye rose and held his wife in a tight embrace. The faint blue sparkles surrounding her parents drew a deep longing from the center of Lara's chest. Would she ever find a relationship even close to the soul-fulfilling love between her parents?

Jaye leaned close to Allyn's ear but spoke loudly, cocking his head toward Lara. "She wants to take time off." He backed away, one hand held dramatically over his heart.

After testing her ankle, Lara stood, reached over and slapped her father playfully on the arm. "You've been around Uncle Tommy too long, Dad." Reluctance wrapped around her, prompting her to hold the secret of Iain even closer. Now was not the time to share him with anyone. The faint concern over her hidden emotions blew away on the light breeze.

She took a long breath, and then kissed Jaye's cheek. "Thanks for the time off, Dad. I've got to get going so I don't lose track of when I came back. There're a couple of things I need from home."

Speculation tinged the violet depths of her mother's eyes after Lara kissed her cheek as well. Allyn smiled gently at Lara. "We'll talk soon, then?"

Feeling she had been caught in a guilty lie, Lara glanced quickly at her mother from under partially lowered eyelids. "Of course, Mom. I don't plan on being away too long." *At least, I don't think so.*

Jaye's deep voice followed her as she headed toward the permanent portal leading to her home in the mortal world. "She'll be fine, love."

"Yes, I know she will."

The prickle of her parent's eyes on her back followed her across the clearing. Lara tried to shrug away the tingles and the guilt. Just the simple omission of not telling them when she was going branded her a liar. It burned between her shoulder blades.

She spent only a few minutes at home. She grabbed a favorite length of plaid to help ward off the manor's chill and a small woven bag. Dumping a few carefully prepared essentials into the bag, she spared a thought to the usual concerns about taking bits of her time into the past. But the tiny clay pot of toothpaste and the pain relievers sewn into the bag's seams had never been discovered or caused problems before.

The lure of her chocolate drawer drew her into the kitchen. A few loose pieces of candy fit perfectly in her palm, but didn't stay there long. Letting the creamy sweetness melt on her tongue, Lara shrugged and tossed a full bag of foil-wrapped comfort into the woven pouch. She'd be extra careful to keep the bag hidden or in her possession.

Quick steps took her back to Faerie. Skirting her grandparent's clearing, Lara made her way to her favorite glade. Her pulse quickened--soon she would return to the past, to Iain.

A quiver fluttered low in her belly and her breasts tingled. Iain made her feel so much, made her burn for more with just the touch of his hand and the brush of his thumb across her nipple. There was no comparison to the fumbling attempts at seduction she'd experienced before.

Younger, she'd been desperate for love, aching to find the all-encompassing passions of her parent's love. The few times she'd hoped she found that fire and succumbed to clumsy seductions had been emotionally painful and disappointing. The completeness she hungered for eluded her each time, leaving her even lonelier.

Would it be the same with Iain? Being honest with herself, she knew she would pursue a physical relationship; she would cross time to be with him.

Lara shook herself. Such behavior was not like her, not in her normal responsible world. She popped another piece of chocolate into her mouth. Perhaps it was time for a change.

The ringing sounds of steel against steel rose from her glade. A tiny frown wrinkled her forehead. She had no wish to talk to anyone, only wanting to return to that secluded highland manor. Pausing under a shadowy overhang, her frown turned to a loving grin. Her brother faced Derrik, a long sword held loosely at ready.

Derrik lifted a long-fingered hand. "Hold, Jayse. Yer sister is here."

Jayse lifted his sword in salute, then turned a brilliant smile toward Lara and wiped a hand over his sweaty face. "Sis, I've been hoping to see you."

Lara's grin froze as she tried to restrain her impatience and moved into the glade. "Glad to see you both, too. Need something in particular?"

"Naw, just wanted to talk. I've got some historical questions."

A wicked smile touched Derrik's lips before he sheathed his sword. He handed Jayse a thick leather scabbard and gave a short bow. "I will leave ye to yer talkin' then."

"Thanks for the training, Derrik," Jayse called after the wide, retreating back. An over-the-shoulder wave was the reply.

Jayse carefully wiped his blade with a soft cloth before he returned the weapon to the scabbard. After wadding the cloth into a tight ball he struggled to stuff it into the hip pocket of his jeans. With a sweep of one hand, he led Lara to the soft mounds of grass at one side of the clearing and yanked her down beside him. He cast a quick dispassionate glance at her low-cut bodice. "Nice dress."

Lara giggled. "You sound just like Daddy. I've got to look the part when I travel." She settled comfortably in the grass; conversations with her brother were never short as he struggled for accuracy in his love of historical re-creation. "So, how can I help you this time?"

Derrik's long strides took him past an alcove off the Queen's main audience chamber. A quiet word stopped his progress, and he turned slowly toward Jaye.

"There are strange happenings, Defender."

"Aye."

"I have one of those proverbial bad feelings. Lara is traveling to a time she won't disclose."

"Yer daughter is a woman grown. Dinna worry." Derrik laid a hand on Jaye's arm.

"Normally, I wouldn't, but for this feeling. I can't shake it." Jaye ran his hands through his hair, then scrubbed them over his face. "The feeling reminds me of the dreams I had before I found Faerie."

Derrik's eyebrows lifted, a swirl of worry filled his eyes. "Have ye had dreams?"

"No, just this gut feeling. I don't know if my concern really centers around Lara, but something..."

Derrik thought a moment, and then nodded. "It is well within me duties as Alastriona to protect the portals. To protect, I must ken. I will return to ye when I assure Lara's safety."

A brief nod and grateful smile sent Derrik back to Lara's glade, a tremor of apprehension added to the tension building across his shoulders.

Aubrian roused immediately from his meditation at the faint zing of approaching magic. He stretched, unknotting tight muscles, and glanced through the overhang of branches. The morning was far gone but, even so, he was somewhat surprised at Lara's quick return. The remembered scent of her passion surrounded him. It was irritating, but not surprising she returned to the human.

Rising to a crouch Aubrian carefully parted the bushes and peered into the sun-dappled open area. A faint shimmer signaled an opening portal. Eager, he leaned forward, anticipation quivering his muscles. He reaffirmed that his decision to delay his return to Faerie until he had Lara's cooperation--he smiled--was the correct action. He would complete the hunt.

The portal glittered open and Lara stepped through. There. She was nearly clear of the shimmer. Aubrian took a slow breath, held, then released it with a soft whoosh as he stood.

And immediately sank back into hiding, belatedly raising mental shields to protect him from discovery by other magic-wielders.

"Alastriona." Bitterness forced the word hissing through taut lips. Aubrian's eyes narrowed when the tall warrior stepped through the portal a few moments after Lara. The Defender glanced around, and then touched Lara on the shoulder. She whirled on him, hands raised in defense.

"My God, Derrik. Don't do that." Her eyes narrowed suspiciously. "What are you doing here?"

"Yer da asked ye to tell him when ye were goin'. Did ye do so?"

Lara's shoulders drooped and she hung her head, but pleading defiance filled her eyes when she lifted her gaze to the Defender. Aubrian licked his lips hungrily. "If you're here, then you know I didn't. Don't tell them, please."

The suspicion slipped to Derrik's eyes. "An' why would ye wish this?"

Aubrian smiled at her submission; soon he would taste that submission for himself. The powerful heat of the hunt returned. "I--I don't know." Lara turned from Derrik and took a fortifying breath. "I'm an adult. I don't need you chasing after me like you did when I was four."

"Aye, ye can take care of yerself. But that dinna mean yer parents can stop worryin'."

"I'll be fine, tell them that. But, keep this time to yourself. Please."

Aubrian relaxed. The implanted suggestion to keep Faerie from discovering him through her remained in place. Perhaps now he could persuade her to take him through the portal to the exact time he desired. He held in a pleased chuckle--events had turned remarkably to his advantage.

"I will keep yer secret--this time." Concerned reluctance filled his eyes before Derrik shook his head. "Allyn will be displeased."

Jerked from his pleasant contemplation of revenge, Aubrian barely withheld a gasp. He crouched lower as Derrik's intense gaze skittered over his hiding place. Allyn?

"I know, but Mom and Dad will just have to get over it."

Lara? The witch's spawn? Small wonder he was drawn to her. Containing sudden joy was difficult; his advantage, and his revenge, grew in proportion to this new discovery. He would find the pleasure denied him by the mother with the daughter. Then return to Faerie and take the mother as well. The man here and the usurper in Faerie would pay dearly for his years of banishment.

The anticipation settled heavily in his groin. Yes, finally he would be satisfied. Turning desire-hazed attention back to the glade, he watched the cursed Defender turn from Lara and step toward the portal.

"Someone comes, Lara. I must be leavin' ye. I will keep yer promise, for the time bein'. Dinna stay out of contact too long, or I will return fer ye."

"Thanks, Derrik. I'll be fine."

"Aye, ye will." Derrik flashed a smile that set Aubrian's teeth on edge. As the portal snacked closed he made to rise, but the presence of another pulled him back into the shadows with a sigh.

The human moved noisily into the clearing and stopped suddenly when he discovered Lara's presence. His overly loud voice caused Aubrian to cringe. The human lout.

"Lara. Why are ye here?"

TWELVE

L ara faced the deep disapproval rumbling through the quiet glade. Iain glared at her. Tired of domineering men who thought they knew what was best for her, she stomped across the glade to stand before Iain and fisted her hands against her hips.

A wide grin split Iain's face. "Yer ankle is better."

Irritation fading, Lara returned the infectious grin. "Yes, I heal quickly." Bold, she let her gaze roam hungrily over his body. Her breathing quickened as his own breaths tightened the shirt across his chest. Sunlight glinted off the deep, soot-black of his hair. The merry gleam in his eyes darkened, and she was lost in the depths of her desire for the man. A step closer and she could touch him, feel the soft cushion of dark hair that curled at the low, even neckline of his tunic.

Iain turned his head to one side at a slight noise. The intriguing contact disappeared, and disappointment flooded through Lara. These were the feelings she had returned for, what she craved. Concern touched the corners of his mouth when Iain turned back to her.

"Should ye have come so far from the manor? Ye dinna wish to reinjure--"

"I said I'm fine." Lara bit back a further tart reply and swallowed past a dry lump in her throat. "What are you up to?"

"Up to?" His shoulders tightened visibly.

Lara gave a vague wave of her hand. "Oh, you know, what are your duties now?"

Relaxing, Iain nodded. "I ken. The festival is but a few days away. Two small fruit trees grow on the hill where the gatherin' is held. I dinna wish for the wee things to be trampled so I shall move them to Mathair's garden." He paused and took a short breath. "Would ye care to visit the hillock with me? We will go slowly."

Lara had to swallow again past that dry, agonizing lump. "I'd like that."

Iain held out a hand. "Come, then."

Unable to take her eyes from his face, Lara lifted her hand until Iain encircled it with his warm fingers. Fiery heat pulsed up her arm. A gasp forced its way between her parted lips and her knees buckled from the intensity.

Iain wrapped her upper arms with his large hands, supporting her. Concern faded as his pupils grew larger, filling his eyes with glittering promise. Lara swayed, her gaze falling into the bottomless well of his desire.

His hands moved to her shoulders to caress with slow, sure movements. He stretched his fingers into her hair to cup the back of her head. Iain tugged gently to tilt her face to his. Reverence filled his kiss. Lara sighed, letting her lips part beneath his. The heat of his tongue slid across her tender inner lip. The fire trailed instantly through her body and she lifted her hands to his face.

The sharp lines of his jaw, roughened by a day's growth of stubble, felt perfect against her palms. Perfect. The flames pulled her closer until she pressed against him to wrap her arms around his slender waist. Encased in the heat, Lara forgot the pain of the near lies she told her family, forgot the reasons to be careful. Forgot everything but the man who fired her with such passion.

Slowly, Iain traced the length of her arms and then reached behind him to take her hands. Easing them from his waist, he stepped back and held their entwined fingers to his chest. Just as slowly, Lara opened her heavy-lidded eyes. Unspoken questions formed in her dazed mind.

"Dinna speak, sweet. We canna do this."

"Yes."

"'Tis no'--"

"I don't care." Lara wrenched her hands from his, aching at the sudden cold that surrounded her. "I want this. I thought you did, too." She returned her hands to his chest.

"I canna deny it, sweet."

"Then why stop?"

"'Tis no' the time." Iain looked around. "Nor the place." When she drew a breath to argue Iain slanted his gently moving lips across hers to return the heat and the flames to her. But it was over too soon, and Lara sighed in frustration.

Iain's voice rumbled from deep in his chest and vibrated against her sensitized nipples. "I must go to the hill. Will ye still come with me?"

If the hills were further from the manor, perhaps he would not fear discovery. That had to be the reason he stopped now. The evidence of his arousal jutted against her belly. Trying to keep her voice from trembling, she whispered breathlessly. "I'd still like to go with you." *Anywhere.*

With a tender smile, Iain tilted his head toward her and dropped a quick kiss on her cheek. Her hand was still in his as he led her from the glade.

Aubrian waited until they were well gone from the area before rising from his hiding place. A frown of disgust twisted his lips. Inhaling deeply, he tasted the combined flavors of the humans' passions and then spat the bitterness against the rough bark of an ancient, weatherworn tree.

Angered that his plans were constantly thwarted, he stomped toward the manor. Before reaching the gates he paused, smiled and turned instead toward the hovel the farmer Edwin proudly called home.

As he suspected, he found Edwin lounging before the rough shack. The lazy man jumped to his feet at Aubrian's soft throat-clearing and glanced around anxiously.

"Is the MacDhuibh wi' ye, Seanachai?"

"Have no fear. I doubt the lord has yet risen from his bed this day."

Edwin motioned to the bench. "Sit then, storyteller. Be there somethin' ye want wit' me?"

"Aye, Edwin. I have noticed you are dissatisfied with life here. And your lord."

Edwin's eyes narrowed. "Nay, master. There be no complaints comin' from me."

Aubrian laughed. "Fear me not, Edwin. I bear no love for m'lord Castantin." He paused to glare toward the distant manor house. "Nor any of the holding."

Fear warred with ambition in the farmer's heavy-jowled face. "Seek ye to overthrow the MacDhuibh?"

Aubrian laughed again, slapping the farmer on the back. His smile turned to a grimace of distaste, and he wiped his palm against his thigh. "No, good Edwin. I only wish retribution. I will regain what is rightfully mine."

"And wha' need o' me, master?"

"Are there others?"

"Others? I dinna ken--"

"Do not be thickheaded, Edwin. You know exactly what I desire. There must be others who wish to no longer languish under the ineffectual lording of Castantin."

Edwin tried to look innocent, but cunning glinted in his eyes and Aubrian nodded. He had made a wise choice in coming to this filthy man. He would not trust Edwin, for he no longer trusted any confederate, but he would use the farmer without regret.

Edwin leaned forward until Aubrian was forced back to escape the stench of the man's rancid breath. "I dinna ken many, but one man may be of help to ye, master. I can take ye to him."

"Who is this one, Edwin? If I deem your suggestion worthy you may lead me to him."

Edwin preened and puffed out his chest. Aubrian bit back derisive laughter that tickled his throat. Edwin rose and paced, nodding to himself. "Aye. We will go to the anchorite."

Aubrian's eyebrows shot up with surprise. A religious man? Ah, the tide turned in his direction once more.

CHAPTER
THIRTEEN

Lara curled her legs under her and watched Iain. After insisting she wait for him under the minimal spring shade of a windswept tree, he had quickly found the first of his young trees nearly hidden by tall grasses. Now he worked at the second, the first lying beside him with the tender roots wrapped in a length of rough cloth.

He had tossed his shirt to one side. Fascinated, Lara watched the play of muscles across his back and shoulders as he dug carefully around the plant with a small hatchet. A smear of dark blue accented one shoulder and then ran down to circle his upper arm. She knew it must be a tattoo, but distance blurred the intricate design.

Reaching into the bag that lay at her side, she pulled out a piece of chocolate and, hiding it from prying eyes, unwrapped the silver paper. The foil rolled into a tiny ball between her fingers and she slipped it back into the depths of the bag. She let the chocolate melt on her tongue, savoring both the sweetness in her mouth and the view of pure male...delicious.

Iain turned toward her, forcing Lara to swallow guiltily. His long strides carried him swiftly to her. He lay his bundled plants to one side, joined her in the shade and then used his shirt to wipe sweat from his face and chest. Lara's mouth was suddenly dry, words hovered thickly in her throat.

Iain took a long swallow from a flask and then offered it to her. Lara took a tentative swallow, and then a longer drink of the lukewarm water. "Thanks."

Iain shrugged and gazed to the top of the hill.

"This is where the celebration will be? What celebration?"

Iain's dark gaze turned to her, surprise sparking the depths of his eyes. "Bealtaine. The first of May."

Delighted, Lara clapped her hands. "I love May Day. Will there be a maypole?"

"An' that be?"

"A maypole? It's a tall pole with ribbons attached to the top. Everybody dances around it, weaving the ribbons down the pole. It's so much fun."

"I dinna ever hear of such a thing."

"Oh, don't tease."

Iain's brows drew together. "I dinna tease ye, Lara." A wicked gleam twinkled in his eyes. "No' about this, sweet."

"Could we have a maypole dance anyway?"

"If ye wish it."

Lara nodded happily. In one fluid motion Iain rose to his feet and pointed to a small stand of saplings. The tall, slim trunks swayed in the light breeze. "Will one o' those do?"

"Perfectly. Then we can stand it at the top of the hill."

Iain smiled. "I shall be leavin' the ribbons to ye and Beitris." Pulling the small hatchet from his belt, he made quick work of felling a slender tree. Then he stripped the branches to leave a smooth trunk. The tree bounced jauntily as he carried it to the top of the hill.

Lara stood and shaded her eyes with a hand to watch him use his hatchet to chop a hole in the sod. She clapped when the sapling held firm and upright. Iain bent to pack dirt firmly around the base of the trunk, stacked a few loose stones around the base and then trotted down the hill.

Without stopping his near headlong rush, he wrapped Lara in

his arms, lifted her from the ground and twirled in a circle. "Do ye need anythin' else, sweet?"

Iain let her slide down the length of his body, holding back a groan of wild pleasure. Excitement brought a pink blush to her cheeks. If simply cutting down a tree made her so happy he would do it every day until no forest remained, then plant a new one to begin again.

The soft, moist fullness of her lips drew him closer. He should not kiss her again, should not let himself fall into the temptation of their heated desires. Lara pulled her bottom lip in between her teeth, released it and then licked the abused area. He was lost, forever lost.

Lara stood on tiptoe and met his kiss with sensuous demands of her own. Her soft lips opened at the brief touch of his tongue, letting him delve into the moist depths. Stroking and exploring her mouth wasn't enough, so he cupped her bottom and pulled her hard against him.

She said yes against his mouth and arched her hips against his. Why should he deny the desire for this golden flame of a woman? Why should he refuse what she was so anxious to give him?

Iain jerked away, shaking his head to clear it. He could not. Turning from the questions and Lara's warm body, he gulped air and tried to calm his ragged breathing. The touch of her hand on his shoulder froze all movement and any thoughts. Lara leaned into his back and her soft, sweet breath brushed past his ear when she spoke.

"Don't deny me, Iain. Please. I won't ask more, for now. Sit with me, talk with me."

Iain nodded slowly and let her take his hand to lead him back to her place under the tree. Lara knelt to smooth the length of plaid material over the uneven ground and sat holding her hand out to him. Would he be able to sit next to her and deny the want, the need? He had no choice.

With his back pressed hard against the rough tree bark, Iain watched Lara from the corner of his eyes. She fussed with the blanket and the revealing neckline of her dress before she turned to face him. A shy smile, but a smile full of sensuous promise, made her face shine. And his heart leap.

Licking his lip, Iain tasted her kiss, and something else. A sweetness such as he had never tasted, a strange, smooth sweetness. "What is this taste? 'Tis wonderous."

"What?" Her violet eyes were wide with confusion. "What are you talking about?"

"The taste of yer kiss that wasna ye."

"The taste..." The realization and mischief that dawned across her face filled Iain's chest with longing so deep it must sink to the core of the earth. "Oh, that's chocolate."

"Chocolate? Where did such a thing come from?"

Lara swallowed and Iain watched the movement of her throat intently. "I brought it from a land far from here."

Iain leaned forward eagerly. "Is there more?"

Lara laughed, and the tinkling sound filled the countryside. "Yes, I have more. Do you have a sweet tooth?"

"Oh, aye. Beitris says 'twill be m' downfall someday. She oft catches me sneakin' sweets from the kitchen."

Lara reached into her bag and then held a small, shiny nugget toward him. Iain took it gingerly from her open palm and held it to the light. He inspected the tiny thing, interested in how the sunlight glinted off it when he turned it first one way and then another. He popped the nugget into his mouth.

Lara gasped and reached out to him, shaking his arm. "No, don't. You need to unwrap it first."

Iain let the chocolate drop from his tongue into his palm and gave her a sardonic smile. "Guid. 'Tis no' so sweet this way."

Taking the candy from his hand, Lara unwrapped it before holding it toward him between two fingers. He leaned forward, chasing her moving fingers, until he could suck the chocolate, and the tips of her fingers, into his mouth. Lara jerked away, but her smile of invitation remained.

"Now, you have to let it melt on your tongue to get the full flavor."

Iain nodded and rolled the chocolate around his mouth. The taste was heaven itself. No sweet, no pastry he'd eaten before came near to the perfection of this tiny bite of chocolate. In order to fully experience chocolate, his eyes closed in bliss.

"Do you like it?"

"Oh, aye. 'Tis heaven."

"That's always what I thought." Lara chuckled then paused. "Would you like some more?"

"Oh, aye." Iain slowly opened his eyes and held out one hand and tried not to look, or feel, like a hopeful little boy. The knowing grin on Lara's face was worth his discomfort. Lara teased him for a few moments, swaying her closed palm over his hand before dropping a few pieces of the sweet into his palm.

He took one and after carefully unwrapping it, slowly placed the small bite in his mouth. Then he smoothed the silver paper on his knee before lifting it to the sunlight. His words were muffled as he spoke around the melting lump in his mouth. "I have no seen anythin' like this before."

Shrugging, Lara unwrapped a sweet for herself. "It's just the wrapping paper. Foil."

"Ah, foil."

Her mouth fascinated Iain as she sucked on the chocolate, the tip of her tongue darting out to brush against her lower lip. The movements were those of a lover's kiss, the touch of desire. *Resist.* He did not understand the word.

Balancing with one arm, Iain leaned toward Lara. Lost in the thrall of the chocolate, her eyelashes rested against the faint pink of her cheeks. And his heart was forever lost to her. Her lips parted as his breath touched them and she closed the minute distance between them with a soft whimper of need.

Iain drew her gently into the kiss and stroked the chocolaty sweetness from her mouth with his tongue. When she sought to extend the contact, he pulled away carefully but curled her next to his side and secured one of his arms around her shoulders.

With a soft giggle Lara unwrapped another chocolate and drew it across his lips, barely touching his mouth. Iain nipped at the passing chocolate and growled in frustration until she let him capture the prize.

Strangely at peace with this golden woman pressed against his side, he smiled down at her.

She traced her fingertip around his upper arm. "Tell me about your tattoo."

Iain choked and leaned forward coughing until Lara pounded him heartily on the back. When he could wave her attention away, he lifted his gaze warily to her face. "Why do ye wish to ken?"

"Why? I guess because it's beautiful." Iain tensed as she continued to trace the fine lines of the design. Her touch burned, and he jerked away from her searching fingers. Eyes cast down, she folded her hands in her lap. "My father has a tattoo, on his leg. I've often thought of getting one, but never could decide on the design."

Taking deep breaths to calm the churning in his stomach and cool the heat of his skin, Iain reached to the side for his shirt. Tugging the loose material over his head covered the tattoo. Lara sighed, disappointment filling her face when she looked up, and he almost removed the shirt again. The memories of the priests' fears and anger when he was younger stopped his hand and forced a tight explanation.

"'Tis no' but an ancient symbol. 'Twas placed there the spring I came of age."

Afraid to look at the condemnation seen so often in other's faces, Iain fiddled with the hem of his shirt. The stylized horse and trail of spiral rings banding his upper arm had once been a source of pride, giving him a sense of place, of belonging.

Slim fingers cupped his chin to lift his face. Violet eyes, swirling brown with concern stared into his. "Why did you cover it? Are you ashamed?"

"Shamed? Nay, 'tis no' the way of it. 'Tis a symbol of the beliefs of m' mother and the ancients of the land. I suffered much derision and punishment with the monks because of it. I have learned to keep it hidden."

"But--"

Iain cut her off with a sideways swipe of one hand. "'Tis the way of the Christ followers." His words were abrupt and he turned his face from her to stare unseeing over the countryside.

Lara rubbed his shoulder softly and guided him back to lean against the tree. Then she wrapped one arm across the tense planes of his stomach and rested her head against his chest. "I think it's beautiful. Someday I hope you'll tell me the meaning."

Iain remained stiff and silent, wondering if she could hear the staccato beating of his heart. Her breathing changed and she relaxed against him. A quick glance confirmed she had fallen asleep. A smile twitched his lips. Aye, he would tell her about the markings; he could refuse her nothing.

Angling his body, Iain settled her more comfortably against his side. With one hand he lay her bag in his lap and rustled through the depths until he found a crackling, clear pouch nearly full of the wonderful foil-wrapped chocolates. He dumped the contents on the ground making a satisfying pile next to him. After carefully selecting one he struggled to remove the foil with one hand. Eyes closed, he savored the sweetness and sighed in contentment such as he had never imagined.

"Lara, wake." The urgent voice drew her from a pleasant, dreamless sleep. Snuggling into the warmth next to her, Lara mumbled a denial. But the voice intruded again, accompanied by gentle shaking. "Please, Lara."

Her eyes opened slowly to a face hovering close, dark eyes swirling with distress. Jerking from the intrusion she knocked the top of her head against Iain's chin.

"Ow." Rubbing at the painful spot Lara stroked Iain's chin with her other hand. "Are you okay?"

"I fear ye have poisoned me." Iain doubled over clutching his stomach.

Poison? What was he talking about? They had eaten nothing

since she returned from the Otherworld. Nothing-- except chocolate.

When she braced one hand against the ground Lara heard a familiar crackle. Glancing down she discovered the crumpled, empty bag and a pile of neatly stacked foil wrappers. She felt her eyes grow wide. Even in the depths of her most lonely chocolate cravings she had never eaten a whole bag at one time.

She patted Iain's lowered head until he looked up at her, eyes glazed. A tiny smear of chocolate hovered at one corner of his mouth. Unable to help herself, she laughed.

"I dinna ken the humor."

"I'm sorry, Iain. Did you really eat all the chocolate?"

Resting his forehead on his knees, Iain rubbed his belly. "Aye. I canna stop...when the sweet is so guid."

"You've done this before?"

"Aye. Once I stole an entire tray of gundy. Beitris was no pleased with me. But I dinna feel this poorly."

"You've never had this kind of candy before. It was bound to make your stomach upset--since you ate it all, you Greedy Gus. And didn't leave any for me." Lara was unable to hold an outraged pout so laughed instead.

Dark eyes glared at her, making her instantly contrite. "I'm sorry, Iain. Surely there must be something in your mother's store of herbs for an upset stomach."

"Aye. But I dinna think I will live long enough to find them."

"Sure, you will." A slight pat on his arm was meant as encouragement. "Maybe the walk will do you good as well." Lara struggled against the tangle of her skirts until she stood over Iain with her arms crossed under her breasts. "Come on, now. Up and at 'em."

"I canna."

Lara stroked the top of his head and then wound her fingers through the soft length of his unbound hair. A steady pressure upwards dragged his agonized gaze to hers. "Yes, you can. The sooner we return, the sooner you will feel better." She smoothed his hair back and leaned to kiss his forehead.

Iain rose awkwardly and stumbled toward the manor, still clutching his stomach. Men were so helpless when they didn't feel good. Lara chuckled and grabbed her bag and the plaid. She turned to follow Iain, and then remembered his small trees.

Cradling them in her arms she laughed again.

Iain paused and turned his head toward her. One side of his lips twitched upward, erasing some of the discomfort from his face. "Ye willna tell Beitris, will ye?"

CHAPTER
FOURTEEN

T he thick sloping stone walls of the broch pressed in on
Aubrian, and he fought the need to hunch his shoulders
protectively. Sitting so he faced the low, thin entryway
did little to alleviate his discomfort while the pungent unwashed
bodies of Edwin and the anchorite further tightened the small
space.

Aubrian had refused the anchorite's offer of drink from the
small barrel set against the wall. Deep in his mind the memory
surfaced of a pleasant taste and the delightful lightness of the
drink. Being able to re-taste those feelings, letting the drink drive
away his concerns and anger tempted him almost to the point he
reached for the offered filthy mug.

No. He would not accept the temptation. Many long years had
passed since drink last touched his lips. Long years of cold,
tortured trembling, fighting the invisible insects crawling under
his skin; years of strange dreams and agonizing pain. Rebuilding
his base of power after the abuse, after the loss and confusion,
had nearly broken him. The visions of his destiny, the rightness of
his actions forced him past the need to lose himself in drink.
Seldom now was the temptation so great.

Aubrian focused on the filth around him and shuddered in disgust. "Edwin speaks of your dissatisfaction, holy man."

The anchorite peered guiltily into his mug. "The feelings are not worthy of my seclusion, and I pray long and hard to defeat that evil."

Aubrian laughed, the sarcastic sound chasing away the last of the drink's temptation. "Ah, holy man, you please me greatly. Do as you wish. Hide your true feelings from others, from your god, but I see into your heart. You wish harm to the lord of this holding."

"No harm upon the laird, but upon the old laird's son. He is all that remains of my disgrace." The anchorite took a long swallow from his mug before continuing. "As the mathair has died..."

Aubrian smiled broadly. Better than he dared hope, the anchorite's desires supported his own. Both would be satisfied by taking Lara.

The anchorite cleared his throat and peered sideways at Edwin. "I have been contacted by others. Warriors from across the northern seas."

"Vikings?" So the longship he had seen far out to sea the day Lara arrived had not passed the tempting shores. Better still.

"Aye, the Lochlannaich have been here, scouting, laying plans to overthrow holdings along the coast."

"You would wish Viking rule?" After facing the Norsemen's powerful destruction on his journeys northward, the thought that a people would welcome the warriors was strange. It forced a shake of Aubrian's head.

"My God is my ruler. Whatever earthly domination I must suffer makes little difference."

"The Vikings have brought destruction to many monasteries."

The anchorite shrugged. Aubrian knew then he'd found another to aid his plans. Perhaps the Viking warriors would play a part as well, with the promise of the spoils of the holding as reward.

Aubrian leaned forward, lowering his voice until Edwin and

the anchorite were forced to scoot closer to hear the impassioned words. "This is my plan."

"M'lady Lara. Ye have no' ridden with me to see me holdin'." Castantin stood to one side of the table, a soft cap twisting in his hands.

Aware that she had not spent much time with the exuberant lord of the holding, Lara smiled up at him. Her lack of interest and praise of his works must wound his great pride. "Today would be a wonderful day for you to show me around, Castan. I've been remiss and am looking forward to seeing your holding. I haven't ridden for a long time, though."

The metal pitcher on the table nearly tipped when he reached for it. Water dribbled from Castan's beard when he drank and Lara chuckled. The empty pitcher rocked on the smooth table, and Castan straddled the bench next to her. "Aye? If ye dinna wish t' ride, a cart shall be provided fer ye. I shall show ye the far reaches of me holdin' then."

"That'd be wonderful. I think I need a wrap, though. Can I meet you at the stables?"

A large mouthful of bread muffled his answer, but his happy nod gave her permission to rush to her room.

The few times she'd seen Iain the past two days had been in the kitchens or gardens, so she took the long way through the manor hoping for a chance meeting. But only Beitris and a young helper, engaged in gossip as they prepared vegetables for the evening meal, occupied the kitchen.

The gardens were empty as well, although the fresh, damp smell of recently turned earth lingered in the pleasaunce. Lara paused in the tiny walled garden. Fragile seedlings were protected from bitter spring winds by small woolen windbreaks. A length of linen shaded another area from the harsh sun. Iain's knowledge of agricultural practices surprised her; many of his ideas were exceedingly modern.

Knowing how impatient Castan could be, Lara turned reluctantly from the garden and practically ran to her room. The length of plaid she'd brought from home was folded neatly at the end of her bed. Tossed around her shoulders it made a soft, warm shawl to protect her from the cool, morning weather.

Castantin nodded in approval when she stepped from the hall and met him in the center of the wide yard. He held the reins of a docile gray mare harnessed to a cheerfully painted two-wheeled cart. A single, decidedly uncomfortable board seat spanned the narrow cart.

"The cart belonged to Iain's mathair. I prefer to ride." Castan made a showy bow. "But this day, I escort me honored guest."

Lara giggled and took his outstretched hand. He tugged her closer, then spanned her waist with his large hands and lifted her to the seat. The cart tipped drunkenly when he jumped up behind the seat, angled Lara slightly to one side and knelt. A sharp snap of the reins across the horse's back lurched the cart into an awkward rocking motion. Lara grasped the seat with both hands.

"Relax, m'lady. Move wi' the cart, no' against the motion."

"I'll try, but I'm afraid I'll tip off my seat."

"Beg pardon, then, m'lady." Castan took the reins in one hand and wrapped his free arm around Lara before taking the braided leather again in both hands. "Ye'll no fall from me cart now. Look ahead, we shall drive the village road to the sea."

Startled by Castan's arms about her and the press of his thick chest against her back, Lara held herself stiffly. Castan chuckled. "Ye need fear naught from me, m'lady. I would no' fight me coz fer yer attentions."

Lara jerked her head to one side to try and look into Castan's face. What had he meant by that? She had tried to be circumspect whenever Iain was around. And in the beginning Aubrian had paid her more attention. Castan gave her a slow wink. He was teasing--she hoped. Still, that fateful leap of her heart at the mention of Iain continued to beat firmly in her chest. Iain... Already the tour was too long away from him. Castan's eyebrows had drawn together, so she pasted on a bright smile.

His smile returned. "Soon we come to the kirk built by Iain's da."

T he small cart raised little dust as it left the yard, but Iain watched until every speck had fallen back to the path. The hard lump that lodged at the base of his throat when Castan wrapped his arms around Lara refused to be swallowed away. It burned, but not so much as the heavy desire lower in his body. That fool body would not allow him to forget the touch of her skin or the fire of her kisses. He could dig through the earth and discover new worlds on the far side, but he could never rid himself of her. Instead, he sighed, he would make small holes and finish planting the medicinals while the golden distraction was away from the manor.

Working in the gardens lost much of its pleasure when Lara was not there to talk with him or work by his side. Iain grinned at the thought of her on her knees--hands covered with damp soil tenderly placing a seedling in its new home. There was no doubt those tiny growths would become the sturdiest plants in the gardens. Her presence blessed his planting.

The Bealtaine celebration was but a few days away, and the holding's planting would be truly blessed. The people gossiped eagerly of the new dance Lara would bring to them, spoke of her presence as the sign of a heavy harvest. Iain shook his head; her presence was surely a bringer of change, but what change? There was a change within him, a new view of his life. A new belief?

Iain continued working, moving without thought until the large tray of plants was safely tucked into the ground. Then he leaned back against the ancient tree and stared into the blue sky. How long would it be until Castantin and Lara returned?

A huff of breath blew his frustration to the wind. He pulled a folded packet of parchments from under his shirt and carefully opened the well-read pages. Spreading them on the bench, he leaned forward to read, occasionally tracing a word with a finger while he deciphered the varied languages. Much of the morning was lost to him while he studied the world of farming.

A lthough impatient with the flow of days, Aubrian was pleased with how well his plan progressed. The anchorite surprised him with knowledge of the manor and had taken him to the perfect location for the culmination of the plan. The Vikings' arrival on the shore was a stroke of well-timed luck, and any damage caused by his departure would be blamed upon the tall, blonde warriors. As would the death of the old lord's son.

Aubrian paused in an open doorway off the kitchen and stared into the gardens. The human was there, as usual. A grin twitched his lips and he stepped outside. Negligent of how he placed his feet, Aubrian passed through the newly planted kitchen garden to the walled inner garden. He leaned against the arched stone entry, crossed one foot over the other and folded his arms across his chest.

Absorbed in the sheets of cramped writing spread before him, the human sat on the ground. Aubrian rolled his eyes to the sky.

"So, Master Iain." He chuckled at the sudden stiff posture and clenched fists of the human. It was so easy to taunt their lower minds. "What are you reading?"

"'Tis naught but methods of plantin' and growin'."

"I see." Aubrian moved to the bench and pushed the pages aside so he could sit. Iain grabbed the parchments before they could fall to the ground and glared at Aubrian.

"Ye, of all, should honor written words, Seanachai." Iain stacked the pages on his knee and refolded them carefully.

"I honor words as tools for my use."

Iain squinted at the storyteller. There was hidden meaning in the simple statement and much left unsaid. "Aye." He stood and placed the parchments within his tunic. "Aye, fer yer use. And what use do ye have of this holdin'? Yer pretty words charm Castantin, yer tales entertain."

Aubrian placed one hand over his heart and bowed his head. "I am, as always, honored by your compliments."

A loud snort was Iain's answer. "I dinna compliment ye, storyteller. Dinna believe all within this holdin' are without wonderin' what 'tis ye wish here."

Mock surprise rounded Aubrian's mouth. "Why, I only wish to entertain."

"Dinna try an' fool me. I dinna ken who ye are, but I dinna trust ye."

"Then we understand each other well." Aubrian stretched and laced his fingers behind his head before leaning back against the tree. "Or shall I say, I understand you all too well. You will never understand the likes of me."

Iain chuckled. "Ye overestimate yerself." He turned away.

"I would not walk away, young master."

The threat in the cold voice lifted the hairs Iain's arms. Fists clenched tightly, Iain halted. "I shall, fer I dinna have more to say to ye."

The soft rustle of Aubrian's rise to his feet was barely audible over the sounds of the busy manor. Iain turned cautiously, one hand reaching for the dirk strapped to his calf. Aubrian poised on his toes, dancing lightly from one foot to the other.

With his gaze intent on the strange actions of the storyteller, Iain waited to draw the dirk. He should not challenge a guest of the holding but could stand no more of the man's veiled insults. Watching the storyteller's shoulder, Iain waited for the slight drop that would signal the reach for the knife at the man's side. Sure of his own reflexes, he was patient. The man's fighting would be as slippery as his words.

Long, tense moments filled the garden with oppression so thick Iain found it difficult to draw breath. Aubrian continued to bounce before him, weaving patterns in the dust with his feet. Would the man do nothing but continue the infernal dancing?

The sound of Lara's voice stopped the dance and lifted the heavy air. Iain took a long, deep breath and held it a moment before letting it out slowly. Aubrian frowned and returned to his place on the bench and leaned back with his hands cushioning his head. Iain eyed him; he acted as if nothing had happened. But, Iain wondered, what had happened? What would have happened without the interruption?

"Truly, Castan. I had a great time. Once I got used to the movement of the cart." Lara's giggle preceded her into the garden. Castan followed closely, carrying a length of plaid material. With a thick finger he traced the crossed lines of white and purple and held the weave to the sunlight.

"I have ne'er seen a finer weave. Or a pattern so pleasin' to me eyes." He sighed and handed the plaid to Lara. "Would that me weavers could create such beauty."

Lara touched his shoulder. "I'm sure they could. Would you like them to see this? Perhaps they could make something like it."

Iain chuckled when Castan's broad smile spilt his beard from his moustache. Happy as a child with a new plaything, Castan took the plaid from Lara and wrapped the material around one hand before holding it to his face.

Aubrian gave a soft sound of disgust as he stood. "I will leave you then, m'lord. I must prepare for my next tale."

Castan started and dropped his hands to his sides. Red infused his face. "Seanachai, I dinna ken ye were here as well."

"Merely passing a few pleasant moments in the sun." Without even glancing at Lara, Aubrian moved past Iain. He lifted one eyebrow, smiled and cocked his head to one side.

Iain turned to watch until he was long within the manor. Then with a bow to Lara and a mumbled excuse to Castantin, Iain hurried from the garden as well, certain the storyteller was a threat to the holding. And to Lara.

FIFTEEN

Pleasant days flew by even though Lara rarely saw Iain. He was avoiding her, and she wasn't sure why. Unless she helped him in the gardens, he kept busy elsewhere. On those rare occasions when they passed in the halls the fires of desire burned deep within her, shortened her breath and brought heat to her face.

As much as she ached for a glimpse of Iain, she literally ran from any chance meeting with the storyteller. His fey presence made her blood run cold, his speculative glances chilled her until she thought she would never be warm again. All it took was a thought of Iain and she was heated through; all memories of Aubrian faded to darkness.

Lara kept busy helping Beitris with the plans for the coming celebration. The word of her maypole traveled throughout the holding and daily new piles of ribbons and narrow lengths of cloth arrived from the small crofts. Lara vowed to use each strip, so she braided many together to make wildly colorful lengths to fasten to the top of the pole.

While they worked, Beitris told her stories, tales of Iain and Castantin as boys and young men. Tears formed in her eyes each time she spoke of the years Iain had been away from the manor, hidden from life within the stark desolate walls of the monastery at Lindisfarne.

Stephen and his small puppy stayed close to her side. He took his new duties seriously and was ready to jump to any errand she may have for him. Lara benefited from his breathless chatting, learning more about Iain's kindness and tireless dedication to the land and its people. She loved her dark Pict more each day.

Love? Lara dropped the supple twigs she was braiding into a crown. Stephen scampered to retrieve it and held it out to her. She stared unseeing at the circlet and took the unwinding twigs from the boy automatically. Did she love the ancient man? Tingling filled her body with the remembered glory of his touch. No, it was only lust.

But, even as she told herself the feelings were only her body's search for release her heart said she was wrong. She would gladly stand beside this man for the rest of her life. His intelligence and compassion completed her in a way she didn't even try to understand. The passion. Now, that was definite frosting on the cake.

Lara ducked her head and grinned at the memory of Iain frantically rummaging through the herbal in his haste to ease the pain of too much chocolate. Unable to enjoy the variety of delicacies at the feast that night, he had suffered silently at her side and carefully wiped the clammy sweat from his face when he thought no one watched. They had successfully hidden the treatment of his sweet transgression from Beitris and had laughed together briefly about it the next day.

But then--then, he left her alone. Did he blame her for introducing him to chocolate and letting him eat the entire bag? Lara shook her head. He wouldn't hold a grudge over something he'd done to himself--would he? No, it had to be something else. Had she been too forward? There she had no idea; and, other than the servants, there were no young women within the manor for her to use to gauge her behavior.

Beitris pushed a basket of cut spring flowers toward her. "Ye must finish yer crown, dearie."

The profusion of colors enticed Lara, and she stroked a few of the soft petals before she sighed. "I'm afraid the flowers will fade before tomorrow."

A deep voice sounded behind her. "Then I will bring ye flowers before the dew fades." Iain stepped past her and perched on a bench next to Beitris and kissed her wrinkled cheek before he ruffled Stephen's hair.

"Ye have no' been in the house much these days, master Iain."

"Aye, Beitris, there has been much to do." The depths of his eyes when he glanced at Lara were so dark she thought of a starless sky stretching into infinity. She savored that infinity until he broke the contact and leaned back with his elbows resting on the worn table behind him. "I dinna wish any duties to take me away from the celebration."

Beitris motioned toward the large basket of braided ribbons. "How are we to affix these to Lara's pole?"

Taking a length from the pile, Iain pulled it through his fingers. Lara trembled in response to the caress of fabric against his skin. A quick toss replaced the streamer in the basket. "Once I take the pole from the ground, ye will affix the ribbons. I will replant the maypole in the proper place." He grinned at her. "All shall be ready fer yer dancin'."

The small black dog sniffed Iain's boots and, begging for attention, rose on his hind legs. Iain lifted the puppy into the air and looked him over carefully.

"Ye have taken guid care of this wee one, Stephen. Have ye named him yet?"

The puppy licked Iain's hand and wiggled franticly, so Iain set him on the floor and laughed as it rooted around Beitris' feet for scraps. Stephen pulled a worn and much-folded piece of hide from inside his shirt. Looking through the coals at the edge of the wide kitchen fireplace, he found a long thin piece of charcoal, knocked it against the stone to create a thinner edge and brought it to the table.

Lara leaned forward trying to see past the boy's narrow back as Stephen bent over the table. Finally, curiosity won and she stood to one side of the boy. His tongue peeked from one side of his mouth as he carefully formed large, shaky letters on the hide.

Amazed, Lara bent closer. "You know how to write?" Stephen finished a letter, placed a large dot after it and smiled up at her. "Aye, m'lady. master Iain teaches me."

Lara glanced at Iain in wonder. Sure that in this time only a few could read or write, she found the generosity it took to find the time to teach a small child his letters endearing. This kindness was filed away in her heart, hoarded with other memories she hoped would last forever.

"Master Iain? What do the letters say?" Stephen held the hide to Iain, who took it by the edges to keep from smearing the charcoal letters. Nodding sagely he looked from the hide to the boy and back again. There were matching happy glints in both sets of eyes.

"Ye make fine letters, lad. Ye have been practicin'."

A faint red crept under the dirt on Stephen's face. "Aye, Master Iain. But, what do the letters say?" Stephen bounced eagerly in his excitement to know.

"Ye made plainly the letters n, o, i, and d. What do ye wish of this word?"

"'Tis the name of me dog, sir."

Iain tapped one finger against the hide. "Ye wish to name yer dog Noid? 'Tis a mightily strange name, lad."

"It be the name I choose. Ye canna make me change me mind." Small fists clenched at Stephen's side and defiance burned in his eyes. He glared at Iain.

"I dinna wish to change it, just wonderin' at the strangeness of it." Iain held the scrap of hide toward Lara. "What'd ye think of the name, Lara?"

But she had heard nothing after Iain recited the letters. Noid? How could there be two black dogs with the same strange name? Her grandfather told her he named his dog Noid because it was a word he had liked the sound of. Two Stephens, two Noids. It couldn't be.

"Lara?" Iain touched her arm.

"I..." Confused, she looked between Stephen and the puppy. "Uh, why did you pick that name?"

"The word sounds guid. 'Tis a fine name, is it no', m'lady?"

"Yes, it's a good name." Lara sank onto the bench next to Iain and bent to scratch the curious puppy behind the ears. Noid's head turned so she could give attention to a particular spot behind his left ear. The exact spot her grandfather's dog always wanted scratched. She gasped and jerked her hand away.

Beitris had turned to the pastries she was preparing for the next day while Iain and Stephen were bent over the hide, as Iain taught his young pupil the first five numbers. No one noticed her confusion. Only intelligent, black eyes watched her as the small dog cocked his head to one side, seeming to smile at her.

B eitris rousted Lara out of the warmth of her bed much earlier than she thought was necessary. The sun had barely risen above the edge of the sea cliffs; the dark chill of the spring night still lay heavily over the holding. Shivering beneath the wrap of her plaid, hoping for something other than thick, gritty oatmeal for breakfast, Lara made her way to the great hall.

When the large bowl was set in front of her, she sighed, and then held her hands over the steaming mixture to warm her cold fingertips. The cereal looked different today, browner. The scent was sweeter, too, full of--cinnamon. Smiling, she lifted a full spoon to her lips; it might be oatmeal, but it was different. The faint taste of apple lay on her tongue as the sharp tang of cinnamon faded.

Beitris watched while she took the first bite, then returned the smile and leaned over Lara's shoulder to add a drop more fresh milk to the bowl. "I used a bit of spice left from making the Gundy and added some chopped winter apples to make yer breakfast more pleasant."

"You have no idea how much better this is." Lara dipped her spoon into the bowl and tried to stir the thick mass. She'd grown up with her granda's favorite oatmeal for breakfast, but never enjoyed it as much as the overly sweet chocolate puffed cereal of the mortal world.

As if summoned by the thoughts of chocolate, Iain entered the hall. The full sleeves of his tunic were gathered by a multitude of ribbons tied at various places along his arms. A length of multi-colored braid wrapped his waist. The ends fluttered around his knees as he walked. Lara giggled and paid inordinate attention to the food in her bowl.

Iain dropped to the bench and inched close to her and reached for the pitcher of milk. The large hall was empty, so Lara took a chance and rested her hand over his.

"Yer no dressed for the dancin'." Iain turned his hand to capture her fingers; warmth spread into her palm, swirled around her wrist and moved up her arm. She could hold hands with him forever. "Ye must be the one to lead yer maypole dance."

"That won't be until later, will it? We still have to hang the ribbons. What about the rest of the celebration? You've never told me much about it?"

Iain played with her fingers. A lump of oatmeal stuck low in her throat; Lara waited breathlessly for his answer.

"'Tis no' but the spring celebration of the old gods, softened by the worship of the Christ. Mostly we celebrate the end of winter. The hard work of spring and summer must begin after this day. Planting and rebirth are important in this harsh land. The simple folk believe the ancient dancin' secures the guid will of the gods, grantin' fertility to the land." Iain's eyes twinkled, the glint softening to a languid promise.

A shallow breath and three swallows later Lara was able to speak. "I understand. That's pretty much what the maypole is all about, too."

"Guid. Then there should be an excellent harvest."

Iain's expression clouded, his eyes becoming hooded and distant. Startled by the sudden change in mood, Lara tried to tug her fingers from his. But his grip tightened until she relaxed. Iain traced faint patterns on the back of her hand.

"I dinna mean to sadden ye. I dinna look forward to this harvest, for it will be me last at the holdin'. Castan is adamant I leave. He willna trust me to remain and no try to take the holdin' fer me own." He shook his head sadly. "I dinna ken. Neither how he feels, nor what I will do."

You could come back with me. The sudden, unbidden thought nearly passed Lara's lips. What was she thinking? She couldn't take him with her, could she? She might change history. Had she changed some future when she was four and brought Bryce home? Yes, without her Bryce would have had no future. But Iain? Her suspicions that the boy Stephen was her grandfather grew as she pieced together family stories and happenings at the holding. And if Stephen were Castantin's son, then where would that leave her relationship with Iain? Struggling to sort out a family tree without pen and paper led her nowhere but to confusion.

Iain squeezed her hand gently, laid it on the table and canted his head to look into her face. He was about to ask a question, one she wouldn't be able to answer. Trying to paste a happy smile on her face she attacked her breakfast with a vigor that would have surprised her had she stopped to think about it.

Speaking around a mouthful of oatmeal, she glanced side-ways at Iain. "So, when do we go to the party?"

The questions were still evident of his face until he glanced to the wide doorway. "Many have already gone to the hill. The 'party' will last the day and well into the night." The dark gaze returned to her. "We can go whenever yer ready."

Swinging her legs over the bench, Lara leapt to her feet and rushed from the table. The large spoon was still clutched tightly in her hand and when she turned to toss the utensil back on the table, she faced Iain. "Then, I'll be ready soon." Grinning at his open-mouthed, stunned expression, Lara ran from the hall before--before what? She slowed her headlong rush. She really didn't understand her own thoughts anymore.

Head down and lost in her confused thoughts, she walked into the solid wall of a body. Arms wrapped around her and held her close to a firm chest. A strange, musty odor surrounded her. "Ah, sweet Lara. How I longed to see you this day."

Shudders ran along Lara's spine. *Sweet* was a totally different word when Iain whispered the endearment than when it dripped from Aubrian's lips.

Aubrian had ignored her during the past week, for which she was extremely grateful. But that one word brought all of the unpleasantness of his faerie glamour slamming back into her memory. She cringed from his touch.

Aubrian laughed, ran the back of his finger lightly down her cheek, turned and walked away whistling a lively tune. Lara stared after him. She knew he was up to something; he had been gone too often from the manor in the past days. And had been far too pleased with himself upon his return.

She'd wanted to talk to Iain about her suspicions, but to do so she would have to tell him about Faerie, and her talent. And since she couldn't even define those concerns to herself, there was no reason to try and convince someone else. The whistles faded, but the aura of Aubrian's presence and the feel of his touch remained a hovering cloud over the promise of a pleasant day.

A ubrian started his day the way he planned to end it, with Lara in his arms. That she shrank away from him mattered not. In fact, he looked forward to breaking her spirit and bending her to his will. She did not yet understand it was his destiny to use her.

He left the manor through a small, seldom-used door leading to an overgrown path to the rocky shore. Waves broke heavily over scattered, wildly angled boulders, the spray cold and salty against his skin. As he jogged along the shore he worked swiftly through bliss-filled contemplation of the day's plans.

A low murmur of hushed conversation underscored the boom of the tide. The visitors were in place. Aubrian slowed his pace and then crouched in the shadows between two large stones until the single sentry turned to gaze longingly into the waves.

Slipping into the only slightly warmer circle around a tiny fire, Aubrian cleared his throat. A tall, blond warrior leapt to his side and pressed a long sword against Aubrian's neck.

"Uh-uh, my friend. That is no way to greet a welcomed guest to your fire." The Norseman paused at the musical tones of Aubrian's speech. "Look away to meet your own death."

The Norseman's heavy brows drew together, but his eyes did not leave Aubrian's face until the nick of a sharp blade against his ribs drew his attention. Aubrian held a short dagger; the razor-fine point had already drawn a thin trickle of blood. Eyes wide, the Norseman backed away, scrambling over small rocks in his haste.

A man stood slowly. "And that is no way to enter the comfort of a friend's fire, storyteller." Not-so-subtle sarcasm filled the final word.

Aubrian laughed again. This was not a day to take offense from these simple warriors. They would serve the purpose he had planned for them. Then, perhaps, he would let them live and encourage them to return with their long-boats to destroy the fool Castan's precious holding. Or, if the mood suited him, he would kill them. It really didn't matter.

"We know the plan, storyteller. You should not have risked our discovery by coming here."

"There was no one to watch. All are busy with their foolish celebration. You will be in place at the appointed time?"

"As I have said, we understand the plan." His callused hand slashed downward in a dismissive gesture. "It is unwise to risk all this for a woman. There are many women."

"Not such as this. There is much she has to offer me, and much more I will take without the offer." The Norseman grimaced at Aubrian's delighted laugh. "So, Viking, you do not share the joy of conquest?"

"Conquest of lands and men worthy of fighting." Light-blue eyes filled with disdain told Aubrian he was not one of those considered worthy. That was a small matter; such comments only sealed the Viking's fate more securely. "There is no glory in what you plan."

"Ah, but there is. Glorious conquest awaits a foe I have long fought within my mind. Now the hunt and the battle come to me on this world, at this time. Here will be the pleasure of conquest, the glory of which you speak. I shall take that glory as due to me and conquer another, and yet another until I am avenged. Until I am satisfied."

Aubrian's feral snarl rang off the surrounding rocks, startling nesting seabirds. The Norseman turned away. "As you wish, storyteller."

B eitris found Lara struggling with the dress they had chosen and laughed. She continued to chuckle until Lara was able to stick her head through the correct opening. Breathing heavily, Lara glared at the old woman and then joined in the contagious laughter. "Well, help me, then. Please?"

Together they got the dress on properly. Lara tugged the neckline higher only to have Beitris smooth it low on her breasts. Nervous giggles erupted as Beitris's aged fingers tickled against her skin. "'Tis not the day for modesty, dearie. Ye'll not catch the lover ye wish if ye dinna offer."

"I'm not looking for a lover." Lara thought she sounded convincing but knew she failed by the speculative look in Beitris's eyes.

"Are ye no'? Ye canna fool these old eyes, what with yer moonin' about when master Iain be away."

"It's no use. He doesn't want me. I thought..."

"Too much thinkin'. From the both of ye. I dinna believe there was one to overthink more than Iain, but ye have outdone him. Dinna think this day, just do." Beitris gave a sly look. "Ye havena seen him starin' after yer back when ye leave a room. A guid tumble's what ye both need."

"Beitris." Lara pretended to be shocked and turned her back to the woman. Could what she said be true? Did Iain really return her feelings? With a soft smile of determination, Lara vowed she would know the truth of his feelings this day. And of her own.

"Sit ye down. Ye dinna need to be coy with me, child." Beitris turned Lara toward a chair and pushed on her shoulders to make her sit. "I will be fixin' yer hair now. Master Iain is no' such a patient man when he has to wait fer what he wants."

Lara tried to imagine the coming day as Beitris wove lengths of fine, colorful ribbon through her hair. A soft scratching at the door interrupted Lara's thoughts and she made to rise. Beitris lay a heavy hand on her shoulder to keep her in place then crossed to the door. Stephen darted inside, his arms filled with an abundance of fresh flowers.

"Master Iain sent these to ye, m'lady." Stephen bowed awkwardly and the flowers tumbled to the floor in a mass of glorious color.

"What are these for?" Confusion made Lara's voice soft and wistful.

"Ye dinna remember yestern?"

At the sake of her head Beitris continued. "When ye were makin' yer crown fer today, ye dinna wish to put on the flowers. Ye feared they would no' be pretty today. Master Iain promised to cut fresh ones fer yer hair."

The heat of a blush covered Lara's chest then moved to her face. "Oh, I--I'd forgotten." She laughed nervously. "I could never use this many flowers. What was he thinking?"

Beitris chuckled. "I dinna believe he was thinkin', unless it was only a wish to please ye. Men have little concept beyond such things."

Lifting a handful of the colorful spring blossoms to her nose, Lara grinned, and then spoke through the flowers. "No, they don't. I'll sure enjoy the excess this time, though."

Beitris's low, hearty chuckle filled the room. She motioned for Lara to sit again and began adding flowers to the ribbons already woven among the riotous golden curls.

"Oh, wait, what about the crown? Where'd I leave it?"

"Never ye mind, child. Ye dinna need it. Stephen, go tell the master m'lady Lara will attend him shortly."

"That sounds so formal." Lara giggled behind her hand, imagining the ways she could attend the tall object of her affection.

Beitris merely continued dressing Lara's hair, humming softly to herself.

CHAPTER
SIXTEEN

Iain froze and stared, open-mouthed. Like a vision from one of Beitris's fairy tales, Lara paused at the top of the stairs; late morning sun streaming through the windows behind her cast her in golden light. She was a creature of flame and he burned for her.

The moment's desire turned to clarity within Iain. In that second he believed.

The airy words, spoken from his mother's deathbed, returned to curl through him. *To find your place in this world, in any world, my son, you must be strong. And you must believe.*

He had held her, desperately pleading for her life, pleading to understand while her final breaths whispered past his ear. Already jaded by the differing dogmas of his home and the monastery, he did not find any belief within him. The small curiosity, the hope that he would come to know the forces calling to him died with the gentle woman.

As he laid her back onto the sweat-drenched bed coverings, Iain had decided that believing was only a key to sorrow. He would not follow any belief.

The past year had been a battle, memories and theology churning together within him. Now the confusion was replaced with a fire so intense, so consuming he had to believe, or die himself.

Lara moved down the steps, lifting her hand to him as she stepped closer. *Believe.* Iain thought his mother meant he must follow one of the conflicting religions, but the sudden clarity of Lara's presence in his world made him understand her true meaning. Only within would he find the strength; all he had to do was believe--in himself.

Taking Lara's hand, he tugged gently; and she stepped willingly into the circle of his arms. The wide violet swirl of her eyes reflected the fire of desire growing to an inferno between them. Tilting her head back slightly, she parted her lips and lowered her eyes until golden lashes lay in crescents against flushed cheeks.

Slanting his mouth across hers, Iain arched her back and crushed her to him with the ardor of his kiss. Lara clung to him, igniting his skin with her frantic touches. The slender fingers that dug into his hair exerted a pressure, encouraging him to deepen the kiss. His tongue stroked deftly into the heat of her mouth, dancing against hers.

He meant to pull away, to end the kiss before he lost his tenuous control and took her there in the cold, open hallway. But as he lifted his lips from hers Lara wrapped her arms about his head to hold him firmly in place. Standing on tiptoe, she forced his head back and drew the moist tip of her tongue along his jaw and down to the hollow just below his Adam's apple.

Breath hot as a midsummer wind scorched his skin as Lara placed tiny kisses along a damp path to his clenched jaw. Mindless of the flowers adorning the golden nimbus of her hair, Iain captured the sides of her head to draw her lips again toward his. The jolt of lightning at the touch carried him swirling into oblivion.

The subtle clearing of a throat above them was as effective as a bucket of cold water thrown over a fire. Startled, Iain tried to step back but Lara clung to him. Her breathing was labored, and he held his own harsh breaths to gaze at her in concern. The desire-glazed smile she gave him calmed those fears. He cradled her against his side and glared up the stairs at Beitris.

The old woman grinned, the wrinkles around her eyes settling into happy lines. "Dinna worry about me, younguns." With one hand against the wall to steady herself, Beitris moved carefully down the steps. "But such is best suited to the end of the day. To ensure the harvest, is that no' correct, master Iain?' His eyebrows lowered at the knowing glint in the woman's eyes. Beitris cocked her head and winked. When she reached their side she leaned close to Lara and whispered loudly. "Mind what I told ye, child."

Deep red flushed Lara's face but she smiled sweetly at the servant. "I remember. You may be right."

Beitris bowed slightly from the waist. "Dinna think I am too old to remember or understand. 'Tis a guid thing." Her gnarled finger stabbed toward the doorway. "Ye had best be goin' to the hill. Dance fer joy and fer the plantin'. Weave yer ribbons down the pole, dearie. When darkness comes, master Iain will light the balefires." Turning on her heel, she moved quickly into the depths of the manor.

"What did she tell ye, sweet?"

Lara gasped, trying to catch her runaway breath. When she'd seen Iain waiting at the bottom of the stairs it had been all she could do not to fly into his arms. She'd known, without any doubt, he would welcome her there.

And he had. Bright fire filled the coal darkness of his eyes before he kissed her. Ah, what a kiss. The impact trembled through her like the resounding electricity of a lightning strike.

If Beitris hadn't interrupted they would still be...and never leave the manor. And she was looking forward to a good party.

"Lara?"

"I'm sorry, what did you say?"

The satisfied glint in his eyes showed he knew where her thoughts lay, and Iain flashed a bright smile at her. "I asked ye what Beitris told ye to remember."

"Oh, she said..." As close as they were to making Beitris's words come true there in the hallway, Lara didn't think this was the time to add more fuel to a fire already out of control. "It was women stuff."

Iain's dark eyebrows rose into the shock of hair that fell over his forehead. Lara brushed the soft hair back and smoothed the shoulder-length strands. She was glad he wore it loose, although the dark strands tempted her fingers to return to the silky length.

He touched her hair, and the soft scent of bruised flowers surrounded them. "I fear I crushed some of yer flowers."

Feeling herself drawn toward him, Lara jerked back and closed her eyes against the sultry desire in Iain's face. They'd never get to the party if they didn't leave right now. "It doesn't matter. Shall we go?"

Disappointment flared past the desire in Iain's eyes but was soon replaced by a merry twinkle. "Of course." He paused for a fraction of a second. "I believe ye will enjoy this day."

T he village priest intoned a loud blessing for the May Day celebration, then accepted a large cup of aged, nearly clear ale and swallowed it down in one long gulp. With a grin and exuberant wave to the assembled people, he promised to add his prayers to the hopes for a warm spring and bountiful fall harvest. His long strides carried him away from the building noise of the celebration.

The anchorite stood beneath an overhang of low branches, watching. Arms crossed over his chest, he scowled as the merry priest passed him. As was his normal practice, the priest ignored the anchorite's presence.

A sigh filled the anchorite's chest. He always hoped for more from others who followed the Christ. Why did his way of worship segregate him so completely from others? Another deep breath strained the thinning, ragged material across his chest. That was the way for those who chose the path of solitude--or who had the role of anchorite forced upon them.

Slipping into the shadows of a small wooded area at the base of the hillock, the anchorite turned to his companions. "I fear this will be a long day of waiting. We canna rush the Seanachai, or his plan."

One of the Norsemen grunted and sat cross-legged with his back braced against a tree. "We are a patient people." He took a dagger from its sheath. "When the chance of reward is great." Finding a thick, broken branch, the Norseman began to strip the bark. Cold blue eyes remained focused on the anchorite as the Norseman worked to slice off a measured length of the wood.

"I thought a man of your calling would be used to solitary waiting." He pointed the dagger at the anchorite and then stabbed it toward the ground. "Sit, holy man. We follow the storyteller's plan. Foolhardy though it may be." The thick, northern accent grated on the anchorite's patience, and he knew the Viking laughed at him.

Turning his attention to the hand-length of branch the Norseman began carefully carving away slivers of wood. The anchorite sat and folded his hands in the aspect of solemn prayer.

But the thoughts rushing through his mind were far from prayerful. Although agreeing to the foolishness of the Seanachai's plan galled him, it was the nearest the anchorite had come to his own revenge on the holding of his birth. He had chosen the ancient broch near the village as his place of contemplation. Then he had watched and waited. Years passed and the anchorite had nearly forgotten the reasons for his long anger.

Until the farmer brought the visiting storyteller to his lonely hovel. The memories of rejection and derision returned. That the old laird or the outland wench he married no longer lived made no difference. Revenge, even shared with other outlanders, would go far in returning the blessed peace of heart lost long ago.

L ara sipped a cup of sweet mead. Unfortunate past experience with a bad hangover had shown her she had little tolerance for the fermented drink. However, the revelers drank freely, lifting their cups and bowls to the sky and then lowering them reverently to the earth each time the kegs were visited. The smell of roasting mutton blew across her senses to mix unpleasantly with other cooking odors and the smells of the people. Lifting a flower to her nose, Lara inhaled deeply, vaguely promising herself to never complain at functions where each woman seemed to wear an overpowering amount of a different perfume.

Iain was constantly being called away by one of the locals or Castantin. Each time, his look of apology tugged at her heart and she gave him kisses of forgiveness when he returned to her side. How would Castan manage to run his holding when Iain was gone?

A deep sigh filled her with sorrow and longing, and she wished she could stay until the time he was forced away. But neither her parents nor the guardians of Faerie would allow her to stay in the past so long. Deep in her mind she knew they were right. The longer she remained, the more chance there was she could adversely affect the time or the people she visited.

The ability to create a time portal was rare and none before had redirected the future. Whether or not such a change would happen was merely a group of theories discussed by those who had never traveled through a time portal. Lara had no wish to be the first to prove or disprove any theory.

"'Tis no' the time for sadness, sweet." Iain spoke close to her ear, and then caressed the lobe with the tip of his tongue.

Quickly turning her head, Lara captured his lips for a lingering kiss. "I'm not sad, just thinking."

"'Tis no' the day fer thinkin'." Iain took the mead from her hand and lead her to the center of a wide, flat area. Expectant faces ringed the area. Confused, she turned her gaze to Iain's smile.

"They willna begin the dancin' 'til we lead them." He shrugged. "I canna change the mind of any of them."

Lara giggled. The curiosity of the people had followed her since her arrival in the past, but even so she was embarrassed to be the focus of the attention. "Do we have to?"

"Aye. 'Twould no' be guid to anger the spirit of the celebration. Ye dinna wish to curse me harvest, do ye?"

"Oh, no. I'd never do that." Lara hurried to reassure him and then poked his shoulder when his face broke into a mischievous, eye-twinkling grin. "You're teasing me."

Unable to hold an apologetic expression, Iain twirled her in a circle. "I am? Dinna be too sure."

Taking her hands, Iain drew her into a swaying dance. Raucous music, played by a few musicians standing to one side and hand-clapping filled the air as they moved around the open space. Dropping one of Lara's hands, Iain turned to another in the crowd and drew her into the dance. Smiling, Lara followed his example. One by one the crowd joined the dance. Laughter and off-key singing of the bawdy words added to the lilting melody.

Lara danced until a tight pain caught at her side and she was forced to move to the edge of the gathering. Iain was soon beside her. He cupped one hand to her side and slid his fingers slowly up and down to ease the painful stitch. But, her breathing would not return to normal. The soft movement of Iain's hand and the other arm wrapped around her waist to hold her close was nearly more than her overly stimulated senses could deal with.

Iain drew her toward the long table where food and drink were offered. Pouring a cup of mead, he wiped the lip and offered it to her. Shaking her head, she moved to lean over the table and glanced around for plain water. A cool stone cup was pressed into her hand. "Ye dinna care fer mead?"

"No, actually I love the taste, but it makes me lightheaded."

Iain rubbed a loose golden curl between his thumb and finger. "But yer head is already light." He leaned to kiss the top of her head.

"No." Her voice shook. "I mean it makes me drunk."

His lips moved in another kiss, bringing teasing tingles to her scalp. "Then ye shall drink naught but water. I willna have ye without yer faculties this day."

The words excited her. Even though she wanted to stay within his arms, she stepped away and stared into the dark depths of his eyes. Lara bit at her lip and laid her hand on his shoulder. "Why?"

The roughness of his callused palm smoothed along her arm until he captured her hand under it. Turning her palm toward his waiting lips, Iain let his mouth linger there. He kissed the tip of each finger. His gaze bored deeply into her soul with each touch, each nibble of his strong teeth. Lara could not withhold the gasps of pleasure as he drew heat to her hand and sent it back as spiraling flames to burn the very core of her. "I wish ye to experience all I have to give ye." The sensuous promise of his words hovered in the air between them. Looping her hand around his neck, Iain offered his mouth to her. All she had to do was lean toward him and accept.

The meeting of their mouths was a jolt of pure pleasure. Lara sank thankfully into the support of his arms. She met the thrust of his tongue with strokes of her own and moaned with the sensation. An answering groan pulled her to her toes, her arms wrapped tightly around him to hold the powerful intimacy between them.

"Ahem."

Covering her flaming cheeks with her hands, Lara jerked away. Iain tugged at the front of his shirt and turned a frustrated glare to the woman standing at the far side of the table. She held a large platter of light-brown goo in her hands.

"Beitris." Shaking his head, Iain planted his fists on the tabletop and leaned over them. His words were breathless and shaky. "Ye have the timing of a saint, old woman."

Grizzled eyebrows lifted merrily. "Time enough for that later, young master. Now ye must pull the candy or 'twill be ruined. And ye dinna wish to face me wrath if ye ruin me hard work."

Lara turned to watch Beitris lay the platter on the table. Squinting at the mass, Lara made a face. The sticky goo looked rather disgusting. Hearing Iain chuckle, she turned toward him. He took a handful of the concoction and began pulling and stretching it.

"May look no' so guid now, but once ye pull it, 'tis a pale

yellow color." His eyebrows lifted in appreciation and sultry speculation. "An' so sweet."

Before she could respond, he turned toward the dancers, lifted
his hands high in the air and shouted. "Yellowman." The music
stopped abruptly, and the people looked toward him. A shout
echoed from the dancers and they rushed as one toward the table.

Drawn into the center of the excited mass of people, Lara was
handed the end of a glob of candy. As she and her partner pulled
the stretchy mess, it began to pale to a light yellow. Trying to
wipe a blob of stickiness from her cheek with an equally sticky
hand, she looked around for Iain. He stood in the center of a small
group that diligently stretched the Yellowman. Laughter and
conversation faded to soft grunts of effort and satisfaction as the
Yellowman grew stiffer and more difficult to pull.

Lara rolled her eyes. This was nothing but an old-fashioned
taffy pull. Around her, soft sounds of triumph told of the
successful completion of the pull. When lengths of candy were
placed before Beitris, she used a long knife to swiftly slice the
Yellowman into pieces. Soon, sighs of delight replaced the excited
chatter as Beitris held out the tray of candy.

Each reveler took a handful of the shiny yellow candy and,
talking softly among themselves, wandered off to shaded resting
places. Iain wrapped his arm around Lara's waist to draw her
away as well.

"Don't you want any candy?" She slid a piece into her mouth.

Although Iain watched her intently as she chewed, he shook
his head and rubbed ruefully at his belly. "I dinna care for any."
Pressure at her waist invited her closer. "There is only one sweet I
desire this day."

Swallowing heavily, Lara gazed into the distance. "I don't
have any more chocolate," she whispered.

"'Tis no' the chocolate." Iain tightened his hold and moved
them away from the table and Beitris's grin. "Perhaps after ye lead
the maypole dance I shall show ye, sweet." He rested his lips
gently against her cheek. "We should rest before the feasting. And
yer dance."

"I--"

An equally soft kiss stopped her words. "Come, everyone rests now. Ye may sleep upon me shoulder as ye did that fateful chocolate day."

Lara nodded.

Iain rested his chin on the top of her head. "My sweet."

Convinced that she'd never fall asleep while pressed comfortably against Iain's side, Lara woke when the late afternoon sun heated her face. Shining brightly in her eyes, the sun was a warm comfort. But her side was cool; Iain had left her.

Feeling bereft and lonely, Lara tugged at the low neckline of her dress and then tried to fluff the crushed blossoms in her hair. Giving up, she removed the broken flowers and tossed them to one side. Laughter drew her attention to the tables. People milled about, holding thick slabs of bread covered with sliced meats. She chuckled; it looked just like a modern barbecue. Except here you really could eat your plate.

Her stomach grumbled loudly, so she hurried to the table and created a thick sandwich. Included in many of the surrounding conversations, Lara smiled and chatted but all the while she looked around for Iain. She was concerned and strangely frightened by the lack of his warmth at her side.

When the people began pointing to the top of the small rise, she turned to see Iain crouching near the base of her maypole, tamping the dirt more firmly around it. Gloriously happy, she started toward him.

The heat of his gaze when she reached the top of the hill burned through her with an intensity that matched the lowering sun at her back. Taking the last of her sandwich, Iain looked sadly at the juices dripping down her fingers.

"Ye have made a mess of yerself, Lara." After taking a large bite of her food, he held the last morsel to her lips. "Ye must no' be so tasty when ye lead the dancin'." Lifting her hand he licked at the juices. Teasing her with his tongue, he sucked each finger into his mouth.

Gasping for breath, Lara took one of his fingers to return the amazing feelings. The rough pads of his fingertips rasped against her tongue and she longed to taste the smoother skin elsewhere, everywhere on his body. She glanced at him through partially lowered lashes. His head was thrown back and bliss touched the corners of his lips. Lara smiled, happy beyond any joy she had known she was able to give him pleasure.

"Time fer the maypole dancin'."

Drawing his fingertip from Lara's mouth, Iain clenched his fists at his sides. Teeth gritted, he ground out one single word. "Beitris."

Leading the revelers, Beitris topped the hill; her innocent grin did not touch the mischief in her eyes. "See,' she said to those following her, "I told ye they would be ready. Time fer our guest to lead her dance."

Taking Iain's hand between hers, Lara stroked his fingers; he needed to relax. She bit back a sigh--much easier said than done. Finally, Iain smiled down at her, tension still evident in the muscle that ticked along his jaw. Turning her toward the expectant people he whispered, "Lead them, sweet. There is but one thing more I must do. I shall join ye later."

"Promise?" Doubt made the word waver as it left her lips.

Fate had not truly been on their side this day.

"Nothin' can keep me from ye, sweet." With that he turned and walked slowly down the hill.

Lara took a deep breath and flashed her most professional smile at the gathering. Their eagerness was infectious, chasing her frustration to the far reaches of her mind. Listening intently to her instructions, many eyed the maypole with curious distrust. When her instructions became clear, heads nodded happily; and the people moved in mass to the pole. So many wished to dance Lara paired them together, then took the last dangling ribbon herself.

Leaving her place in the circle, Lara crossed to where the small cluster of musicians waited expectantly. After a few moments conversation, she bid them to play any lively tune. The sun was low on the horizon when she returned to her place and the dancing began. With only a few mishaps at the beginning of the weaving pattern, the people fell into the steps with the ease of those who danced regularly and exuberantly. The colorful ribbons wove down the pole. The laughter of the participants was contagious and the musicians laughed until they could barely play. Soon only the steady rhythm of the bodhran kept the dancers moving.

The last, short bits of ribbon were woven within the tangle of dancers, who were determined to leave no ends dangling. Lara laughed with the rest as they stood around the banded maypole with their arms around each other. She loved this easy camaraderie. If only Iain were there to share it with her, the moment would be perfect.

Preparing the balefires took little time, but Iain dawdled over the task. He should have placed them earlier in the day, but had not wanted to leave Lara's side for a moment. The sounds of laughter and singing from her maypole dance carried down the hill on the slight breeze. Closing his eyes, he ached to be dancing with her. Now that he finally believed, how could he be apart from her?

The crone sidestepped next to him. Her clouded eyes held wisdom he had never taken the time to see before. Nodding at his placement of the balefires, she lay her wrinkled hand on his arm. Her claw-like fingers squeezed his flesh.

"Ye should have accepted the call of the horned one this Bealtaine. 'Twas ye he wanted, no' the other. The way will be difficult now, fraught with danger. The three mean naught, dinna let them turn ye from yer path. Heed the call; dinna let the false horned one's desires stand before ye. Believe.

Releasing the pressure on his arm, she was gone more quickly than Iain thought possible for such an elder. As usual, her speech was twisted and riddled. He sighed, frustration ripe within him. What did her words mean?

Castantin entered the clearing, assisted by two equally unsteady servants. Surely, these were not the three of which the crone spoke. Castan stood unsteadily behind one of the piles of brush and waved one hand. "Go. Bring me people."

Iain rolled his eyes. The people were Castantin's only when it pleased him. After lighting the torch set into the soft ground, Iain lifted it high into the dusk and trudged back to the maypole. He briefly admired the brightly colored twists of ribbon adorning the top of the hill, then searched through the throng of people for Lara. The last rays of sunlight glinted off the fine gold of her hair to steal his breath away.

The air filled with anticipation, and the laughter and conversations ceased when he drew near. Taking Lara's hand he shook his head briefly to forestall her questions. Silent, the people followed him from the hill, the aura of the sacred descending over them. Iain vaguely recognized the ancient feeling, but his thoughts focused on Lara.

Walking beside her was torture. She was flushed from the success of her maypole dance, and damp straggles of hair stuck to her cheeks and forehead. His agonized thoughts spurred his imagination to spread the pleased pink to cover her entire body.

The feel of her sweat-slicked skin beneath his...

He stumbled, and Lara caught at his arm, pressing the fullness of her breast against him. Biting back a groan, he led the silent parade to the clearing surrounded by thick woods. The three piles of dry hay and branches he had prepared lay ready. The balefires would call the old ones to grant the successful future harvest. The bright flames would then announce the one chosen to portray the ancient horned god. A quick glance to one side passed quickly over the small knot of hopeful young women. One of them would be chosen to lie with the horned one that night.

A tingle of misgiving ran across his shoulder blades to settle in the center of his chest. The priests ignored this remnant of the old ways and smiled behind their hands at the superstitious peasantry. But something of this night felt wrong.

Castantin climbed unsteadily to the top of one of the pyres. "Ho, me people. The sun is near set; the moon rises from the sea. A full moon to bless the gatherin' and me lands." He pointed over Iain's shoulder.

The silver fullness of the rising moon drew a gasp of appreciation from the crowd. "Coz, light the fires." Castan fell backwards off the prepared bonfire as he waved for Iain to continue.

Iain gave Lara's hand a squeeze and thrust the head of the torch deep within the first balefire. Sharp crackling sounded as the dry hay caught and flared into the dark. Moving in a circle that mimicked the flight of the sun through the sky, he lit each of the fires in turn, finally tossing the torch into the last with a wide flourish. A cheer filled the clearing, and then echoed away into silence as the people awaited the horned one.

The day had been spent in seclusion, planning, scheming, building anticipation to a fevered pitch. Aubrian felt the call of the moon, though it was still hidden behind the sea-washed horizon. Full and powerful, the silver disk would rise

in support of his plans. Had it been so few days since he vowed
Lara would be his by this night?

Tossing off his clothing, Aubrian donned a short leather kilt
and tightened the wide belt. Barely long enough to cover his
semi-aroused state, the soft leather rubbed against him sensuously. Disappointed he had to cover himself at all, Aubrian sighed
and reached for a small pot of deep blue paint.

Creating the design without a way to view his progress irritated him, but his skin remembered the feel of the pattern and
his heart flew with the renewal of power. The tortured knotwork
on his chest flowed into a blue line rising the length of his
arched neck to connect with a mask of blue already painted over
his eyes. Aubrian paused to revel in the power flowing through
him.

The years since he called upon this much power had seemed
eons long. The culmination of his pain-filled waiting, the long-
awaited satisfaction of his body, and his revenge was near. His
erection grew firmer, making a tent of the kilt.

Aubrian laughed in delight, the image he presented filled his
senses. The horned one would be long remembered after this
night.

He lifted his head and inhaled the cooling night air. It was
time. A hint of silver moonlight glinted along the edge of the sea
and the golden sunset behind him sent deep shadows dancing
through the trees. The muted rustling of the gathering neared--he
must be in place soon.

Moving with faerie grace through the trees, he surprised those
waiting for him. The anchorite scowled and dropped his gaze
from Aubrian's face. When the gaze touched upon the fullness of
his body, the anchorite paled and turned away.

The Norsemen elbowed each other's ribs and joined Aubrian's
pleased laughter. Taking the final steps into the small clearing,
Aubrian glanced around regally, his head high, hands fisted
against his lean hips. "I make a fine god, do you not agree?"

The Vikings' continued laughter covered the anchorite's
breathless grumbling.

"Silence, all of you. It is nearly the hour of my destiny. Are you prepared?"

The anchorite bowed toward Aubrian but refused to lift his eyes higher than the bare knees. "We are ready."

One of the tall blonds moved to Aubrian's side. "We do not agree to leave our weapons behind. It is not the way to glory."

"Ah, but you will leave them. The horned one needs no weapons other than those he carries upon his head." Aubrian pointed to the large rack of antlers resting against a tree. "You are here merely to make sure none follow the god and his chosen. The people will fear you, if they even recognize your presence. The frenzy created by my appearance eases your duties."

The Norseman turned to his companion, rolled his eyes and canted his head sharply back toward Aubrian. The other shrugged and moved into position at the far side of the clearing.

Darkness claimed the clearing, for the moon had not yet risen high enough to illuminate past the tall trees. An echoing cheer rose nearby; then, pregnant silence lay heavily over the land. Aubrian gave the anchorite a shove and stepped forward, lifting the antlered mask to his head. Though disappointed the heavy half-mask covered the beautiful blue markings on his face, Aubrian realized there would be only one to see him in all his godlike glory. Aubrian renewed his pledge to the bright circle of the full moon. Lara would be his.

C heering with the rest after Iain lit the last bonfire, Lara tried to follow his progress back to her. But he was lost in the darkness between the bright fires. The gathering pressed around her, and someone grasped her hands to pull her into a circle moving slowly around one of the fires. Glancing over her shoulder as they moved she could see circles forming around each fire, the slow stomp of many feet pulsing like a living heartbeat.

Lara had taken part in similar events at Renaissance faires with her brother or at Faerie celebrations, but this dance created a life of its own. Flowing through her blood, the ancient call threw her head back until she stared into the full moon. Gasping at the shadowed face and the rotund beauty, she lifted her arms, tugging those of her neighbors with hers. The pounding in her ears was loud in the otherwise silent clearing; the merry crackling of the fires filled her. It was as if she came alive in the dance. Each sense tingled with electric vibrations. The dance was exciting her and bringing her to a strange and increased state of arousal.

She looked frantically for Iain. He needed to be beside her; it was his fault she felt this way. Heat followed the ancient call in her blood, burning her from the inside out. His touch was the only way to end the burning desire.

Finally, firelight highlighted the deep black of his hair. Dancing in another circle Iain caught her eye, smiled and winked. Then he was gone in the silent swirl of bodies.

A single, wordless shout rang out. The circles froze, each person turned slowly toward the open triangle between the fires. A poorly dressed priest waited there, arms lifted high above his head. As he slowly strode past each circle, his eyes glittered emotion that brought tremors to chase each other along Lara's spine.

The priest fisted his hands and shouted. "He is come."

A collective sigh followed a gasp of anticipation when a man, barely dressed in a leather kilt and wearing a horned mask, moved beside the priest. Legs spread, arms crossed over the design painted on his chest, the bulging evidence of his virility was proudly displayed. A collective sigh rose from the women.

Lara stifled a giggle. True, she was impressed, maybe even intrigued. The man had to be throwing off pheromones at a fierce rate; the girl next to her was nearly panting.

Wanting only one man, the man who had marked her as his earlier with burning kisses, Lara turned from the spectacle, looking for Iain. Let the horned god plant magic with one of the willing girls--she would cultivate her own relationship with the man she loved.

Stumbling on the rough terrain, Lara lifted her fingertips to her mouth. She desired Iain and ached desperately for a physical relationship with him, however brief. Pain centered in her chest--however brief. The question rose again. Did she love him? Could she come to love someone in such a short span of time? Two weeks wasn't that long, and she hadn't even been with him that whole time.

People surged around her, turning her toward the masked man. Women of all ages vied for his attention. Lips held tightly in a firm line, the man ignored the flirting and shook off the caressing hands that moved under his kilt and over his chest. Fascinated, Lara watched his eyes dart from one woman to the next. She would wait and find Iain after she saw who was honored and chosen by the god.

She had taken many steps toward the horned man before she recognized the undeniable force dragging her forward. Faerie glamour--directed at her. Cold blue eyes glinted under the horned mask. Aubrian. Trying to twist away even as she moved closer, Lara struggled to form words to chase the glamour away. But the hounds were silent.

Aubrian's smile glistened with predator's intent and he pushed the other women away. The world stopped when he stepped forward and reached for Lara's hand. She was unable even to shake her head to show the denial in her heart. The palm that cradled her hand was damp and soft; her skin crawled as though a thousand ants crawled over her.

The priest's voice shot through the night. "The horned one has chosen. May the union bless the plantin' and bring bounty to our harvests."

Unable to return to Lara's side after lighting the fires, Iain joined one of the circles. The dance had brought them close many times before he finally caught her eye. He found himself entranced by the bounce of her hair as she stomped around her fire. The mixed cool silver light of the moon and the

golden flames surrounding her tightened the knot in his chest.
When the one chosen to portray the horned god arrived Iain
vowed to spirit Lara away to a private haven and show her how
deeply he loved her.

*Ah, sweet, I do love ye. Mathair, I understand, and I believe. You
would love her as well.*

"He is come." Iain's eyes narrowed as the voice of the
anchorite announced the horned one. The reclusive holy man had
not joined the Bealtaine fires in the long years he existed in his
lonely hovel. Unease settled, immobile in the pit of Iain's
stomach.

Although he tried to breach the distance between Lara and
himself, the anxious rush of women and curious groups of men
constantly held Iain back. Catching sight of the horned one, he
nodded in vague approval; the man was certainly well versed in
the part he played.

The lump in Iain's chest sank to his belly and grew until he
could hardly breathe. Unable to move closer he could only watch
as the man held out one hand to Lara and she took it.

Holding her tightly against his side, the horned one lifted one
fist in triumph.

"The horned one has chosen." The anchorite's words grated
through Iain's pain. He struggled against the crowd but he could
not get to Lara, could not wrench her from those wrong arms. The
small tide of humanity turning to carnal celebrations kept him
from Lara.

Helpless, he watched the horned one lead Lara toward the
trees. The fake god stopped under the dense overhang and turned
Lara to face him. The moonlight brightened around them as if
blessing the union. The horned mask turned toward Iain and the
icy eyes locked onto his. With a swift, graceful movement the
mask dropped to the ground.

The madness and triumph in Aubrian's face forced Iain to take
an involuntary step back. The storyteller's eyes held Iain's while a
lewd grin twisted Aubrian's lips. Grasping Lara's chin, he lifted
her mouth to his for a brutal, punishing kiss. Nodding to him as if

in polite acknowledgement of a friend, Aubrian turned Lara and disappeared into the dark trees.

Limp with despair, Iain fought to understand why Lara would respond so enthusiastically to his lovemaking, and then go with another. She couldn't respond to another as she did to him, could she? Strength began to flow back into his muscles. He knew she could not. And had not, for she did not react to the Seanachai's kiss. When he led her away her movements lacked their usual grace, as if she fought against each step.

You must be strong, my son. Remember.

Iain shook off the now-familiar echo of his mother's voice. In doing so he also shook off the lethargy. Moonlight led him from the circle of balefires. The horned mask lay forgotten at the edge of the firelight. Iain snatched it up as he passed and nearly dropped it when tingling jolts of power surged up his arm. His shoulder throbbed, and he turned the mask over and over in his hands. There was no clue to the source of the unusual power. Holding the mask by one branched horn, Iain began the careful tracking of the false god who had taken the woman he loved.

Deep in his mind, almost beyond the range of his inner hearing, Iain recognized the baying of hounds. Confused, he turned one way, then another under the thick, wooded canopy, searching for signs leading to Lara. The baying faded when he faced one way but grew stronger when he turned the opposite direction. Letting the hounds guide him, Iain rushed through the shadowed forest.

Suddenly, two large, thickly built men appeared before him. Slowing to a walk Iain moved to go around them, but they angled to block his path. Iain straightened and peered through the darkness.

Their clothing was odd; heavy metal breastplates covered their chests, their yellow hair and beards braided. Lochlannaich? Iain took a deep breath. The holding had been lucky. This close to the sea, they had not yet been visited by the marauding Vikings. His hopes that the area would avoid the warriors dashed to pieces on the bracken-covered ground.

"What do ye wish here?" Iain spoke slowly in Latin. Eyebrows raised, the men looked at each other. One stepped forward and spoke in a heavily accented version of Iain's native tongue. "You will not pass."

"I shall. I have no argument with ye unless ye deter me from me task."

"You will not follow the storyteller." The Viking patted his side searching for his weapon. His hand fell on an empty scabbard and he gazed skyward with a minute, disgusted shake of his head.

"I shall, if I so wish." Iain stepped forward clutching the sharply horned mask before him.

The second Norseman spoke rapidly in his own flowing language and gestured anxiously into the dark woods. A soft, urgent discussion followed. Iain waited impatiently, trying to circle the men but even as they spoke they moved to continually block his progress. Each moment that passed increased the need to move, to find Lara. Finally, he held his ground, knowing to fight both warriors would end in his defeat.

The Norseman turned back to him. "For a woman, this is foolish. We no longer desire a part. We will not return to these shores...for now." Without waiting for a response they loped past Iain and disappeared.

Shaking from the strange encounter and the urgent need to find Lara, Iain followed the faint path of Aubrian's passage. The baying hounds sounded closer; he did not question the knowledge they led him to Lara.

The cacophony of sound ended abruptly as Iain bent to enter a secluded bower.

Aubrian held Lara close, grinning as her hands reached under the kilt. The soft, jerky movements of her caress wrenched a cry of denial from Iain. Aubrian turned his head, his expression possessive and triumphant. "Leave us. She is mine."

"She is no'."

Aubrian leaned his head to one side. "Think you not? She has always been mine." Touching Lara's cheek, he drew her lowered gaze to his. "You are mine, Lara. Tell him."

Tremors of agony shook Iain while Lara's face turned slowly toward him. Moonlight glistened off the damp trails of tears covering her cheeks. Fresh tears hovered thickly on her lashes, and a strange emotion Iain did not understand filled her eyes. She did nothing but stare at him, pleading.

"Tell him." Aubrian shook her shoulder roughly and Iain took a quick step forward.

Lara's head began to nod, the muscles in her neck taut in protest of the up-and-down motion. Her eyes closed, a painful struggle evident in her face. Full, bruised lips formed a word without sound. *No.*

Intent upon Iain, Aubrian did not see her response. Backed by the baying hounds, Iain took another step forward. Cautiously closing the distance between them, he wondered how he could defeat the storyteller weaponless. Hand-to-hand combat had never been one of his skills. The mask shifted in his fingers, power throbbing up his arm. He had a weapon, one Aubrian sought to use against him. Determination grew stronger within him.

"So, you still do not believe." Iain jerked at Aubrian's words. His teeth ground together, his muscles bunched for an attack.

"Hmm, then we must show him, my dear." Aubrian physically drew Lara's gaze back to his. Iain's eyes narrowed-- this was how the Seanachai controlled her. Through his narrowed gaze Iain saw a faint shimmer pass between them. It was as if one of Beitris's tales of the fey otherworld came to life before him. He wished he had paid more attention to the old woman's stories.

Aubrian pushed on Lara's shoulder to force her to her knees before him. "Show him." Pressure from his fingers dented the fair skin of her neck as he lifted his kilt and pressed the tip of his erection against Lara's tightly closed lips.

The exalted grin he flashed at Iain faded when he did not gain entry to Lara's mouth. The fingers tightened. "Show him." Body stiff and unresponsive, Lara's eyes were squeezed shut and tears slipped past her lashes. A tiny trickle of blood from a corner of her mouth joined the trailing tears. Aubrian shook her, snapping her head back. "You are no better than your mother."

Lara crumpled to the ground and began to sob loudly. As if a spell were broken Iain leapt forward. With one of his hands wrapped around the antlered mask, he raised it high for a swift, downward slice. His other fingers curved, grasping, aching to find release around the storyteller's proud neck.

Laughing and taunting with waggling fingers, Aubrian bounced lightly out of the way of Iain's headlong rush. A gasp ended his laughter as the god mask sliced into one arm and lay a long strip of flesh open. Blood welled and dripped to the ground. Covering the wound with his hand, Aubrian laughed again--the sound, shaky and less defiant. "You may have won this night, but she will be mine. And willingly. It is my destiny." He turned and disappeared beneath the trees. His cold laughter faded into the distance.

Iain's unfulfilled anger seethed through him until it escaped his lips in a primal roar of rage. He thrust the horns into the night sky, and the rage erupted once more before he took long strides to follow the Seanachai. Blinding red flashed before his eyes.

He froze mid-stride at the barely whispered sound of his name. Panting, he willed reason back into his body. He had not lost control in such a way since his youth. Then, the anger had so frightened him he refused even the mock battles of training. Now, the anger was freed and he did not know how to control it. Seething hatred pounded through him and he started again after Aubrian.

The soft, musical voice, the memory of his mother and the cries of the hounds returned. *The evil will not return this night.* The mask slipped from his unfeeling fingers. *She needs you. Go to her.*

Lara lay curled in a tight ball; silent sobs shook her violently. Her pain filled him, and pushed his anger into a concentrated lump he could easily return to the safe recesses of his mind. He stumbled to her side and knelt, hesitating to touch her.

"Lara? Sweet?" He brushed golden hair back from her face.

Lara cringed away from him. "Don't touch me. Please, don't"

Taking a deep breath to calm the fresh rise of anger Iain bent almost double so his face was close to hers. "Aubrian is gone, Lara. But I am here fer ye," he whispered.

Lara's hands muffled her voice. "I know he's gone. I can feel it. But you can't touch me."

"I canna comfort ye if I canna touch ye, sweet."

Lifting her head, Lara gazed into Iain's dark, concerned eyes. The heat of anger glimmered behind the concern and she shrank back into her ball. Why would he even still be here after what he'd just seen? What she'd done?

One finger brushed lightly over her cheek, then his palm cupped her chin. Struggling against the touch she scooted further away. "Please, don't. How can you bear to touch me?"

"I dinna understand. Why dinna ye wish to be comforted? I ache to hold ye, sweet."

"After what I just did?" Lara's dry sobs wracked her already-trembling body. She wrapped her arms around her knees, holding her disgrace tightly within her.

"Och, ye did nothin'. 'Twas all the storyteller."

A faint hope flickered. "How...how do you know?" Lara let him take her hand without pulling away.

Iain softly stroked her fingers. "I dinna...ye were...he controlled ye someway. Dinna laugh, but it was like tales Beitris tells of otherworldly powers."

Lara gasped and then tried to hide her surprise at the truth of Iain's words. "But, the things he made me do, I couldn't stop. I couldn't."

"Aye, then his power must be strong. I shall protect ye from him, I willna let ye away from me side." Iain paused. "Will ye let me hold ye now?"

Lara scrambled to her knees and fell into his arms, knocking them both to the ground. Sprawled next to him, Lara let him mold her against his side with soft strokes down the length of her back. With her head resting on his chest, she listened to the low, comforting beat of his heart. As if she were a captured princess, her handsome prince had rescued her.

The tempo of his heartbeats changed subtly, the passage of

his hand became a sensual caress. Tiny fires burned along her spine. Seeking to extend the contact, she arched into his hand. When she lifted her head to gaze into his face, the breath died in her lungs. The intensity of longing he let her see before glancing away started a fresh flow of tears.

"Lara, what is it?"

"Nothing." She glanced around the bower and shuddered. "Can we leave this place?"

Iain sat cross-legged, lifted her into his lap and smiled. "Aye. Close by is a tiny spring. 'Tis said ancient druids once blessed the water. Perhaps the holy properties will wash some of yer pain away. Would ye like me to take ye there?"

"Will there be anyone else there? I don't think I could face anyone right now."

"I dinna think so. Few ken the existence, for 'tis hidden well and near the center of the holdin'. There are no farmsteads nearby."

"I would love to wash my face." The mundane action might help calm her although she knew she could not scrub her face hard enough to erase the memories of Aubrian's touch. Lara patted her hair; she must look a mess. Iain's company would soothe her tattered soul as well.

Iain lifted her to her feet and gallantly wrapped his fingers through hers.

Lara gladly followed Iain through the moonlit forest until the tinkling sound of water intruded on the agony she fought to keep from her memory.

After pushing aside thick, overgrown bushes, Iain gestured for her to enter a small grassy area. A tall rock formation with deeply carved circles covering the surface walled one side of the clearing. Bushes enclosed the other three sides, making a tiny forest room with only the sparkling night sky for a ceiling.

Delighted, Lara stepped closer to the clear spring. A bubbling spray of water gurgled through a small fissure in the rock, creating patterns of ripples in the otherwise smooth surface of the pool. Kneeling carefully at the rocky edge, Lara dipped one hand into the water and brought it to her mouth. It was cold and refreshing, with a slight aftertaste of the salty ocean.

Iain chuckled. "So close to the sea, perhaps a bit o' the salt seeps into the spring. That taste, 'tis said to bring healing." Dark brows drew together and lifted before he tugged at one of his sleeves. It ripped from the shoulder seam. A grimace of concentration wrinkled his face as he tried to untie the ribbons that still bound the sleeve to his arm. With a sigh of relief he held it out to Lara.

"Use this to wash yer face, sweet."

Amazed that he'd ruined his shirt for her, Lara could only stare. So, Iain knelt beside her and dipped one end of the sleeve into the water. Lara closed her eyes while he wiped the grimy tearstains from her face and brushed the cloth carefully along her lashes. She ran her tongue over her lip and tasted the coppery tang of blood. Iain then took great care in wiping her lip and soothing the cold water over the tender surface. Her lips parted.

The caring ministrations stopped suddenly. When Lara opened her eyes, Iain had looked away. His chest rose and fell rapidly; the damp sleeve crushed tightly in his fingers. Touching his bare arm jolted the electricity between them to life. The desire in his heavy-lidded gaze turned her insides to quivering oatmeal.

"Thank you, Iain. I do feel much better."

"Aye, I think ye ken I would do aught fer ye."

"Would you...could you fully wash away the memory of those awful moments with..." She shuddered, and Iain wrapped both arms around her and cradled her head against his chest.

"Ye dinna need to say more, sweet. What can I do?"

Lara kissed the skin exposed by the low vee of his shirt. She spoke so softly, not even sure herself if she actually said the words or only thought them. "Make love to me."

EIGHTEEN

Torn by desire and concern for the fragile woman in his arms, Iain peered into her face. Her eyes were closed; a smile softened the remnants of pain from her features. Great joy burst through him. She had not asked him only to lay with her. Her words demanded more than a Bealtaine mating. *Make love to me.*

Treasuring the subtle differences of a few words, Iain brushed her lips with his own. "Aye, sweet. If that is what you...truly desire."

"Love me, Iain."

"Here? 'Tis no' the soft bed I would wish fer ye."

Lara's fingers searched through the tangles of his hair until she grasped his ears to tug his lips closer. The soft movement of her lips against his cheek was near his undoing. "Here. Anywhere. Only...now."

Claiming her mouth with tender pressure, Iain nibbled on her lip and strove to wipe away the attentions of another. Lara clutched his shoulders and then gave a gentle push. Confused, Iain inched away.

A twinkle had returned to the darkened violet swirls of her eyes. "Beitris won't show up again, will she?"

Iain's hearty laugh crumbled the last tentative vestiges of his reserve. Tracing the curve of Lara's jaw with the back of his finger he shook his head. "I think this is how she planned fer us to end the day. Her interruptions merely stoked the fires."

"I'm stoked." Lara giggled at his startled expression and then tried unsuccessfully to hold a serious demeanor. Iain leaned closer. Lara's breath whooshed out in frustration when he stopped with his lips nearly touching hers and turned his face to the side.

"Perhaps the grass will be more comfortable than this rocky ledge."

"You think so, do you?" Lara shoved until Iain fell sideways. He grabbed her and rolled until she lay beneath him. Struggling against the intense pleasure of his weight, Lara was not ready to let him have the upper hand. "We're not yet at the softest grass, big boy."

Twisting, she modified one of Derrik's self-defense moves and ended the move straddling Iain's chest. Her hair fell around his face when she leaned to kiss his firm, smiling lips. Extending what she thought was going to be a brief kiss, Lara angled her way off Iain's body and curled against him when he turned to his side.

"There. Here. I mean, we're here."

"Aye." Iain plucked at her curls, straightened one and let it bounce back softly. "Ye are a nickum quean."

"What? I'm what?"

Iain kissed the tip of her nose. "A mischievous." The side of her mouth received the same thrilling treatment. "Young." The other side of her mouth felt the tingling pressure of a kiss. "And definitely woman." Full pressure parted her lips beneath his; she accepted the tentative gift of his tongue with a deep moan of pleasure.

Life. It was as if he gave her life with his kiss. The burning began, winding a path from her lips to her breasts. Did he feel the heat? She arched with a cry and pressed her breast more fully into his palm. He teased her by drawing small circles over her skin. His hand left a trail of fire across it.

Needing to return the heat he gave her, Lara tugged at Iain's shirt. Rising to one elbow, he smiled and yanked it over his head. Still held in place by the ribbons tied at his elbow, the soft crush of material hung down one arm. But with another tug on the sleeve, the shirt was gone. Iain's firm chest and the dark blue tattoo at his shoulder were exposed to her avid gaze.

Assisting Lara to a sitting position beside him, Iain traced the low neckline of her dress and loosened the ties at the back of her neck. The bodice pooled around her waist; she held herself still under the intensity of his gaze.

Lara ran her fingers lightly through the dark hair dusting Iain's chest and paused to tease the flat buds of his nipples. Rising to her knees, she wrapped her arms around his neck and rubbed against him. The crisp hair cushioned and tormented her skin. Becoming incredibly aroused, she moaned and arched her back.

Iain attacked the curve of her neck with his lips, nipping and then soothing the length with his tongue. He pushed the dress down over her hips. She shivered in delight when he cupped her bottom, brought her closer and set her against the firm bulge of his desire. She wiggled, fitting her body to his.

"Be still, woman, or ye'll finish me." Lara immediately ceased wiggling and leaned back.

"If you didn't have those silly pants on..." Drawing a finger lightly along the top of the braided ribbons he still wore as a belt, Lara barely touched his quivering skin and smiled coyly at him.

Growling, he pushed her unceremoniously to the ground and struggled to his feet. Lara helped him pull off his boots and unwrap the straps binding the bottom of the each pant leg. By the time she finished and lay back in the soft grass, he was able to step from the clothing, naked and gloriously aroused in the moonlight.

Returning to her side, Iain took a long, slow breath. "We could still..."

Lara shook her head. "I could not. Love me." Her fingers

wrapped around him and stroked his length with a strong, gentle pressure. Then she shivered and bit at her bottom lip. Iain captured her hand and reluctantly eased the warmth away.

"Ye dinna have to do aught ye dinna wish."

Swallowing heavily, she curled one hand into his hair and returned the other to stroke his heated length. "I know, Iain. Chase away the bad memory. Give me you to remember."

Lara could have him; he would gladly give her memories leaving no room for others. Their lips melded together and he spread the golden mass of her hair around her shoulders. When he looked down at the fire brightening her eyes, Iain's body responded, growing even firmer, seeking the scalding heat of his sweet.

He had to touch her, to taste every inch of her, but the urgency would not allow his leisurely explorations. The pressure of her fingers drove him to the brink of sensual madness. "Sweet, dinna touch me so. I willna be able to wait."

A hint of innocence widened her eyes even as she stroked him firmly. "Wait for what?"

Her delighted giggles as he rolled so she lay on top of him pleased him greatly. Her small hands burned along his skin to tangle in his hair. The slow dip of her tongue into his mouth as she rubbed her breasts over his chest pulled the same eternal rhythm from his hips.

Rolling again, he settled with one knee between her legs and arched to suckle the dusky tip of a breast. Scraping lightly with his teeth, he drew sharp cries from his sweet. The sounds of her pleasure brought his own low cries, building his joy to a barely controllable peak. When his mouth moved down the side of her breast and up to the other waiting nipple she gripped his head tightly to hold him in place.

Resting his hand against her belly, Iain felt tiny tremors flowing lower, racing to the core of her womanhood. He followed the trail with his fingers and curved his hand over her hip and into the soft curls. Parting her folds, he dipped his finger into her moist heat and grazed his thumb across the nub of her desire.

Lara's breath came in short, sharp gasps. Firmly suckling her nipple while circling his finger within her, Iain sensed the beginning of her release. Her shoulders lifted from the ground to press his mouth tightly over the tip of her breast. Then her hips arched and she rubbed against his teasing thumb.

Slipping his free arm around her shoulders, Iain supported her as she rocked against the double sensation. Lifting his head from her breast, Iain held her tightly and captured her pleasured cries in his mouth.

Unable to give either of them pause, Iain braced himself on his forearms, cradled the wild tossing of her head with his hands and entered her with one swift thrust.

A sharp, gasping intake of breath centered Lara's shattered senses on the final joining of their bodies. The air left her lungs with a whispered, "Oh, yes." Iain moved within her and she gasped again.

Restless, she moved her hands over his back and shoulders. She stroked and teased his sweat-slicked skin. Reveling in the powerful way he filled her with each stroke, she cupped his buttocks and traced the thrusting muscles.

He slowed, circled his hips, and pulled nearly free. Wrapping her legs around his hips, Lara pressed him into her. "Don't you dare leave me," she gasped.

"I waudna, even if I could." The low whisper tickled her ear and was soon followed by the moist heat of his tongue. His thrusts became long, powerful, and increasingly more rapid. Gazes locked, the fires blazed higher in the darkness of his eyes, matched by the burning spiral within her, her desire tightened with each meeting of their bodies.

Consumed by the flames, Lara let the sparking fires carry her beyond herself, beyond reason and thought. Iain's heat burst into her and he cried out. Her cries followed his, rising to burn the cool face of the moon.

• • •

S cowling, Aubrian set up a small camp near the windswept coast where he had first discovered Lara. He had returned secretly to the manor to retrieve his pack and left as quickly through the old seaward door. The human's anger made it unsafe for him to remain in comfort despite his control over Castantin.

He trudged along the beach. Raising his fists in anger, he screamed at the tiny speck of the Norsemen's ship riding the waves far from shore. Although he had not expected the strangers to keep Iain from him, a longer delay would have served his purpose well. The agonized pain filling the human's uncultured face was a balm to the disappointment at the interruption.

Rolled in a blanket, Aubrian laced his fingers behind his head and stared into the sky. The path of the moon had nearly bisected the sky; he could smell the coming dawn.

This should have been the day of his triumphant return to Faerie. The anger blossoming in his chest forced him to sit and rest his arms on his knees before he took slow, deep breaths.

Fate, and the cursed Alastriona, would rue the day they stepped in the way of his destiny. Ah, but the satisfaction awaiting with the destruction of the human here and the usurper in Faerie pleased him greatly. The daughter was nothing, only a tool to use to get the mother.

Scooping up a handful of small stones he began tossing them toward the sea. Chasing seabirds from their search of the dark tide made him laugh. A plan formed as his thoughts were tossed about like a piece of driftwood and froze the smile on his face.

Lying back, Aubrian closed his eyes. A few days were needed to implement the new plan. He had been gone from Faerie a short time in his ages-long lifespan, a few more human days would make no difference. When the sun was high he would visit the sniveling anchorite.

· · ·

ain snored lightly, waking Lara from her sated slumber. Wincing, she pulled a sharp stick from under her hip and snuggled against Iain's side. His arm lifted to hold her possessively, but he did not wake. Even though the moonlight had dimmed, there was still enough light for Lara to see clearly. She cheered silently for the pollution-free past.

Watching Iain sleep brought a tiny smile to her lips. The hard, worried angles of his face had softened; only the growing stubble of the next day's beard marred the smooth surface. She rubbed her cheek and hoped the imprint of each whisker marked her as his.

A chuckle shook Iain's chest and he smiled. Lara kissed his cheek. "You're not asleep. Faker."

His eyelids lifted languorously, offering her the chance to fall into the emotion-filled depths of his eyes. "Ye are well?"

"Of course, silly. Why wouldn't I be?"

Iain hesitated and then wrapped both arms around her. Lara's eyes widened and she felt the heat of a blush cover her naked breasts. But no unpleasant memory intruded on their seclusion. "Oh."

Chuckling, Iain sat and pulled her onto his lap. He rapidly grew firm beneath her bottom. Lara leaned into him and nipped at the taut skin of his neck and chest. So intense was her sensuous attack she forced Iain onto his back.

Straddling Iain's thighs, Lara continued exploring and tasting the planes of his chest. She sat back slightly to admire the ridges of his abdominal muscles and run her fingers lightly over his quivering skin.

The evidence of his arousal bobbed against her belly, the length teasing Lara with sensual promise. She slapped his hands away when he tried to drag her up his body. Although she ached to return to the pleasure of his kisses, there was something she wanted more. Lifting her hips, she guided him into her waiting heat. The unison groan as she lowered herself to sheath him completely was the only sound in the still glade.

Held in timeless suspension, Lara gasped in surprise at the intensity flowing through the connection of their bodies. Then she leaned forward and began to arch her hips to take his length deep within her. She ran her hands over his chest to knead tight shoulder muscles.

Her mating was fast and hard, driving them both to the edge of a great fiery abyss. Trying to slow her desperate movements, Iain grasped her hips. But she covered his hands with hers and slid them up her body until he cupped the fullness of a breast in each palm.

His callused fingers twirled her nipples. A second wildfire blazed within her. The two fires burned, swirling closer until they slammed into each other, becoming an inferno that blasted her flying into the sparkling abyss.

Barely able to draw breath, Lara collapsed against Iain's chest. Satisfied, she looked up into his tense jaw. His teeth were gritted together, his eyes closed tightly. She stroked his face and he throbbed within her. The pulsing was a match to the beat of her heart.

By tugging on one of his shoulders, Lara managed to pull Iain on top of her without losing his heated presence at her feminine core. Able now to wrap her legs about his waist, she opened fully to him. With a sigh, he thrust into her and held himself still before ravishing her mouth with frantic kisses.

Iain set a varied pace to draw Lara into renewed passion. Her inner muscles convulsed and tightened around him and his seed poured into her. The silence of their release was absolute and profound.

Lara could hardly bear the beauty of the moment that brought tears to her eyes. Iain nudged straggles of damp hair from her forehead and kissed away her joyous tears. Lara tasted the salty skin of his chest and savored the male essence that lingered on her tongue. A breeze blew across the spring and over their bodies. Lara shivered.

"Are ye cold, sweet lowe?"

"Now what are you calling me?" Confused, Lara wondered if

she had been in this time too long, making her aunt's translation spell weak. He couldn't be calling her an artificial sweetener.

"Ye ken 'sweet'?"

"Of course, my wonderful chocolate lover."

Iain's eyes brightened. "'Lowe' is but flame. Ye are m' darlin' sweet flame."

Lara sighed deeply. She'd never been called anything so beautiful before. It made her feel... "And you make me burn like I am on fire. I can't imagine any way to quench that fire, except to be with you like this."

"Does it help?" Iain stroked the side of her breast with the back of his fingers.

"Help? It depends on what you mean by help. Being with you makes me feel...like... I don't have the words. Do you understand?" Lara knew her expression was hopeful, and that he would understand. How could she tell him now that she loved him when she would be gone in a few days?

Lara shivered again. Iain reached for her dress and slipped it over her head. "Ye are chilled. We must return to the manor, for the night will become cooler still before the dawn. Yer room will be warmer when I build a fire."

Lara waggled her eyebrows at him. "That I don't doubt." Pulling his pants over his feet and up the length of his legs, Iain pretended outrage. "I meant in the fireplace." He looked at her sideways. "Unless ye have another fire in mind."

"I don't think that fire will ever be far from my mind. Or my body."

"Ah, sweet, ye do torment a man."

"Only one man, darlin'."

After slipping his boots on, Iain stood, adjusted his belt and then lifted Lara in his arms. Leaving the torn remains of his shirt beside the bubbling spring, he carried her into the forest and toward the manor.

Lara squirmed but kept her arms wrapped tightly around his neck. Iain paused and looked down at her. "Ye are the hardest woman to carry, sweet."

"I am perfectly able to walk. Put me down."

"I dinna wish ye to stumble on unfamiliar ground. Ye may re-injure yer ankle."

Lara tapped him on the top of his head and pulled herself higher to match her mouth perfectly to his. The silky dance of their tongues left her breathless.

"And I don't wish you, keeper of the flame, to tire yourself out by carrying me all the way to my bed."

Immediately, Lara's feet were on the ground. Iain held her close for more leisurely kisses before taking her hand to guide her rapidly toward the dark shadow of the manor, into the dim hall-ways and through the doorway of her room. With his back braced against the closed door, Iain glanced meaningfully at the fireplace.

"Would ye care for a fire, m'lady?"

Lara had already crossed to the bed and tossed her dress to one side. She turned to him with arms spread wide. "Not there."

NINETEEN

L ara stretched, enjoying the pull of tired, pleasantly overused muscles. She lay facing the door and shivered because her back was cold. When she reached to pull another blanket over her, she realized she was alone on the wide bed.

The brief instant of panic faded at the dim memory of Iain's face looming over her. He had told her he would return soon. Snuggling deeper into the covers, she tried to relax enough to fall back asleep; she'd never been much of a morning person.

The night had been long, but not long enough. Lara thought she would have enjoyed more than the few scattered moments of sleep she and Iain allowed each other before turning again and again to the fire and need. She might have enjoyed the sleep, but exploring Iain's body and satisfying the constantly renewed passion was definitely more pleasurable.

A tiny flame curled low in her belly and the now-familiar tingle of sensual anticipation swirled through her. How long would it be before Iain returned? Catching her lip between her teeth she worried at the fullness. Each moment with him was precious; there was little time left. She'd never stayed this long in one period of the past and the concern drilled into her by her parents was surfacing.

The door creaked open slowly. Lara smiled and sat up, holding the blanket to her chest. But it wasn't Iain. Beitris poked her grizzled head into the room and then tiptoed through the open door.

Lara sank back against the cold wall and tried to school her expression to hide her disappointment.

Beitris stomped toward the bed and stood with her hands resting against ample hips. "Where be Master Iain?"

"Iain? Wh--why would he be here? I've just woken up."

"Don't be coy, child." Beitris grinned to soften the rebuke in her voice. "I waud be sore disappointed if the night dinna go as planned."

"So, you did manipulate us." Sinking back under her covers, Lara returned the servant's grin. "Thank you."

"Aye, bless yer meddlin', old woman."

Iain entered the room with a large tray balanced in his hands. He leaned to kiss Beitris's wrinkled cheek, set the tray on a low stand beside the bed before he drew Lara into a leisurely embrace. His broad smile melted Lara's already limp bones. Iain rose, wrapped an arm about Beitris's shoulder and angled her toward the door. He hurried her across the room and then touched his lips to her forehead.

"I dinna believe we need aught this day. Have Stephen leave meals outside the door. There is no emergency great enough to disturb us, at least until the morrow. D'ye ken?"

Beitris patted his cheek. "I have already planned it so. The boy will wait at the end of the hall should ye need him." She sent a quick glance back at Lara. "I dinna expect to hear from ye until the gloamin' meal."

"'Tis me pleasure to do yer biddin'." Iain bowed and pushed the door firmly behind her, nearly catching her voluminous skirts. The sounds of her delighted chuckle returned through the closed door.

Lara scooted to one side of the bed and held up a corner of the blanket to invite Iain to join her. He shook his head. "There are times a man needs more than his woman. I must break my fast." After stirring the coals in the fireplace, he laid a fresh log and watched until the small flame caught in the dry wood.

Lara curled beneath the covers. She was hungry, too, but not necessarily for food. Would she ever get enough of him? She hoped not.

A rumble sounded from her stomach. Iain grinned toward the fire. "Ye need yer strength, sweet. Ye will join me."

"What I need is sleep." Her stomach growled in argument. Sitting up, she wrapped a blanket around her and swung her feet to the cold floor. "Okay, I can't fight both you and my stomach."

Iain enveloped Lara in his strong arms and held her tightly before settling her in the chair before the fire. With the tray repositioned to one side, he sat at her feet. He peeked under the cloth covering the tray, lifted one eyebrow and then removed the cover with a flourish to expose a fresh loaf of dark bread. He ripped off a chunk and held it out.

Inhaling the warm, yeasty smell aroused another vigorous complaint from her belly. Biting into the firm texture was a special treat, and Lara chewed slowly. When Iain handed her a thick slab of cheese, she smiled a thank-you.

"But isn't it the time for the morning meal?"

Iain spoke around a large mouthful. "Aye."

"There isn't any brose?" Her tone wasn't very hopeful.

Slicing a wrinkled apple with his dagger, Iain handed her a thick piece and shook his head. "Ye dinna seem to enjoy porridge, so there is none fer ye this day. I could return to the kitchens...if ye desire."

Lara slapped her hand over his shoulder when he made to rise. "Don't you dare. I've had my fill of brose, and those dry old oatcakes, as well."

Trying to look offended, Iain handed her another slice of apple. "The end-of-winter larder is no' well stocked. There are no fine foods to offer ye." He uncovered the final dish.

Lara clapped her hands and reached for the light, honey-coated pastry; but Iain captured her fingers with his instead. The deep black of his eyes darkened further as his pupils enlarged. The pastry was forgotten as he pulled her from the chair to the floor next to him. Casually unwrapping the blanket, he let his gaze wander over her body until she was shivering from the heat. Longing was palpable and desire thick and heavy in the air between them.

Arching her back over one of his arms, he touched his lips to the hollow at the base of her throat. "I have waited too long fer a taste of my sweet."

They didn't leave Lara's room that day--or the next. Long hours spent in Iain's embrace brought her to life, and set Lara free in a way she didn't try to analyze. There was no logic in her love for him, only fear knowing how empty her life would be without him.

As they talked through the dawning of each day she knew she could not walk away from him, but neither could she find a way to stay at his side. When she watched him sleep through the darkest hours of the night, she practiced many different ways to tell him good-bye, never believing the near-flippant words herself.

She didn't want much, only forever. And then she feared that would not be enough. Each touch, each glance branded her--even when their passions were momentarily sated the flames remained.

Lara inched from Iain's side and crawled from the bed. After slipping a thin chemise over her head, she tied the neckline ribbon and watched the smooth rise and fall of his magnificent chest. She had to tell him but doubted the fact she loved him would be much of a surprise. Would he become angry when she said she had to leave? Or would silent bitterness fill her empty soul? If only she could ask him to return with her. There was no place for him in the holding; Castan was making him leave, anyway.

The light of another morning filtered through the heavy hangings to lure her to the window. Parting the drapes, she stared into the pale sky. The distant sounds of the folk of the manor waking to their daily chores increased her concern and fear.

The thick material swooshed back in place and she returned to the bed. She lay with her cheek propped in one hand and closed her eyes against the tempting sight of her ancient lover. If she took him from this past she could risk altering any life he may have away from the holding. Torn in two, Lara let silent tears roll down her cheeks. What could she do? Why was there no one to help her?

Iain's gentle hands cradled her face. "Why d'ye weep, sweet lowe?"

Lara's eyes opened to deep, loving concern. One of her tears was suspended on his finger. As he studied it, the droplet caught the light of the fire and was fractured into a thousand tiny sparkles. Her tears dried. Was this to be her fate?

Would her love disintegrate so completely?

Sniffing loudly she cast a tremulous smile Iain's direction. "Just a woman thing, I guess."

"'Tis a convenient excuse to me mind, darlin'. Ye shall tell me when ye can?"

Fresh tears flowed at his tender concern. Iain opened his arms; and she rested her head on his chest, her tears caught by the soft, cushioning hairs. He stroked her back and inched her closer to his side. "Lara?"

Lara grimaced at the dampness left on his chest when she lifted her head. Dabbing at the evidence of her tears with the full sleeve of the chemise, she looked into his face through blurry, tear-filled eyes. "Yes?"

"Ye have brought me somethin' I never believed existed fer me world. I dinna know how I can tell ye." Iain turned his head so he looked past her into the dying embers of the fire. Slowly, the intensity of his gaze returned to her face.

"Sweet, I love ye."

Silence met his admission. The stunned look in Lara's tear

glistened eyes ripped vicious holes in the heart she had so recently filled. Had she no idea how he felt? Why did she not speak?

Lunging forward, Lara rained kisses on his face, and her hair tangled around him. Frantic, her lips skimmed the surface of his skin, bringing with her touch a new burning, a new fire.

Breathless, she held his face in her soft hands, her fingers making tiny, prickling patterns on his temples. "I didn't know how to tell you either. I love you, I will love you forever."

"Sweet? 'Tis true?"

"True." Lara grinned through her tears. "For you, I would give up chocolate."

Having no words to compete with the soft teasing, Iain took control of her mouth. His tongue danced against hers.

When he thought he could form the words, he spoke against the softness of her cheek. "Ye love me this much?"

"And more." Lara pushed away the blanket covering him, stroked her fingers along his body and followed her touch with the sweet fire of her kisses. When she dipped her tongue into his navel Iain shuddered, grasped her shoulders and encouraged her to face him.

"Aye, and forever." As he pushed the loose neckline of the chemise from her shoulder Iain wondered why she bothered to dress.

TWENTY

"Iain." Heavy thumps against the door jerked Lara and Iain from their entwined slumber. Iain held a finger against her lips and they waited silently, hoping the intruder would go away.

The door slammed against the wall as Castan shoved it open. He strode into the room and stood at the end of the bed with his hands fisted and arms folded across his chest. After a smile of appreciation for the smooth expanse of Lara's skin, the big man's gaze moved to Ian and he frowned.

Iain tossed a blanket over her and sat on the edge of the bed. "What in bluidy hell are ye doin' here, Castan?"

"I need yer help, coz."

Lara curled behind Iain and peeked over his shoulder. A quick look at her bright-red face had him quaking in anger. "We were no' to be disturbed."

"'Sbeen three days."

"So?"

Castan lowered his arms and turned away. "I canna handle Edwin. I dinna ken what to do wi' his continued complaints."

Iain stood to face his cousin. "'Tis yer holdin', m'lord Castan-tin, hold it."

"Aye. But ye must show me."

Lara scooted further into the shadows along the wall. The flush had not faded from her face and her eyes were wide with swirling emotions. Concern for her blazed like wildfire through Iain. "Later." Iain pointed to the door. "Out. I shall dress and meet ye in the hall. Have Edwin there. I dinna wish to be away long."

Castan nodded meekly and took a few steps from the bed. He stopped, turned and bowed to Lara. "Beg pardon, m'lady Lara." The door closed quietly behind him.

"I dinna wish to leave ye, sweet."

Lara giggled, the sight of her naked love confronting and backing down his fully-clothed cousin struck her as extremely funny. The giggles turned to full laughter and she forgot her own embarrassment.

Iain growled and leapt onto the bed to corner her against the wall. One of his hands braced him while he touched the tip of Lara's nose and tapped lightly. "Ye find this humorous?"

"You have to admit..." Lara caught her breath and covered her face. "What if he had come in earlier?"

"Then he would have seen a different flush on yer skin."

"Oh, my g--"

Iain kissed her, slanting his lips over hers in tantalizing patterns. When they were both breathless, he eased away and tugged the blanket back up over her shoulder.

"If I dinna go he shall return. An' see much more." After a swift kiss on the tip of her nose, he was off the bed. Dressing took only a few moments. He gave her a look of such longing she wondered again how they would ever survive a parting.

A spring breeze blew the curls over Lara's face. Pushing them behind her ear, she rested her back against the wall. The wide window ledge was the perfect place to wait for Iain's return.

Maybe she'd be able to talk him into taking a walk. She'd taken time to explore the beach and, somehow, thought along the sea might be a good place to tell him. Before, when she thought all they had together was the result of physical lust, it would have been easier to leave him. Painful, but easier.

Iain confused the issue by confessing his love. That had made it easier to make her own declaration. How much did this change things? She would never find another love like this, doubted another man could ever bring such a blissful rise of passion. Did his love run as deeply as hers? She'd never know. Lara sighed and lifted her hair off her neck to let the breeze cool her skin.

There was little activity in the courtyard. Only the low mumble of voices through the hall's open doors disturbed the early morning. It sounded like an angry discussion that would last a long time. Undoubtedly, the servants had their ears pressed to the hall's thick doors.

Sliding down from the ledge, she tugged at the hem of Iain's shirt. She loved wearing the soft fabric. Lifting a wide sleeve to her nose, she inhaled the pure male essence of him. It was as if he was caressing her; and since the shirt hung to mid- thigh, it was long enough to protect her modesty. As if she had any left after Castan barged into the room. Knowing Iain was angry enough to break stone with his fist, she hoped he would give Castan the dressing down he deserved.

A few apples remained on the tray by the fireplace. Suddenly hungry, she stood before the fireplace chewing slowly. The embers reminded her of Iain, the deep black of his hair and eyes, the red-hot burning desire he created between them.

Laughter turned to a sob and caught in her throat. Would she ever be able to look at the coals of a barbecue again and not think of Iain?

The door creaked softly. Lara dashed the tears from her cheeks and stared intently into the fireplace. Beitris must have known Iain was gone and came to see if she needed anything. Only him.

"I'm glad you're here, Beitris. I need someone to talk to." With the old woman's store of fairy tales and loving knowledge of the man, perhaps she would understand and be able to help Iain. The warmth of another body moved behind her.

A hand clamped tightly over her mouth while an arm snaked around her waist to pull her back against a firm body. Hot breath flowed past her ear.

"I am exceedingly happy that you are glad of my presence." The arm tightened, pressing on her ribs until she could barely draw breath. "Even if I am not that worrisome old woman." Aubrian twisted her head around until she could look into wild, icy eyes. Facing the madness that must have lain dormant before, she struggled; and his fingers tightened painfully.

"You will come with me now." Lara tried to bite at the fleshy palm over her mouth and then swung one leg back to unbalance her captor. Aubrian laughed, angling his body so she couldn't reach him with her frantic defensive movements.

"Ah, sweet Lara. There is nothing you can attempt that I do not already know. This will be enjoyable. I dislike a willing conquest."

Slumping weakly, Lara hoped a new ploy would work. Aubrian moved until she was pressed against the rough stone wall, held in place by the length of his body. She gasped at the pressure of his hips against hers.

"As I have said, nothing you try." He pulled a mercifully clean rag from beneath his shirt and stuffed it into her mouth and then angled his lips to tease the corner of her filled mouth.

Lara choked at the touch of his tongue and shuddered at the evil that surrounded him. She tried to push the rag from her mouth.

A length of braided ribbon appeared in Aubrian's hand. "Do you recognize this, my dear?" Giving her a wink, he wrapped the length around her head to secure the gag. Another banner from her maypole was twisted around her wrists. After he tied a loose knot, a half-smile preceded the quick jerk that tightened the binding painfully. The gag muffled her agonized moan. "Now, Lara, you will come with me."

Lara shook her head, trying to will defiance into her expression. The glint she received in return from the faerie's eyes frightened her even more than his hold on her. This time her muscleless slump was not feigned.

Aubrian caught her shoulders, bent slightly to slip one arm under her knees and lifted her unresisting body easily. "Now, my dear. We shall leave this place. You will call for a portal to your time and return me to my rightful place in Faerie."

Confused, Lara thought it best to play along with the madness. If she didn't find a way to escape, Iain would search for her. Even with Aubrian's fey powers, Iain would defeat him. She knew it.

The faint baying of hounds intruded on her fear. The sound brought a brief moment of hope. Until Aubrian shook her roughly. "There will be no distractions. I use no glamour upon you, the hounds can not reach us." He shook her again. "Send them away."

Lara tried to plead with him, but she didn't know how to reach through the madness. Always sure of herself, she had never bothered to learn to call the hounds, or how to refuse their assistance.

"Do it." The shaking scraped her confined tongue against her teeth and she tasted the coppery metal of her blood.

Please. Go away. She didn't know if she spoke to the hounds or to Aubrian, but with the sudden silence Aubrian relaxed and carried her through the doorway. Twinges of canine presence remained, comforting Lara with the knowledge of possible rescue.

Stephen lay crumpled in a heap at the end of the hall; his furry black puppy whined and licked his face. The fear Aubrian had seriously injured the boy strengthened Lara's renewed struggles.

"Be still, abomination."

Lara froze. Abomination? Aubrian had professed to desire her, tried to force that lust on her many times. How could he call her 'abomination'?

Aubrian paused by the boy and prodded him with the toe of one boot. "He will sleep. He is not harmed, yet. Do not force me to make his gentle sleep permanent."

Lara turned her face from Aubrian and stared unseeing through a shimmer of tears. She kept still, barely daring to breathe, afraid any movement would bring on a violent madness to harm Stephen.

Shoving the boy further into the deep shadows at the base of the wall, Aubrian gave the small body a hard kick. Puppy growls sounded and Aubrian gasped. Off-balance, he stumbled forward, banging Lara's head against the wall. Pain further glazed her vision and she struggled to focus on the black mass hanging from Aubrian's calf. Lara gave a silent cheer for the sharp teeth of the protective little Noid.

Aubrian dropped Lara's legs and held her upright with a vice-like grip on her shoulder. Grasping the puppy by the scruff, Aubrian lifted it high into the air. Panic and fear for the small animal overrode Lara's personal concerns and she pounded her bound fists into Aubrian's chest. When his fierce expression turned toward her, she lifted her hands in supplication and looked meaningfully at the squirming black bundle.

"You plead with me? For this?"

Lara nodded and tried to speak around the gag.

Aubrian tossed Noid against the wall next to Stephen. The dog gave a small whimper and curled next to the boy. His bared teeth glistened white against the black fur, but he did not advance.

Aubrian hefted Lara securely into his arms, and then let his lips linger against her forehead. "I find your pleading a powerful aphrodisiac, my dear. You will plead for another life soon, and I will be satisfied." He spoke softly before his cruel laughter rang and she renewed her struggles.

He carried her from the manor and boldly into the yard. A cart waited near the open gate. He tossed her into the two-wheeled vehicle, then climbed in and knelt at her side, using one of his knees to pin her against the rough wood. A long, thin splinter imbedded itself in her upper arm. The pain helped refocus her fear and anger. Her muffled cries were ignored as Aubrian slapped the rope reins and the cart jerked into motion.

Fighting to deny the darkness that hovered at the edges of her consciousness, Lara focused on the pain caused by the bumping, swaying movement of the cart. She could not swallow and hoped the roiling of her stomach would not force the rising bile any higher in her dry throat. How would Iain find her far from the manor? Her silent tears fell and dampened the ribbons binding the gag to her mouth.

The cart lurched to a stop and Aubrian eased to his feet. Freed from the pressure of his knee Lara took a careful, deep breath and winced at new pain. Some of her ribs must have been bruised. When he rolled her from the cart and into his arms, the split wood broke off, leaving a sliver deeply embedded in her arm. A warm, wet tickle moved across her skin.

Aubrian spoke to someone and Lara angled her head trying to see. But Aubrian moved with her, keeping his compatriot hidden. "Take the cart. You know what to do. Return to me here. When the farmer returns as well I shall set the plan in motion."

When the mumbled response came, Aubrian's spine stiffened with a jerk. His eyes flashed like sun off a glacier and a muscle ticked in his cheek. "You will do as I say, anchorite. Do not think to cross my plans. Do not fear for your reward, it will be justly deserved."

As the cart rolled away Aubrian smiled down at her. "A diversion, my dear. Now, let me show you to your chamber. You shall rest there until the appointed time."

Lara twisted wildly, kicked her feet and tried for a release from the cold touch of his body against hers. Aubrian gave her a look of cool appraisal and she froze. "I shall not take pleasure with you here, my dear, but as a celebration of my return to Faerie. There is one I wish to witness the moment I take you." Heat rose in his eyes. "Then I shall have her. At last, the witch will be mine."

He kissed her forehead. "And the usurper of what is rightfully mine will be no more." A deep breath of satisfaction lifted his chest. "Look upon your chambers, m'lady." Aubrian turned and motioned with a jerk of his head.

They stood before a wide field of scattered stones arranged in a precise fan pattern. Each stone stood as high as Aubrian's knees and lead to parallel, thin upright stones. A huge, rounded pile of boulders rose behind the uprights.

Aubrian moved swiftly across the field of stones and through the uprights. The ground sloped steeply downward. With each step he took, it became colder--and darker. Lara closed her eyes but still felt the darkness closing in on her, trapping her. The dark had never before bothered her, but the ancient structure stole the breath from her lungs.

"Welcome, my dear." Aubrian dumped her unceremoniously on the littered ground; something jagged and sharp sliced into her palm. The fresh pain made her jerk her hand away. The thin wood slipped deeper into her arm. Opening her eyes wide did little as she tried to find any recognizable feature in the total darkness.

Aubrian took her bound hands, as sure in the darkness as in full light. There was a brush of prickly rope against her forearms and then she was pulled to her knees and forced to cross the floor. Aubrian grunted when she held back, fighting the dark pressure. The rope jerked and she fell face forward, her arms stretched out in front of her.

"It will do you no good to resist. The rope is affixed to a pole. You have not the magic to free the knots I placed there. You will wait until my return."

The echoes of his passage up the slope were amplified in the dark. Lara tried to scream but the muffled sound tightened the ribbon cutting into the corners of her lips. She couldn't even manipulate the gag past the ribbons to push it from her mouth. Needing some small security, something to ground herself with, she moved carefully through the darkness, using the rough rope to find the pole. She leaned against the wood, rested her forehead on her knees and closed her eyes against the darkness.

Iain, help me.

CHAPTER
TWENTY-ONE

Frustrated by Castan's thickheaded lack of understanding and the farmer's foolish, time-consuming demands, Iain stomped through the hall. The scowl softened to a smile of remembered pleasure as he neared Lara's room. A glance through a high window showed him the fine warm sunlight of a shining spring day. Perhaps it was time they left her room, for a short while. He would take her walking along the sea. There would be no better place to reaffirm the love he had for the flame that brightened his life.

He chewed on the inside of his cheek. There was nothing he could offer her, although Castan had broadly hinted at having him remain at the holding. Would Lara stay with him? She was traveling when she came into his life. If he were to leave, would she go with him? The scowl faded completely. Traveling with the feisty, golden-haired woman would be a joy, indeed.

He took the stairs two at a time. He would ask her to share his life, forever, as his wife. Then he would make love to her in the soft sand at the edge of the sea. Body rising like the tides, he jumped to the landing.

Stephen curled against the wall and had the young dog tight against his side. Iain smiled; the boy took his duties of guard seriously. There would be some fine reward for the child, and a large joint-bone for the dog. Careful not to wake the pair, he moved down the hall and into Lara's room.

He knew instantly she was not there. After taking a deep, ragged breath he coughed. The air was tainted. Scanning the room he moved cautiously to the fireplace. A half-eaten apple lay on the floor; a scuffle had disturbed the soot spilling from the front of the fireplace. A tiny flame rose from the nearly cold embers to lick the blackened stone. *Remember, my son. Go to her.*

Spurred to action Iain rushed to his rooms, jerked his seldom-used weapons from their resting-place and ran into the hall. Kneeling beside Stephen, he shook the boy to wake him. The brown eyes opened slowly but remained glazed and unfocused.

"Master? What d'ye need?"

The slurred words narrowed Iain's eyes. He ran his fingers lightly over Stephen's scalp. There were no telltale lumps, so perhaps someone had drugged the boy. Iain would gain no information from him. "Sleep child, ye have done yer duty. I will send yer grandmother to ye."

Eyes already closed, Stephen nodded. "If ye need..."

Iain patted the thin back and lay Stephen carefully on the floor. "Aye, young sir. I shall call." Turning his attention to the dog he received a tiny lick on the back of his hand. Intelligent canine eyes peered up into his. "So, young Noid. D'ye know who did this? D'ye know where my sweet has been taken?"

Noid gave a sharp yip and scampered down the crossing hall-way. Pausing outside the chambers allotted the storyteller, he scratched at the door and whined. Iain crouched and patted the dark head. "'Tis as I suspected. Return to Stephen and guard him well."

The puppy gave another yip and scooted back down the hall. Iain entered the stuffy, closed rooms. Aubrian had not been seen since his disappearance at Bealtaine. Now he had returned only to spirit Lara away. Iain knew deep in his pain-filled heart she was no longer in the manor.

He found Beitris in the kitchen garden. He told her of

Stephen's condition and offered reassurances that he did not think the boy would suffer any permanent effects from his misadventure. Iain questioned the few servants he found on his rushed path to the courtyard. He now knew from the casual comments that Edwin had arrived in a small cart. But when he left the manor, he was on foot. Always dissatisfied with life and searching for an easy way, Edwin must have formed an alliance with the storyteller.

Anger flared in Iain's chest and he ran toward the stables. No whinny welcomed him. The wide gate to the pasture stood open and the horses were grazing on the far side of the hills. The stableman was gone, as well, and a partially cleaned harness lay in the dirt. Aubrian had planned well, for Edwin would not take such action on his own.

Iain drew a deep breath. The long sword weighed him down; and, since he had never seen Aubrian handle any blade beyond a dagger, the two-handed weapon would likely be a hindrance. Close fighting enabling him to win against the Seanachai suited Iain's style, and personal vendetta. He laid his sword carefully among the practice weapons and with a grim smile began to run, a loose-limbed lope designed for distance. Eyes focused on the ground, he searched for signs of the cart's passage.

The image of Lara's distress drew him forward when despair and shortness of breath threatened him with defeat. He stopped at the top of a low rise and searched for the cart tracks he had lost on a patch of rocky ground. Aubrian could be hiding in any of the small clumps of trees that dotted the landscape. Iain took a deep breath--and smelled fire.

A curl of smoke rose from behind a nearby hill. Spreading too wide to be the smoke from a campfire, it made him shake with renewed anger and energy. He ran.

Nearing the source of the fire, he slowed and drew the dirk from the sheath bound to his calf. An old cart sat in a narrow patch of dirt cleared of any vegetation. The blaze was hot and he could not get close enough to look within. There was no smell of anything other than the burning wood. Another distraction set to delay him. Prints, human and equine moved away from the site taunting him onward.

The cart collapsed in on itself sending sparks high into the sky. The remaining small pile of crumbling wood began to burn itself out. Anxious to be on, Iain furiously kicked dirt over the flames and circled the fire until he was sure there would be no further burst of flames to scorch the nearby grass and scrubby trees.

Turning to the easily defined prints, Iain wiped sweat from his face with the back of an arm. The way was too clearly marked, begging him to follow to some trap. He paused, and then took a step forward. There was a soft whisper of prayer behind him and he turned. a heavy branch swung toward his head.

"I am not accustomed to this physical activity," the anchorite whined. "He is heavy. I could barely pull him onto the horse. It would have been easier to use the cart."

Edwin clapped the priest on the shoulder. "Then how would ye have gained his attention? See how the plan of m'lord Aubrian unfolds?"

The anchorite lifted his eyebrows at Edwin's easy use of title when referring to the storyteller. Irritated by the farmer's attitude, the anchorite continued. "I had to hit him again, twice, when he began to regain consciousness. The violence is more than I bargained for."

"Och. Ye complain too much. 'Tis no wonder ye are a secluded one. No others waud bear yer complainin' fer long." Edwin grabbed the back of Iain's shirt and dragged him from across the horse's back, then stepped back to let him crumple to the ground. Edwin slapped the nag's rump and sent her trotting away.

"M'lord Aubrian will reward ye, anchorite. Ye ken?"

"Aye. I fear fer that reward. We may have bargained more than we ken."

Edwin laughed. "I will take master Iain's shoulders, ye the feet. Together we make light work of takin' him to the Seanachai."

Grunting, the priest bent and lifted the dead weight of the old laird's son. Positioning himself between the feet, he held one ankle in each hand. Edwin lifted Iain's shoulders and walked backwards, glancing behind him periodically to guide their way.

A subtle change in the breathing of the man they carried drew the priest's attention. Iain woke once more, but gave no outward sign. Weary of the manipulation, tired of the anger he thought would dissipate with his actions, the anchorite chose to keep his own counsel. The dread of impending doom returned to hover over him like a storm cloud. He did not care for how the day had turned. Once the young master was delivered, he would no longer aid the Seanachai.

An urgent need to return to his broch and the reassurance of prayer swelled over him. The anchorite stumbled and he nearly dropped Iain's feet. One of Iain's eyelids lifted a mere slit. Checking the direction of Edwin's gaze, the anchorite gave a brief nod and pressed his lips together. The eye slid shut and their burden gave a soft sigh.

Iain wrapped his anger into a tight ball and stored it deep away. He forced himself to remain limp and unresponsive, though he doubted Edwin would be perceptive enough to notice any changes as the anchorite had. Sure the old priest would betray him no further, he waited.

"So, you have finally completed your mission." Aubrian's sarcastic tone clenched Iain's teeth together. It took all his will to not wrest himself from his captors' arms and wind his fingers around the mocking man's neck.

The anchorite was a strange, quiet man, keeping to himself in the way of his kind. The force of his words surprised Iain. "Aye, storyteller. And now I am done. I shall assist ye no more."

"That is of no consequence. You may go, gladly." There was a brief pause. "With my blessing."

The anchorite snorted and dropped his burden. Jarred by the sudden impact of rocky ground Iain gasped.

A finger touched Iain's eyebrow then pulled his eyelid open. Aubrian's face loomed above him. "There is no need for subterfuge. I knew the moment you woke, human. Edwin, let him go."

Suddenly released, Iain could not control the fall and his head landed against a large rock. The world swam before him once again. Ruthlessly, he held on to consciousness, shaking his head carefully to clear his vision.

Aubrian lifted his head by the hair. "Did you have to damage him so much?"

The anchorite's sarcasm matched Aubrian's. "He did not come willingly."

Shoving Iain away, Aubrian laughed. "I imagine he did not." Unerring in finding the tender lumps left by the anchorite's branch, Aubrian tugged again on Iain's hair. "The object of your search is here, but will not be for long. Do you wish to see her?"

Iain reached for his dirk, but found only an empty sheath. Tensing his muscles to leap at the mocking storyteller, he froze when a point of cold metal touched his neck. Edwin leaned forward to press the knife into Iain's skin. A tiny droplet of blood welled and trailed down his neck. "Ye will do as m'lord Aubrian decrees."

Feigning the relaxation of his tense muscles, Iain lifted one eyebrow at the storyteller in speculation. Aubrian smiled and shrugged.

The anchorite cleared his throat nervously. Aubrian spoke without turning to the man. "I would ask but one more thing of you, sir priest. Guard the entrance while we are within. I will return, bringing the rewards for your actions this day."

The old priest turned his back to them and stared into the distance. "As you wish."

Motioning to Edwin, Aubrian moved gracefully to stand beside a set of parallel stones flanking a dark rectangular opening. Edwin yanked the unresisting Iain to his feet and shoved him toward the stones. Furious, Iain straightened his back and moved forward stiffly. Had they treated Lara in such a manner? The tally against the Seanachai grew longer. Another shove sent him stumbling over the rock-littered ground.

Glaring at Aubrian, Iain vowed revenge for the continued transgressions. Evil as Aubrian was, how could the storyteller put his sweet, golden Lara in the darkness of the ancient cairn? When Aubrian reached for a torch, Iain bit back a cry of despair. Had he not even left her light? How frightened she must be, how alone.

Alone. The word trembled through him like a premonition of coming evil. His hands lifted toward Aubrian, fingers clawed and clutching for the storyteller's smooth throat.

"Now, sir. You will never see the lady fair if you anger me." Aubrian stared at the end of the torch and it flared to life.

Iain gasped, his hands fell to his sides with a loud slap. How had the storyteller done such a thing? Iain had always discounted magic as a way to dupe the innocent and gullible. But this? Iain shook his head. This vision must be due to the many knocks his head had received. No, Lara brought magic into his life. Why should manifestations by the storyteller be any different? *Believe.*

Iain allowed Edwin to prod him forward without resistance. Mulling over what he had seen, he followed the light through a long winding passage. The way was narrow, and with a man before and one behind there would be no chance for gaining control. Impatient, he waited, and hoped the strength of the ancient place would fill him as it did on the day of his passage into manhood.

They passed through a wide chamber littered with the remains of Iain's ancestors. Sending a brief apology to the ancient ones, Iain chewed on his lower lip. When he had explored the cairn as a curious young lad, he had never gone past this point. A deep calm, a stillness welled over him. It felt as though the ancient spirits gave their approval of him, yet the touch of those spirits sent chills racing through his body. Somehow, all his doubts and wondering, all his confusion over what there was to believe in, culminated in this spot, in this time. With Lara.

A large, flat stone partially covered a meager opening in one wall. Aubrian handed Edwin the torch, rubbed his hands together briskly and then laid one upon the stone. It rolled easily to one side. Aubrian braced his arm across the opening, reached back for the light and thrust the flame into the darkness.

When she heard scrabbling and scraping to one side, Lara tensed, fearing some wild beast or vermin would attack her. Knowing how she must smell of blood from the cuts, she feared a predator would easily find her, even in the total darkness. She steeled herself for an attack.

Trying to locate the source of the noise in the echoing darkness was difficult, but Lara set her back against the pole and faced the direction from where she thought the sounds came.

The bright flare of firelight blinded her even more surely than the darkness. She gave a muffled cry at the flash of pain and held her bound hands over her eyes. Multicolored spots danced in her vision, tears ran from her abused, stinging eyes.

"What have ye done to her? Ye bluidy bastard."

Iain. Reaching out toward the beloved voice exposed her sensitive eyes and she jerked her hands back to her face. A sob made its way through the gag as the light burned and she could not look for Iain's face.

Aubrian's pleased laughter pressed into her heart and made her cower. Keeping her eyes tightly closed, she reached for the doubtful security of the pole she was bound to.

"I shall kill ye, storyteller."

"I doubt that, human. But, see, I have brought you to your love. I grant you this time, a few stolen moments for your farewells. When the day is gone, she will take me to my rightful land. There, finally, she will be mine."

A dry snap sounded and the tight binding around her mouth dropped away. Thankful tears filled her eyes as she dragged the soggy rag from her mouth and tossed it toward Aubrian's laughter. Lara's dry voice croaked her denial. "I will never belong to you."

"Ah, the abomination speaks. Do not defy me, or the human dies where he stands."

"No." Lara's soft, whispered denial echoed off the smooth stone walls.

"No? I do as I will, abomination."

Curiosity momentarily overcame her fear. "Why do you call me that?" Opening her eyes a tiny slit, she was able to make out three bodies standing in the bright circle of torchlight.

The slender form she recognized as Aubrian took one step and paused, as if considering her words. "Perhaps I should tell you. Then you will tell the human who--no, what-- you really are." At his signal, the largest form stumbled forward and landed noisily on hands and knees in the clutter of debris. An orange glow hovered over him and he did not move.

"Tell him." Aubrian kicked the crouching figure who curled in a protective ball. Mumbled, unintelligible curses filled the chamber. Aubrian laughed again.

"I don't know what you mean." Lara lifted her chin and tried for bravado but failed miserably as her traitorous chin trembled.

"Speak your farewells to the human. Then think on who you seek to defy." Aubrian's voice deepened and the shimmering power expanded to fill the small chamber. The sounds of the third man rushing back through the darkness brought a pleased smile to Aubrian's lips. With another snap of his fingers the orange glow was gone and only the torch remained to give light to the dark chamber.

"You are probably nothing but a renegade, banished for some slight you don't even acknowledge." Lara fought to keep bravado in her voice.

Iain moved, struggling to his knees.

Knowing the faerie would not hesitate to use the glowing orange power against him, Lara stretched her arms toward Iain. "Iain, please don't. We'll get out of this later. Don't anger him now."

"Wise words, my dear. For I am no commoner of Faerie whom you seek to defy. Think back on your family's history. I do not doubt the tale of your father's rise to power is a popular one at feasts and celebrations." The words were ground out between tightly clenched teeth.

Confusion clouded Lara's thoughts. What did those stories have to do with anything? Iain inched closer; the warmth and strength of his nearness gave her the courage to continue her bravado. "What could you possibly know of my family?"

Snorting with disdain, Aubrian pulled the stub of a candle from beneath his shirt and lit it from the torch. "I would not leave you without light, so you may remember the countenance of the one you will never see again." He placed the candle in a niche on the wall and passed through the entryway.

As the stone moved slowly to cover the opening he spoke. "I have not always been Aubrian. Perhaps you would know me by my true name, the name of a prince of Faerie." The stone had nearly covered the opening. Only the tiny candle flame remained to cast flickering shadows around them. "I was--I am--Feidhlim."

TWENTY-TWO

T he stone settled into place. Iain peered at Lara and
moved closer. Afraid to touch her, he dangled his arms at
his sides. Her eyes were wide and glistening in the
wavering candlelight. Words formed on her lips but fell silently as
her head shook from side to side. Finally, unable to resist holding
her and comforting her pain, he lifted his arms.

Lara stared at him, ignoring the comfort he offered. "My God,
Iain. What have I done?"

"Ye have done naught. It is Aub--"

"No, no. You don't understand. I've done something terrible. I
don't know how to fix it."

"I dinna ken what ye mean." He feared for her and was afraid
the darkness and cruelty had touched her mind. Taking her in his
arms, he held her stiff, unresponsive body.

"Oh, oh, God. I've destroyed you, too."

Iain grasped her upper arms. A cry of pain loosened his hold,
but it also shook the madness from her eyes. Blood had soaked
and then dried on the sleeve of his shirt. His shirt? The absurd
pleasure of her wearing his clothing brought a foolish smile to his
lips. Lara angled her arm as if trying to keep the material from

touching her skin. Iain stilled her restless movements with a touch.

Silently, he lifted the sleeve and probed the wounded area. Lara gasped, "I think there's a sliver in my arm. From the cart. It hurts."

"Aye, and it will hurt more as I pull it from ye." His careful touch found a tiny end of wood protruding from the flesh of her upper arm.

"Do it. I can't reach." Lara held up her bound hands.

Iain kissed her fingers before focusing on the sliver. Unable to grasp the tiny bit of wood with his thick fingers, he covered the area with his mouth and gently scraped his teeth along her skin until he caught the wood. With a quick jerk of his head, the bit of wood fell into Lara's lap.

Her eyes were tightly closed and her lip held between her teeth when Iain caressed her cheek. "'Tis gone, sweet."

"It doesn't matter. It was punishment because I've destroyed many lives by being here. I should have never returned."

Fumbling with the knots binding her wrists, Iain gave increasingly angry grunts of frustration. The knots looked simple enough, but each time he loosened a twist of the binding, it tightened unmercifully in another spot. "Ye have no' destroyed me." He tossed his hands in the air. "Och, I canna free ye."

"It's his magic. Don't you see? You'll never be able to untie my hands. I doubt you could even cut through the bonds. He has unbelievable power," she added under her breath.

"Power? Tricks, perhaps."

Lara grabbed Iain's shirtfront and shook him slightly. "That's why he called me an abom...abomination."

"Ye make no sense, sweet." Perhaps she had also been knocked unconscious and was now unable to think clearly.

Lara took a deep breath and faced his confusion. She had to make him understand. Maybe by saving his life she could right a little of the terrible situation she'd gotten them into. To do that he had to know, to understand.

"This will be difficult for you to believe, Iain. I am not fully human." Lara leaned away from him and caught her upper lip between her teeth.

"Dinna tease at such a time, Lara. We must escape." He made an attempt to rise but she grabbed his hand and pulled him close. Angled so she could look directly into his eyes, she lifted her hands. Stretching her fingers to capture his face, she held him in place.

"Please, listen. This is hard to say, and I need to do it quickly before he returns." *Or I lose my nerve.*

"I come from another time."

Iain stared at her, eyes narrowed under lowered brows. Glad of the flickering darkness that covered the heat of embarrassment crawling across her face, Lara's voice shook. Her words were a breathless rush, spoken before she could change her mind. "I live far in your future, but I am able to travel to just about any time I choose."

His response was flat, the words evenly spaced. "And how d'ye do that?"

A rise of anger further heated her face. Iain spoke to her as if she were a child--or crazy. A sigh escaped along with her anger. Of course he thought she was delusional. Who wouldn't? The best thing she could do was to tell the truth and let him believe as he would.

"I have the ability to create a sort of doorway between times and places."

"I see. Why d'ye think ye have this talent?"

"I don't think I have the ability--I do. It's an inheritance from my father because..." Lara paused. This was going to be even more difficult. "Because I'm part Faerie."

Iain's look spoke volumes and effectively closed the cover on Lara's faint, unacknowledged hopes.

"Ye are too golden to be fey."

An edge of hysteria echoed around the stone chamber following Lara's laughter. "It has nothing to do with looks, Iain. You and Castan are from the same clan yet you are so different. Why should I be darker to be fey?"

Iain shrugged away the flush that covered his cheeks. "'Tis the notion of the religious men. Why dinna ye escape with yer skill?"

Lara hung her head. "I tried. I couldn't. Aubrian's power is too great. You felt it, didn't you?"

Iain seemed reluctant to answer. Finally, the word drawled out of him slowly. "Aye. 'Tis a strange compelling force."

"That's it--faerie glamour. Oh, my God, Iain, what have I done? He's Feidhlim."

Iain ached to comfort her and take away the agonized pain contorting her features. Her normally clear eyes were a muddy mix, dry as if she no longer had tears to cry. Ignoring those haunted eyes, he gathered her against his chest and smoothed a hand up and down the tight column of her spine.

"And what does that mean, sweet?"

Lara slid her hands between them, pushed back and stared up at him. "Mean? It means he was banished from a faerie clan. It means I stumbled across the one who nearly destroyed my parents. It means I've given him a way to return and finish what he started before I was born. No one in the clan will have any idea he's coming, so they won't know to fight him."

Lara's words, flowing faster and more urgently, suddenly stilled. As she grasped the front of his shirt, her tears returned to glisten in her eyes before trailing down her face.

"It means I've killed my parents."

She shuddered back into his embrace, and he held her as if their very lives depended on it. He had felt the strange power but could not begin to understand. The orange glow had held him cringing like a coward, unable to help Lara, unable even to lift his head. Earthbound claims to power he understood. The spiritual power of the old ones and the newer church were within his comprehension. But this?

Muffled against his chest, Lara's words fell hopelessly into the silent tomb. "I've got to stop him, I just don't know how. How?"

"We could--"

When she jerked away from his comfort, Iain was torn by the loss and the rejection lying deep in the pit of his stomach. Her eyes were clear; the words sharp, filled with a new determination that startled him.

"You will not. I must do this alone." Then her gaze softened, the color of her eyes settling to the deep violet that pulled him inexorably toward her. Hands flat against his chest, she held him away. "I can't let you get involved. He's too powerful. He'll kill you, too." Lara traced the tight cords in his neck with her fingers. "I would never be able to forgive myself."

As he took a breath to refute her statement, she lifted her hand until the tips of her fingers rested gently against his lips. The love she had confessed to him that morning glistened in her eyes and her face glowed in the flickering candlelight. The brief rejection faded from his memory as he ran his tongue over the pads of her fingertips.

A shudder passed through her hand. Taking advantage of her unspoken invitation, he drew her to him and covered her mouth urgently with his own. The kiss was fierce, protective and shattered him completely.

"Ah, sweet," he whispered against her cheek when he could tear his lips away. "I believe."

The tangled golden mass of her hair was soft against the skin of his palm as he guided her lips back to his. Her tiny sigh lengthened the contact until both were breathless. Cupping the sides of her face, Iain held her gaze. He willed the intensity of his determination to convince her.

"I willna let any harm ye, sweet. Nor yer loved ones."

Lara shook her head and his hands fell away. Why didn't he understand there was nothing they could do? Aubrian--no, Feidhlim held all the power. Their lives were held captive in his hands and would mean nothing to him once she opened the portal.

"He will do what he wants, Iain. He's full faerie, I'm only a quarter."

Iain caressed her jaw with the back of a finger. "But he can no find the way without ye. That gives us power, sweet, a leverage against him."

"Leverage?" Lara laughed bitterly. "There is no leverage, nothing we can do. He's blocked any chance I had to call for help, to even let others know he still exists."

She wanted to pace; it always helped her think. But the rope fastening her to the post was far too short for much movement. Instead, she sank willingly into Iain's comfort and sniffed loudly.

The vibrations of Iain's chuckles beneath her ear filled her with contentment, and somehow lulled her to accept what fate had presented her. A faint thought, telling her opening a portal would be the right thing, sparkled in the back of her mind. Ignoring the tantalizing thought, she had to force her lips to form words.

"I don't think this is a laughing matter."

The vibrations ceased, but the pleasurable tingle in her mind remained. That wasn't right, but she couldn't explain why.

Iain's chest lifted once before he spoke. "It is no'. But here is where I began my manhood, here where an old one placed the tattoo upon m' shoulder. An' now, perhaps, 'tis the place where I end me life. There is a strange irony."

"Your life?" A niggling worry penetrated the pleasant haze surrounding her. "What about your life?"

Iain held her by the shoulders and peered into her face. "If ye believe I love ye, my sweet fire, then ye must believe I shall let no one harm ye. Aye, I have felt the Seanachai's power. It may well be I shall die to protect ye."

"Why do you need to protect me?" Lara winced as her words slurred together. Such a strange, unreadable emotion filled Iain's face. She couldn't understand why he was concerned and longed to touch him to erase the lines of pain and worry deeply imbedded between his eyes. But her arms were so heavy, as if weighed down by cool water.

Instead, she smiled dreamily at him. "You know I'll be just fine."

Squinting at her through eyes narrowed to slits, Iain clenched his fingers convulsively on her shoulder. She showed no reaction to the pain. Maniacal laughter echoed between his ears. *You see, human...I have won.*

Unable to control his rage at the intrusion of his mind, Iain's bellowing roar ricocheted from one side of the chamber to the other. He stood, holding Lara tightly against his side. "Show yerself, ye bluidy bastard."

The voice in his head was silent, the cold nothingness after the laughter even more frightening. The rage became battle madness and he thrust Lara away, stalking the perimeter of the chamber, striking the smooth rock walls until his hand was bloodied.

The dulcet tones of Lara's voice seeped through the madness. "I can't help myself, Iain. I must do as he says. You'll be safe if I do as he says." The words trailed off into a soft, singsong repetition.

Ashamed by his lack of control, Iain shuffled to Lara's side. She had not moved since he pushed her away. Her eyes were wide, the dark pupils huge as she stared unseeing past him. Ignoring the pain in his hand, he held her upper arms and bent to look more closely into her face.

The flicker of candlelight was the only life in her features. Her lips moved and soft words passed them, but there was no emotion, no essence of his fiery Lara.

Iain shook her until her head flopped loosely from side to side. Then he crushed her to his chest and cupped the back of her head to hold it gently against the rapid beating of his heart. The singsong monologue continued, muffled against his shirt. The rage blossomed but he contained it, wrapping it into a tight ball of energy to be focused on the storyteller.

Lara shrugged his hands away and stepped back. She was silent, even though her lips still formed words. She trembled violently, her muscles jerking as though she fought a vigorous battle within herself. The need to help her shoved away Iain's anger and the pain. How could he fight one who could control her mind and body? What help could he offer her against an insidious foe?

A brief thought flashed through his tortured mind of his mother ending the hysterics of a woman who had lost a child.

"Sweet?" There was no response. "Forgive me."

With strength fueled by desperation and tempered by love, Iain lifted his open hand and slapped her.

TWENTY-THREE

The haze faded quickly from Lara's mind, leaving only the echoes of Aubrian's delighted laughter. One side of her face burned, the nerve ends tingled angrily. She lifted her gaze to Iain's face.

When her eyes met his, the intensity skittered away to a point over her shoulder. Then his face colored brightly and he ducked his head. He mumbled and shuffled his feet in the dirt.

Holding one palm to the heat in her cheek, Lara took a halting step forward. "What is it?"

He fell to his knees, wrapped his arms around her hips, and nestled his head against her stomach. His broad shoulders shook violently and the deep timbre of his voice cracked with a sob. "Ah, sweet, forgive me."

Confused, Lara tried to pull away, but Iain's arms tightened convulsively. So she caressed the soft length of his hair. "Of course, my love. For what?"

From a tear streaked face, Iain's eyes pleaded silently, begging for understanding. Her heart tripped over itself and she thought it would break with the pain reflected in his face.

"I would never hurt ye, sweet lowe, but I dinna have a choice. Ye were under his spell. I could no' reach ye any other way."

"I don't understand."

"Och, I dinna ken...Lara, I shall never strike ye again." Iain crumpled weakly before her. "I could no' stand the pain."

Finally understanding the hot stinging of her cheek and the absence of Aubrian's emotionless mind touch, Lara cried out and knelt awkwardly beside Iain. Cradling his face between her palms, she lifted and held his reluctant gaze.

When she was sure he would not look away, she searched blindly for his hand. The tight binding on her wrists made her actions difficult but she refused to look away. His hands were cold against her palms as she wrapped her fingers around his. Only a gentle tug was needed to lift his hand, but as his palm neared her face he froze. His hand trembled between hers.

An anxious expression accompanied his whispered words. "When I was a boy, my mathair attended a sick child. The child dinna survive and the mathair became distrait. It frightened me, for she would no' stop her wails of sorrow. Mathair slapped her. I suppose the shock startled her from the hysteria. I dinna ken then how such a thing could be." Desperation returned to his eyes. "Ye were held by...him. I struck ye when I remembered Mathair's actions."

Lara pressed his hand to her cheek and tried to still his violent trembling. "You did the right thing, you know. I needed help. I couldn't fight him by myself. He drew me deeper and deeper into his will." Lara turned her head to kiss his palm. "Thank you. Once again you have saved me."

"Lara, dinna ye ken? I struck ye. In desperation and part...in anger."

"You weren't angry at me, were you?"

"Never."

The shocked exclamation brought a soft smile to her lips. "Knowing me, I find that hard to believe." She waved away any other claims he may have made.

"At this point, it doesn't matter why you acted as you did. Only that you acted and returned my mind to me. Thank you, love."

"I dinna deserve yer love."

"That may be, but you have it. And you always will." Cold seeping into her bones made tight muscles protest as she swiveled to scan the chamber. "We have to find a way to get out of here."

A hint of normal humor touched Iain's eyes and erased much of the guilty desperation. "The sweetness of yer kiss would do much to ease me guilt."

And give me something to remember. Oh, Iain. He's going to take me away from you. How will I bear it? I've lost you, and I'll lose my family to him. What am I going to do?

Tears stung the back of her eyes. Blinking furiously, Lara lifted her arms and eased her bound wrists behind his neck before snuggling closer to his chest. His strong, comforting arms wrapped around her. Iain's soft breath warmed the chill from her body as his lips melded with hers.

Knowing she couldn't afford to lose herself in the kiss, Lara struggled gently to pull away. Rejection flared in Iain's eyes before he covered his reaction with a wry smile. His hands slipped from her back. Lara's arms tightened around his neck. "Don't leave me, Iain. I need to forget what's going on, for a few minutes. Talk to me, please."

"Aye, sweet. Ye wished to ken about my tattoo. Perhaps, since here is where it first adorned my shoulder, here may be the place to tell the tale."

Lara nodded, lifted her arms from around his neck and pushed at the open neckline of his shirt exposing the shoulder. Tracing the deep blue design with her hand bound was difficult; the fist following her finger covered the design as soon as she traced it. She made a soft sound of frustration. "This looks like a chalk horse in England."

"True? Ye have seen a similar design?"

"Cut into the sod so white chalky stone creates the symbol. It's called the White Horse of..." The words trailed away; she couldn't remember where the Neolithic creation was located. She gave Iain an embarrassed grin. "I don't remember just where it is. Why a horse?"

"'Tis but a symbol of an ancient clan."

T he summons distracted Jaye from the pleasurable study of his wife's body. "Not now," he murmured against her taut nipple.

Allyn's fingers stilled, tangled in his hair. "Not now?"

The urgent repeat of the Queen's summons jerked him to a sitting position. His eyes closed as he listened. His brows lifted in surprise and then lowered in anger.

A deep sigh ended the contact. Allyn wrapped a sheet around herself and rose. "It's Lara, isn't it?" She bent to gather the tumbled pile of their clothing.

"The Queen can no longer sense her presence." Hoping to reassure Allyn, Jaye amended his blunt statement. "It's as if the way were blocked in some fashion. The Queen fears Lara unwittingly discovered some new power. Even the hounds are baffled and unable to locate her.

"How are we going to find her, then?"

Jaye smiled and watched Allyn struggle into her clothing before he pulled on his jeans. "I asked Derrik to follow her after her last visit home. She was reluctant to name the time where she traveled. I just wanted to keep track of our precious child. As long as she has not left, then we'll find her."

Allyn grinned at her husband's possessiveness, but her own worries for their daughter's safety turned the grin to a frown. "And if she has?"

"At least we have a starting point to track her from. She does leave that unique pattern through the flow of time, you know." A forced smile failed to mask his concern.

Stepping into her shoes, Allyn leaned forward to catch his hand. "Let's get going, then." He struggled to button his shirt with one hand as she pulled him across the room.

Derrik leaned against the wall opposite the door when it slammed open. Allyn stopped her headlong rush and looked at him pointedly. "How long have you been here?" She stumbled forward when Jaye ran into her back.

Derrik held out one arm to steady her. "Moments only. Come, the Queen waits and the Alastriona have gathered."

"It's that serious?"

Derrik cast a quick look at Jaye and received a minute nod in return. He took a slow, deep breath, hesitant to further concern his closest friends. "Perhaps."

"What a touching sight."

Stiff-backed, Iain angled toward the mocking voice, shielding Lara with his body. His shirt hung from one shoulder with Lara's hands resting against the tattoo. The stone had moved silently, and Aubrian stood in the open doorway. Edwin danced from foot to foot behind him, the nearly gutted torch in his hand.

"Aye, m'lord Aubrian. Touching, indeed."

Aubrian lifted one hand to forestall any further comments from the farmer and a look of pure hatred and disgust crossed his finely chiseled features. "Enough, Edwin. Take the girl, but gently. I would not have her harmed. Yet."

Chuckling merrily, the dirty farmer propped the torch with a small pile of rocks and entered the chamber. At a flowing sign from Aubrian the braided ribbons binding Lara's wrists fell away. But before she had a chance to react to the sudden freedom Edwin pinned her arms behind her. Hot, stale breath raised goosebumps on her neck.

Iain rose slowly to his feet. His gaze darted quickly from Aubrian to Edwin.

"Uh-uh, Iain." Edwin slid a jagged-bladed knife from his belt and held the dull edge against Lara's throat. Grazing Lara's skin with the honed side as he turned the knife, Edwin grinned at her startled gasp. "Spite of what m'lord Aubrian tells ye, if'n ye come closer she will die."

Forcing the tense muscles across his shoulders to slump, Iain took a step back. He turned his head from the terror of Lara's captivity toward Aubrian and cleared his throat. One eyebrow lifted and Aubrian gave a lazy shrug.

"It's okay, Iain." Lara's voice was calm and steady despite the cold metal pressed into her skin. "I understand what I have to do. If I can't save my parents or my clan, at least I know you will be safe." She turned a harsh gaze to the smirk on Aubrian's face. "Aubrian, your honored word as Faerie. You will not kill him, or allow another to do so."

Aubrian blinked, lay his palm over the center of his chest and inclined his head slightly.

Amazement at his sweet's determination kept Iain speechless. Aubrian caught his eye and the other eyebrow lifted along with the corners of his mouth before he repeated the hand-over-heart gesture. The pleased smile caused more pain in Iain's gut than Edwin's knife ever could.

"Nay, Lara, ye canna."

Edwin's surprised grip slipped from her arms, and Lara moved to touch Iain's cheek with her fingertips. "I can, and I will. I'll return to you if I can, my love." Turning on her heel, she marched past an amused Aubrian and into the next chamber. Edwin gave Iain a hate-filled glare and then followed her at Aubrian's gesture, snatching up the torch as he passed.

The soft, echoing thuds of their footsteps quickly disappeared. Iain stared at Aubrian and tried to force frozen muscles to move him forward. The fists clenched at his side begged to find satisfaction in marring the smooth planes of the storyteller's face.

"You will not be able to move until I release you, so you may cease your struggles." Appraising him like a horse on the auction block, Aubrian paced slowly around Iain. Iain half-expected the faerie to pry open his clenched teeth and peer inside his mouth. He shuddered.

"'Tis a shame we will not meet in battle, human. I would enjoy honing my skills with the meager challenge. But, instead, I must prepare for the return to my true place, my true destiny."

"Ye'll no' take Lara."

"Oh, but I will." Aubrian snickered. "Again and again until I grow weary of her."

Iain growled his rage and his muscles cramped with the strain of forcing movement. The storyteller patted his cheek.

"Unfortunately, I did promise not to harm you. I will not dishonor the faerie way, though others have done so before me. You will, of course, die of natural causes, already buried within your tomb. Fitting, don't you agree?"

"Ye will no'."

"I do as I will, and it pleases me to think of you wasting away deep in the cold darkness. With each breath you take until your last you will think of Lara beneath me, of her taking the thrusts of my pleasure deep within her." Aubrian cocked his head and laid one of his fingertips against Iain's brow.

Pictures flashed through Iain's mind; Lara writhing under the Seanachai, accepting the pain he offered, begging for more. Denial choked in his throat.

"M'lord," Edwin's voice bounced into the chamber from far up the passageway. "'Tis nearly time."

The vision was gone abruptly, leaving Iain drenched in cold sweat. His straining muscles were released, and the sudden freedom dropped him to his hands and knees. Aubrian stood over him and grasped a thick handful of hair to pull Iain's head back. His voice lowered to a menacing rumble.

"Here you will stay with only your memories, until you die. Such is the fate of those who would thwart my destiny." Iain fell to one shoulder from the force of Aubrian shoving his head away. The Seanachai passed quickly through the opening; and the stone rolled silently into place, settling with a soft, hollow thunk against the wall. The dying flame of the small candle flared once and total darkness enveloped Iain.

. . .

E dwin held the limp woman tightly, facing her toward the setting sun. Lara did not struggle, knowing it useless. She would find some way to stop Aubrian, either within the portal or after they reached the Otherworld. No, not Aubrian-- Feidhlim. She shuddered, calling the evil by its true name.

Feeling the cold of his presence behind her, she closed her eyes and prayed that even he would hold some faerie honor and not harm Iain. No matter how her life turned, whether she lived or died, she would be content knowing the man she loved survived. And if a miracle should happen, if somehow she could defeat Feidhlim, she would return to this time.

If only she could have had a few more moments.

"No, my dear. Spend no thoughts on the human. Your fate lies in another direction."

"Yes, I know."

Stale breath rushed past her ear as Edwin gasped and his hold slipped away. Startled, Lara stepped away and prepared to run. Aubrian's hand on her arm froze her in her tracks. He forced her to turn toward him.

Edwin lay crumpled on the ground with the bright red of his life soaking into the dry dirt. The haft of a slim knife quivered in the center of his back. Aubrian gave her a negligent, dismissive spread of his hands. "He was no longer needed. Come, we must begin."

Lara shook her head and covered her mouth against the rise of bile in her throat. How many would die because of her? She should never have come to this time. Then she sighed. How could she have known who she would meet in this past?

Aubrian patted her shoulder and then let his hand trail down her arm in a gentle caress. "A sight you will come to know, my dear." Fingers tightened around her tender wrist. The pain of her raw skin was less terrifying than his caresses. "Yes, a sight you will see often as I take my rightful place as a ruler of Faerie."

Biting her tongue to keep back the fierce denial burning through her, Lara stared as Aubrian's eyes glazed over.

"My rightful place. The pleasure of removing the usurper will be mine. How he will suffer for daring to take my place." The blue eyes cleared and he looked into the distance before turning the icy gaze to Lara. He touched her cheek with the back of his finger.

"For, you see, my dear, you are the spawn of the usurper and the human witch who bespelled me so long ago."

"Yes, I know." The words cracked as she struggled to control the threatening tears.

"And you know as well much of my pleasure will come from you."

Lara nodded and tried to tear her gaze away, but his cold fingers held her chin in a firm grip.

"And with the witch, your mother."

Her denial was a bare breath of air past her lips. Dread consumed her until every muscle, every nerve ending trembled in response. The dread turned to fear, the fear to anger. "You will not touch my mother."

Aubrian laughed. "I do as I will. Who will stop me? I underestimated the usurper's untrained power, but never again. I have perfected my skills, honed my strength knowing one day, in some way, I would return to the Otherworld. None will ever again stand against me." Lara's teeth rattled as he shook her fiercely. "No one."

Trying another tack, Lara lowered her eyes and pleaded softly. "I will do anything you ask if you leave Mother alone." Inwardly, she cringed, hating the childlike, submissive quality of her voice. If only it fooled Aubrian.

With his palm cupping her chin, Aubrian lifted her face. He was close, too close. His lips descended and claimed hers roughly, tongue prodding, forcing entry to her mouth. Lara swallowed instinctive cries of disgust and held herself stiff and unresponsive.

Aubrian chuckled and squeezed her chin. "You will do what I wish in any case, my dear. Although I find I do enjoy your, um, reluctance. Yes, I enjoy it a great deal."

Lara bit her lip to keep it from quivering. She would give him anything he wanted. She held back a sigh. Except the portal that might end the lives of those she loved. But if she refused, he would kill Iain. She hadn't really believed Aubrian would honor the faerie vow he took so glibly. The possibility he still had some sense of goodness, some honor, was the only hope she had. If only she could somehow change this past and thereby change the future.

Aubrian angled her to face the setting sun, wrapped his arms about her waist, and rested his chin on her shoulder. "It is time, my dear." He bit her earlobe, the sudden pain drawing her attention fully to him. "Form the portal. Now."

W asting no energy on the screams that hovered at the base of his throat, Iain took a tentative step, keeping his arms stretched before him in the soul-numbing darkness. If he didn't turn himself around he would eventually touch the stone-covered opening. Perhaps he could push the stone away. And save Lara.

Despair darker than the blackness he strained to see through threatened to crush him to the ground. Lara was gone, gone willingly with the other. He took a difficult step forward. Why should he bother, if she did not want him, anyway? Castan would be well and easily rid of him. Would any mourn him or wonder at his disappearance?

His shoulders shook until trembling encompassed his entire body. The despair forced him to his knees. The constant beating of his heart, the pulsing in his ears reminded him Lara had not been willing, but only appeared so in a foolish attempt to save his life. Was that life worth saving?

The cairn was a holy place, the final resting of those who came long before him. Did they listen to his silent pleas? Would the gods come to his aid? The old ones, or the newer one god, it did not matter. At that moment there was no belief within him.

How could he believe when the spark, his golden flame, had

been wrenched from him? Longing for one glimpse of the woman he loved filled him, and he ached for the simple joy of one look from her before the darkness claimed him forever.

There had to be a way.

A miniscule glimmer sparked above the spent candle. The tiny flame flickered before fading back into the darkness. Iain blinked. Did the darkness bring visions? Did his imagination toy with his tortured thoughts? The soft touch of his mother's voice caressed him. *Believe, my son.*

Fists clenched at his sides, teeth gritted with the strain of his words, he cried out. "Believe what? I dinna ken. Show me." The echoes of his words faded to a whisper. "Help me."

Do you believe in nothing that you are unable to see?

"Mathair?"

You know, deep within you, what you must believe in. For you are my son and carry my blood within you. The fates blow you as they will, but one constant remains. You. You are the constant, Iain. You the strength, you the belief itself. Believe and change the direction of fate. Believe and choose: death, or life and love.

Iain shook his head. "I am belief? Aye, the darkness has made me daft." He lurched forward toward the darker outline of the doorway while the brief glow of candlelight remained.

Standing before the smooth rock that covered the doorway Iain closed his eyes and tried to believe. In his mind he visualized his escape. He could save Lara. But his heart, the depths of his soul did not believe. He knew he could roll the stone away. But he did not believe he had the strength to move the ancient rock. He knew Lara loved him. He believed.

Flaring brightly in the darkness, the tiny flame burned spots before his eyes in the returning darkness. Once more Iain felt the touch of his mother's presence. *Patience.*

A soft scrabbling sounded on the far side of the door. Pressing his back to the cold stone, Iain waited as the scratching became louder, and the tumbling of small chunks of rock became a waterfall of sound.

A thin sliver of light appeared, slowly growing in width. The grunting of a man's struggle against the heavy stone filled the chamber. Iain shook his head, not daring to accept what he saw.

CHAPTER
TWENTY-FOUR

A small torch inched through the narrow opening, followed by a metal-clad head. The shining horned crest glinted in the torchlight and sent sharp sparks of brightness to blur Iain's vision. Iain recognized the man and crouched into a tense defensive position. A Norseman. Was he rescuer or intruder?

The Norseman's icy eyes scanned the chamber and a grimace of disgust crossed his face. He held up an open palm and faced Iain.

Iain took a deep breath, leapt from his crouch and tackled the Viking to the hard ground. The torch sputtered in the thick dust but remained lit. Straddling the intruder's chest, Iain lifted a fist but the force of his blow was halted against the flat surface of a large palm.

"Hold...friend."

Keeping his fist raised, Iain peered into calm blue eyes. Brows lowered, he tried to analyze the Norseman's expression. He paused a moment too long.

With a lithe twist, the man tossed Iain to one side like a damp rag. Rolling, he kicked out at the grinning advance of the Norseman. The chamber wasn't wide enough for him to easily regain his feet, so he put his back against the wall and lifted his hands defensively before him. He tried to inch himself upright before being attacked.

The Norseman stopped a few short steps from Iain's position and lifted an open palm once again. Bending to one side while he kept his eyes trained on Iain, he retrieved the smoking torch. Once free of the dust, the small, bright flame burst forth.

"At another time I would enjoy this game. It has been long since I have had a clever opponent." The Norseman spoke carefully, enunciating each word. His bright teeth glistened in the torchlight.

Iain blinked mightily, trying to clear his suddenly blurred vision. What was the stranger talking about? He must get past the Viking to save Lara. There was little time left and the clarity of the knowledge left him breathless.

The Norseman angled his body to enable Iain to see a clear path to the narrow doorway. He pointed. "Come. Follow. The storyteller plans evil for your woman."

Iain nodded slowly but kept pressed against the solid wall. Was this another trick?

The Viking squinted one eye. "You do not trust me. That would be wise--at another time. I offer my help as friend against a common enemy." He spat into the dust. "The storyteller damaged my ship. Far from the shore, we began to take in water. My great ship floundered as we returned to your shores. There is no glory in his subterfuge, no glory in revenge, but I seek retribution for the time my warriors spend in repair."

Iain remained silent, eyes narrowed and moving quickly between the doorway and the Lochlannaich. His focus was jerked to the Viking when the Norseman slapped a hand against his breastplate.

"I am leader, my honor is beyond dispute among my people. It is as I say. The only part I play is your release from the place of the dead. How you deal with the storyteller for his sacrilege against your ancestors, against your woman is not my concern."

A wave of the torch toward the door set Iain in motion. The instant he trusted the strange, yellow-haired man, his decision was made. A single nod brought a smile to the Viking's lips and he turned to lead the way from the cairn.

When the darkness lessened and Iain could sense fresh air, the Viking extinguished the torch and pressed a finger to his lips. Together they crept forward into the light of the dying day. The Viking motioned, making Iain understand the storyteller-- and Lara--were over the next hill. Before Iain could rush in that direction, the Viking grasped his arm and tugged him around the side of the cairn.

Iain gasped at the sight of the breeze lifting the hem of the anchorite's ragged robe. The man lay face down, one arm wrapped around a jagged stone. The hilt of a short sword poked skyward, the blade embedded deeply in the man's back. Shoulders slumped, Iain turned away. There was no doubt who had killed the old priest. Was there no end to the Seanachai's depravity?

The Viking moved in front of Iain and shook his head. He pointed to the sword.

Iain's denial was swift and vigorous. Silently, the Viking placed one foot in the center of the anchorite's back and yanked the sword free. Holding the shoulder of the blade carefully just below the guard, he offered the grip to Iain.

Hands lifted in refusal, Iain backed away. A deep frown marred his smooth, high forehead when the Viking shook the sword at him. Reluctant, Iain took the proffered blade and stared at the blood-covered tip. A heavy hand fell to his shoulder. At his glance, the Viking gave a sympathetic look and then pushed him toward the hill.

"Go," he mouthed.

Iain nodded. "My thanks."

The Viking smiled and offered his arm. "To glory, friend." After clasping forearms with the Viking, Iain turned to the low rise separating him from Lara. Hesitant to announce his presence, he bent lower with each step toward the top of the small hill until he was crawling carefully through the waving grasses. Taking a deep breath, he peered through the low brambles guarding the crest.

The scene below crushed Iain's already deeply bruised spirit. Aubrian held Lara possessively, turning her toward the setting sun. A quick glance behind showed the Lochlannaich disappearing into the woods. The faint sounds of the sea tempted Iain. Perhaps he should follow the Norseman.

His eyes were drawn inexorably back to Lara. Despite what he saw, he could never leave her with the Seanachai. Aubrian's arms rested about her waist and he bent to lay his chin on her shoulder. The air was heavy, even the birdsong silent and waiting. Iain's nerves vibrated with the unnatural stillness.

Excitement tinged the storyteller's words drifting to Iain's hiding place. "It is time, my dear."

Iain closed his eyes, wishing to sigh away his pain. *Look, my son. Does she act to him as to a lover? Believe.*

Unable to turn away even though he commanded the action from his cramped muscles, Iain recognized Lara's stiff posture. She held herself frozen as Aubrian nuzzled her neck. A smile of relief tugged at the corners of his mouth. She did not wish the storyteller's attentions.

Highlighted by the setting sun, Aubrian's teeth glinted as his mouth neared Lara's ear. She jerked away with a soft cry. One hand covered her ear and shock made her eyes wide.

Aubrian pointed to a spot in front of them. "Form the portal. Now."

Clutching the already bloodied sword, Iain vowed to cover the stained blade with the life of the Seanachai. Iain would join the evil man in any number of hells to save Lara the pain settling in her wide, tear filled eyes. He rose to his feet and drew breath to shout his challenge.

Aubrian turned, keeping one arm firmly wrapped around Lara's waist. "You have escaped the barrow?" He looked Iain over from head to foot and smiled when Iain lifted the blade and took a long stride forward.

"I have not the time to deal with you again, human. Since you lay claim to the affections of the abomination, then you shall witness the fulfillment of my destiny. It may prove a more fitting punishment for your interference." He shook Lara and pushed her forward.

"Aubrian, no." Lara's firm voice halted the advance both men. "Leave him be. You have no quarrel with him."

Eyebrows lifted in surprise, Aubrian turned his face toward Lara. "Have I not, dear Lara?"

Lara shook her head fiercely, her sunlight curls whipping across her face. "No. You don't."

Iain's step forward was halted mid-stride by Aubrian's lifted hand. An orange glow surrounded his stiffly spread fingers, grew to form a large sphere, then flew toward Iain. The fine hairs covering his arms lifted as the glow surrounded him. Another step forward took him to the edge of the glow but he could go no further. Retracing his steps, but keeping his eyes on Lara, Iain backed into a hard, tingling force. It was the same at each side.

Lara twisted from Aubrian's grasp, elbowed his side and struck out at him. Aubrian's fingers closed tightly to his palm.

Lara's head snapped back when the purely physical force of his blow met her jaw.

Iain cried out in rage and terror and pounded against the orange walls of his prison. He hacked at the barrier with the sword until the edge was nicked and blunted, and then used the pommel to attack the resistant glow.

Aubrian held Lara by one wrist and laughed. "You once held something I desired. That alone is enough to create the quarrel with you. Now, you seek to defy me in my hour of triumph. For that, you should die as I had planned. While earth did not hold you, my power shall. And when I am gone from this world the power will fade, shrinking in upon itself until there is nothing left but the crushed remains of your miserable body."

Iain leaned his shoulder into the barrier and pounded with his fist. *Believe in yourself, my son. Believe in the blood bond we share. Believe.*

Planting his feet firmly against the pliant earth Iain shoved again. The sphere moved. Intent on placing Lara a certain way in the last glow of the sun, Aubrian didn't notice. Ducking his head to hide a triumphant smile, Iain sent a silent prayer of thanks to his mother's spirit and pushed again. He moved forward easily.

Jerking to a halt and holding the glow in place when Aubrian turned toward him, Iain held his breath. Would the Seanachai notice he had moved nearer? Aubrian glared and spoke urgently to Lara.

"Now. Open the portal now. Too much time has been wasted."

Lara shook her head and stared defiantly at Aubrian. Iain silently cheered her rebellion. But her mutiny was short-lived, for Aubrian turned her toward Iain, flicked two fingers and the sphere shrank noticeably. Forced to bend slightly within the glow, Iain's pride turned to loud, angry curses.

Aubrian laughed and returned Lara's face to the crescent of sun that remained hovering over the horizon. Her shoulders slumped in defeat and there was a slight tremor in her voice when she began speaking unfamiliar words. Iain inched the glow forward.

A shimmer touched the air in front of Lara, and enlarged when she moved her fingers in an intricate pattern. Aubrian leaned forward eagerly as a vast, heavily wooded area appeared centered in front of her. The wavy edges of the trees solidified and Aubrian took a step, dragging Lara by one arm.

Even as Iain drew breath to shout and force himself to Lara's side, a second shimmer appeared, the edges bouncing away from the first, shooting multi-colored sparks high into the darkening sky.

Two men leapt from the second portal, pausing only a brief moment before separating to rush Aubrian from opposite directions. An intense flash of orange sent both flying backwards; thick, acrid smoke surrounded them.

Aubrian's maniacal laughter rang out. The fine hairs on the back of Iain's neck lifted. Smoke parted before the Seanachai as he moved toward a blond man struggling to stand. "So, you have found me, Alastriona. And brought the usurper." Aubrian stood, legs spread, arms folded across his chest.

A faint baying of hounds touched the edges of Iain's attention, growing steadily louder while he slowly moved his bubble toward Lara. Panic, anger, despair and hope chased each other across Lara's face. Who were these men to her? Tamping down the sudden rise of jealousy made Iain stumble, drawing Aubrian's attention.

Aubrian's light brows drew together and a deep furrow formed in his forehead. "How dare you. Even now you defy me?" He lifted both hands, but instead swung around to deliver another blast of power that drove the blond to his knees.

Lara screamed. "Derrik, no, he's too powerful." As Aubrian turned toward the other man, so did Lara. "Dad, don't."

Aubrian waggled his fingers at the one Lara called "Father." The movements taunted and motioned the man forward. Blue sparked around the man, and intense concentration froze his features until a wave of power flew from him. Aubrian chuckled as sparkling blue flowed around him with only the barest lifting of his hair.

Lara wailed and covered her face with her hands. "Daddy."

You are the strength, my son. Believe.

Warrior rage filled Iain. The Seanachai had harmed his woman, harmed one she named kin. Would harm no one again. With a roar that echoed within the tingling confines of Aubrian's power Iain lifted the sword. Crying Lara's name he slashed down, shattering his prison into thousands of orange shards that disappeared with faint popping crackles.

Three steps later Lara was cradled against his side. He angled the sword protectively before them. She would not look at him but sobbed into her hands.

"There's nothing you can do, Iain. He's going to kill all of us."

"He shall no'."

"You can't stop him. If Derrik's and my dad's power is no good against him--"

With the orange power balled and swirling around his hands,

Aubrian advanced toward them. "How did you escape me again, human? What secrets have I yet to learn? Ah, no matter." His hands lifted.

Behind Aubrian, the one called Derrik motioned for Lara's father to move back slightly as he minutely adjusted his own position. Iain caught a finger movement from Derrik and stepped to one side and slid Lara behind him. There was something familiar; something logical about the position of the three men.

The hair on Iain's arms stirred when the portals shifted and moved closer to each other behind him. There was shouting and the far-off baying of hounds sounded closer. With one arm angled behind him, he held Lara against his back. The warmth of her body flowed into him, bringing with it renewed determination.

"Lara," Derrik called, "ye must help."

She shuddered, sniffed and took deep breaths to try and control her tears. Iain doubted the others heard her whispered reply. "I can't. I've done too much already."

Instead, Iain nodded, crouched slightly and held his weapon with both hands. A brief frown crossed Derrik's features before his hands lifted shoulder height at each side. Lara's father did the same.

"Lara. Now."

"Lara. Now." Aubrian's sarcastic repetition of Derrik's calls yanked Lara from her misery and her head snapped up.

She stepped from behind Iain. "I'm ready." Moving in front of him, she paused to touch Iain's hand and then lifted her fingers to stop his protests. "I have to, Iain. Remember, no matter what happens, I love you."

Iain's soft response was a puff of air against her fingertips. Lara turned and matched the pose held by Derrik and her father. Sudden, lightning-bright flashes pulsed from Derrik's fingers and met the blue of Jaye's power. Lara became a conduit for the powers, binding them together to surround Aubrian.

Derrik smiled grimly. "Ye are contained, Feidhlim, ye will no' escape."

"So you may think, Defender." The orange glow filled the triangle surrounding the laughing faerie. His power concentrated on Lara and pushed at the flow of binding.

She was the weak point; her limited Faerie powers usually only worked in creating the time portals. Concentrating on holding the lines, she didn't notice when Aubrian moved until he stood directly in front of her. Smiling.

"You cannot control the power, abomination."

Lara gasped, the lines wavered. Fingers of orange mist curled toward her head and hands. She glanced frantically toward Jaye, her fear growing at the lines of strain deeply etched in his face. Derrik's eyes were closed; beads of sweat covered his forehead. They couldn't help her. Her hands began to lower in defeat.

"No, sweet, dinna give in to the Seanachai." The sword clanged against the rocky ground behind her and Iain's large hands wrapped around hers. He held her arms straight out from her shoulders. "Ye must believe we can contain him."

Another voice, a strange, soft, woman's voice echoed Iain's words. *Believe.*

Lara nodded and bit her lip to force her concentration. Power flowed into her hands and transferred to the man who pressed his body tightly against her back. His tense muscles vibrated and she felt rather than heard his low groan.

Aubrian screamed defiance, gathered strength and sent shot after shot of power toward them. Somehow, Iain absorbed each blast, grunting softly with the impacts that rocked them back. Lara supported his weight when he leaned into her. He was weakening and she didn't know how to help.

Derrik and Jaye moved closer, tightening the triangle of power. Iain whispered in her ear, "I canna...no' much longer..."

Baying hounds burst through a portal, circled the triad of power, and snarled at Aubrian. Anger and frustration fueled the evil power and he increased his attack. Orange blasts came in a blur until Iain's fingers loosened from hers and he sank to the ground unconscious.

Aubrian's delighted laughter was cut short by the slap of Derrik's heavy hand on his shoulder. Whirling to face the Defender, Aubrian began a fierce chant to increase his power. The frantic words were silenced by the very human reaction of Jaye's fist against his jaw.

Staggering back, surprise widening his eyes, Aubrian tripped over Lara's extended foot and landed hard on his back. Derrik planted a boot in the center of Aubrian's chest and leaned heavily on his knee until Aubrian gasped for breath.

A phalanx of Alastriona rushed through the portal. Derrik released Aubrian into their control after yanking Aubrian's arms behind his back and wrapping his wrists with silver bands. Jaye tightened the bands with a tired smile. Moments later, Aubrian achieved his desired goal. Feidhlim had returned to Faerie.

L ara shook off her father's concerned, restraining hand and knelt at Iain's side. She stroked the hair back from his face and caressed the familiar, beloved planes. A smile twitched his lips and his head turned to press a cheek against her palm. But he did not wake.

She took his hand and held it against her breast before she placed a kiss in the palm. Angry red and blistered burns covered his hand. Gently touching the other hand, she found open blisters centered in the palm. How much pain had he endured to save her, to save her family?

"Dad?"

Jaye knelt beside her. "Yes, darlin'?"

"Heal him, please. We couldn't have captured Aubrian-- Feidhlim--without him." Lara broke into tears. "He was going to kill you and Mom, he was..."

Jaye wrapped an arm around her shoulder and cuddled her to his side like he had when she was a young child. "I know." Lara slipped her arms around his neck and he dried her tears with the hem of his tee shirt. "We owe this young man a great deal, more than we can ever repay. My small healing will do little to erase the debt."

Lara leaned away from her father. Should she tell him now? Tell him she was going to stay in this time with Iain, with the man she loved more than life itself. She felt the pain Iain took for her, finally letting the fear reduce her muscles to jelly.

Concern for her father touched Lara's heart; his fight with Feidhlim had drained him. Did he have the strength to heal the terrible burns? Jaye took both of Iain's hands between his. A frown furrowed his brow and he gave Lara a quizzical glance before closing his eyes to concentrate. The burns healed slowly, but when Jaye released Iain's hands they were whole and unharmed.

Lara kissed her father's cheek and then bent over Iain. She took his hands and willed him to wake. In answer to her silent summons, his eyelids fluttered. Suddenly, his eyes flew open and he jerked to a sitting position. "Sweet?"

"I'm here. Everything's fine now."

"The Seanachai?"

Derrik stepped forward and offered a hand to Iain, who paused only a moment before accepting the assistance.

Unsteady when standing, he allowed Lara to wrap her arms around his waist to support him.

"Feidhlim has been taken to the faerie conclave. His punishment will be swift, and fierce."

Iain rubbed his forehead. "Feidhlim?"

"He was Aubrian in this time. He's been an enemy to my family since long before I was born." Lara sighed. Not too many people got to meet, then defeat their childhood nightmare.

Iain nodded slowly, turned to take her in his arms, and crushed her against his chest. Lara accepted the ferocity of his embrace and returned it twofold. Looking into each other's eyes they spoke at the same time.

"I thought I lost you."

"I feared ye were lost to me."

Derrik touched Lara's shoulder. "We must go, the portals have been open too long. The Queen wishes to hear yer tale." He turned away.

Lara chewed on her lower lip before she turned to her father's expectant gaze. "I'm staying here. With Iain."

Derrik spun on his heels. "Ye will return to Faerie. Ye dinna belong here."

"I do, Defender." Her voice softened. "Uncle Derrik, I love him. Daddy, please understand."

Iain stepped around Lara, placing himself between her and the men. "If she dinna wish to go with ye--"

Jaye lifted one hand. "We will not fight you. We owe you too much, including the life of my darlin' daughter. But she must attend the conclave."

"Aye?" Iain's arms folded across his chest. "And ye dinna plan to let her return here. She willna leave."

Derrik's lowered eyebrows had cowed many faerie, but Iain stood firm against the powerful gaze. Lara swayed on her feet. Jaye was at her side in a moment, catching her as she slumped weakly to the ground.

He glared up at Iain. "You would deny her the healers? After what she has been through? And you claim to care for her?" Jaye lifted Lara in his arms and turned his back on Iain.

Lara's voice was a weak whisper. "Daddy, that's not fair." Jaye walked toward the portal, his back stiff with repressed anger. Iain took a step to follow but Derrik's hand on his upper arm held him mid-stride. "Ye willna move until the portal closes." Derrik followed Jaye into the shimmer.

Iain struggled to move, but he was once again held in place. His muscles strained and his joints popped painfully as he fought the magic containing him.

Lara reached both arms back, stretching over Jaye's shoulder. "I'll be back, I promise. I love you, Iain."

With a voice frozen as his body, Iain could not answer, he could only watch his sweet being carried from his life. *Mathair, help us.*

A cool breeze caressed his forehead. Freed, he rushed forward,

Lara's name poised on his lips. Their eyes met once before the portal closed between the two worlds and Iain stumbled on empty air. On his knees, he pounded the turf and cried Lara's name again and again until despair and exhaustion overcame him and he crumpled into sleep in the cold Highland night.

CHAPTER
TWENTY-FIVE

Crowded with representatives from the widespread
faerie clans, the Queen's audience chamber was hot
and stuffy. Lara huddled near the back of the room in a
small alcove, wishing the ordeal to be over so she could be well on
her way back to Iain. Luckily, the gathered officials ignored her
after she gave her report and kept their attention focused on the
small circle cleared in the center of the floor.

When the undulating throng of people moved Lara stared at
Aubrian's still, silent form. No, she needed to call him by his true
name. Feidhlim. Lara shuddered at the surfacing memories of his
control. Ruthlessly, she pushed them away and centered her
thoughts on Iain.

What was he doing? Would he really wait for her? Would he
even want her when she did return? So many questions whirled
through her mind; she didn't hear the soft footsteps preceding
Derrik to her hiding place.

"Lara?" His voice was hesitant and worried.

Lara spoke without raising her head. "What do you want,
Defender?" Perverse pleasure mixed with guilt flowed through
her as he winced away from her cold question. One day she would

forgive Derrik, but not now. The resentment from his betrayal was too fresh.

Derrik turned on his heel without speaking, leaving her to her thoughts. "Good," she whispered then immediately wished she was not so alone.

A path cleared between her and the circle where Feidhlim was held. He lifted his head and turned toward her. His bland expression brightened and he bowed slightly at the waist, acknowledging her. Then evil settled in his eyes as he scanned the gathering, self-satisfaction reflected in his features.

A soft hand pressed comfort on Lara's shoulder. She scooted to one side of the hard bench to make room for her mother. Allyn settled close and took Lara's hand to rub warmth into her cold fingers. Tears filled Lara's eyes. "Mom?"

Allyn gathered her daughter in her arms. She used one hand to cradle her daughter's head while the other rubbed soothing circles on Lara's back. "Don't worry, Lara. It will be over soon."

Lara accepted comfort, but not the comfort her mother believed she offered. Knowing the conclave would soon determine Feidhlim's punishment, Lara sighed. She wasn't concerned. Except to know that as soon as the punishment was carried out she would be free to return to the past. How was she going to tell her mother? Lara bit back sobs as the silence of the conclave announced the presence of her aunt, the Queen.

Alastriona moved to stand shoulder-to-shoulder around the power circle holding Feidhlim. Three of the tall, wide-shouldered faerie knelt, allowing the Queen to see the captive.

"You were once honored among the clan, among all the clans. Dishonored, you caused your own banishment, yet you have returned. You have attempted harm upon my heir, and upon the child of the one chosen to bring closer the two worlds of human and faerie. There is no remorse within you; the hate in your eyes reveals your thoughts. The conclave, disbanded for human centuries, has been called to determine final punishment."

Feidhlim drew breath, his brows drawn together, anger simmering visibly within the tense trembling of his shoulders.

The Queen held up one hand. "You will not speak in my presence."

Drawing air into his lungs, Feidhlim prepared to do just that. A frozen lump lodged in his throat while invisible hands clutched at his neck and extracted his ability to speak. He waved his arms angrily at the Defenders while his mouth opened and closed soundlessly. Stopping again before the Queen, he glared, mouthed obscenities and then lowered his gaze to the floor.

The bitch Queen stole my voice. She will pay doubly. Doubly, I vow. Attempting to school his expression, Feidhlim looked into the Queen's eyes. She merely lifted one finely arched eyebrow and turned away.

Bitch.

Faerie nobles moved to the far end of the hall and gathered around the Queen when she sat on a low chair. Their hushed voices created a tense undercurrent throughout the hall. The Alastriona turned their backs on the captive and Feidhlim wished he could spit through the power encircling him. He marked each faerie, committing them to his long memory. There was always a way, always a pathway to his destiny. Nothing they could do would halt the advance of his power, of the claiming of rights fate owed him.

His gaze landed on Derrik, standing against a far wall, arms folded across his chest. Derrik acknowledged the intent in Feidhlim's look as though he could read the thoughts burning through his mind. Derrik turned away to face the Queen.

Drawn by the desire still knotted low in his belly, Feidhlim found the alcove where Lara huddled with the witch. Swirls of aching need coursed through him as he watched the witch comfort the daughter. He would have given the witch more than the usurper ever could, more than any human ever imagined. Allyn met his eyes coldly, helped Lara to her feet and angled her so she would not look toward him by chance. Lara and Allyn left the chamber arm-in-arm.

Rustling from the conclave brought his attention back from frustrated desire. The Queen rose. Members of the conclave backed away, exiting the hall through narrow doors. The Queen crossed the wide, empty hall. Once again the Alastriona knelt before her as she leaned toward the power bubble.

"Would that I could argue against faerie law that prohibits your death at our hands, but I can not. The worlds of human and faerie would be well rid of your presence. You would be mourned by none. Alas, I cannot order your death, for to do so would rain our punishment upon the one chosen to deliver the blow."

Derrik stepped forward. "I would accept--"

The Queen's lifted hand prohibited further speech. "Well we know your dedication, Alastriona. But you are needed; your life will not be wasted on one so worthless."

Derrik stepped back to the wall, his stance casual in the formal setting. Feidhlim smiled to the floor. That one would pay as well for a long list of transgressions. The Queen's silence drew his gaze.

"I speak now the punishment determined by the conclave of the clans. You have shown scorn for the human world, for human accomplishment. You shall be returned to the human world, forever."

Feidhlim dropped his gaze to hide his elation. The world of humans was tolerable, their weak minds and wills easy to control. He would find another way to return to his destiny, another way to visit revenge upon those who wronged him.

"The time of your banishment will be of my choosing, the place far from any Friends of Faerie."

There are ways, my Queen. *You are have not defeated Feidhlim.*

"One final punishment." The Queen paused until the silence of the hall echoed back upon itself, setting Feidhlim's teeth on edge. "You shall be stripped of power. You will become mortal. As with all mortals, you will eventually die." She turned away.

Feidhlim's silent scream went unnoticed. He thrashed against the power binding him, pounding his fists into the barrier. The few remaining members of the Queen's court followed her, and the hall emptied silently. Only the ring of Alastriona remained.

Feidhlim slid to his knees. The bitch could not. He was once the chosen. He had been the heir. She dare to turn her back on him? She could not take his power. No one could take the power he controlled, the strength continuing to build within him. But even as he denied, the soft tingles of magic flowed from him, every pore in his body seemed to open, loosing the power. Faint streams of orange caressed his skin as if to say farewell and hovered around him for a long moment. The flow rose through the invisible walls of his confinement and oozed into a thick stone amphora held by two serious Alastriona.

When the orange drift was contained, Derrik stoppered the container with chiseled stone and sealed it with a thick layer of dripping wax. The jar was cradled in a silver stand and chained against the wall.

Exhausted, alone and helpless, Feidhlim collapsed into a loose pile on the floor. He screamed silently into the stones until a hand snaked through his hair and roughly jerked his head back.

Although he tried to mask the feelings, Feidhlim sensed from Derrik's triumph the defeat was etched deeply in his own eyes.

"Come."

"No. I do not accept the false punishment." Feidhlim spoke, surprised when sound issued from his throat.

Derrik laughed, a mirthless sound. "Ye have little choice. Come willin' or I will drag ye. And be pleased to do so."

Feidhlim struggled to his feet, keeping the white-hot anger turned within. Fighting the warrior without magic led to nothing but further defeat. He would find a way to regain his power.

Derrik prodded him with the tip of a long knife and forced him into motion. Once free of the hall Derrik forced Feidhlim swiftly through the sylvan woods to a secluded glen. He slapped a hand on the renegade's shoulder and turned him to face the Alastriona's wrath.

"I should still kill ye, an' face punishment m'self."

Laughter bubbled in Feidhlim's chest. He let it escape, poking Derrik's chest with a finger. "But you will not, will you? Unable to go against the wishes of your precious Queen? Unable to give up the pleasures of your human lover? What a shame. Do your duty,

Defender. Send me away. I vow I shall return. When I do, you and the ones you protect are mine."

A knife pressed into Feidhlim's side and he jerked away, covering the shocking pain with a hand. Hot, wet blood seeped through his fingers.

Derrik spoke calmly while wiping the tip of his knife with the hem of Feidhlim's tunic. "I send ye to a time, to a place where ye will no' be able to find yer way back. Ye will harm none under m' protection. Ever."

The electricity of a forming portal lifted the hair on Feidhlim's head. He backed from the wildness in Derrik's eyes, fear making him stumble. "You would not--"

"Aye." Intent only on pushing Feidhlim through the portal, Derrik advanced a step.

Feidhlim turned and frantically scanned the surrounding forest, searching for a route of escape, although without magic he could not stand against Alastriona power. His glance focused on a sharp, short glint to one side of the clearing. The flash of a familiar face quickly hidden behind a tree brought a tiny, pleased smile to Feidhlim's face.

So, members of the Nechtan-Cattee had survived the scourge of the half-human usurper. Feidhlim turned from Derrik and took a deep breath. Giving a minute signal toward the hidden watcher with a flick of his fingers, Feidhlim stepped through the portal into the human world.

A somber celebration brought the fey clans together. A people who disliked the strictures of punishment had forced discipline on one of their own. In the faerie way even the most doleful moments became a celebration, for the long threat to the clan was over.

Lara paused in the entry of the now-empty audience chamber. She sighed, frustrated at having to wait for the Queen to return from the gathering to give her permission to return to the past. Never before had her parents insisted she receive specific permis-

sion to use a time portal. She supposed they were hoping the
Queen would refuse. Not even that would hold her to this time
when the one she loved waited so long ago.

The silken swish of soft fabrics announced the Queen. Lara
bent her knees in a low curtsey. "My lady aunt."

The Queen laughed softly and lifted Lara to face her, drawing
her into a loving hug. "We are alone, no need for ceremony. The
troubles caused by the renegade are over. He is gone."

"Yes, Aunt, I know. I have come to ask--"

The Queen covered Lara's lips with slender fingers. "I know
why you have come. You do not need my permission." She smiled.
"I only wanted a moment to say farewell."

"Then I can go?"

"Of course. I would not strive to keep you here when your
heart lies elsewhere. I may not know the beating of a human
heart, but I understand as much as I am able. You will return?"

"When I can. It may be hard to live in the two times but I'll
figure out how. I can't leave my family, either."

"Then all is well." The Queen kissed Lara's cheeks and
smoothed back the mess of tangled golden hair. "Go, then, and
find your happiness."

"Oh, I will, I will." Lara returned her aunt's soft kiss and
dropped another curtsey. Filled with insane joy and laughter, she
turned to run from the hall. The green forest called, her glade was
waiting. And beyond the glade--Iain.

A healer rushed into the hall, whispered urgently to the
Queen then gestured behind him. The Queen called out, "Lara,
hold."

Frowning at the delay, Lara fisted her hands on her hips and
turned back to face the Queen. She swallowed her impatience and
lowered her gaze. "My lady?"

A void of silence filled the hall, only the shuffling of feet broke
the quiet. Lara looked up to find her parents beside the Queen.
The Healer continued his frantic whispers, gesturing toward Lara.
A sudden lump of fear settled in her stomach.

Her father's face held a bemused expression while joy and

sorrow battled in her mother's features. The Queen turned toward her. "I rescind my permission. You may not use a time portal, Lara."

"What? You said I could go. Mom, what does she mean? Dad?" Lara stomped her foot in confused frustration. "You can't stop me."

The Queen pointed to the healer. "Tell her."

The ancient faerie stumbled over his words. "You cannot use the portal. We do not know what will happen."

"I've traveled through the portals all my life. What's different about now?"

The healer hemmed, hawed, and watched his toes draw patterns on the stone floor.

Lara stamped forward until she was nose-to-nose with the healer and crossed her arms. "Tell me."

Looking between the Queen and Lara's parents, the healer took a deep breath. "It has never been done. We do not know the harm it may cause if you travel through time now."

Lara tapped one foot impatiently.

The Queen touched the healer on the shoulder in order to move him to the side and took his place before Lara. "You carry within your body a child of faerie blood. We will not risk the life of the child or the life of the mother within a time portal. The portals are closed to you."

"Closed? A child? Wha--?" Lara's eyelids fluttered closed, and she slumped to the floor at the Queen's feet.

TWENTY-SIX

Cold seeped so far into Iain's bones he could barely move. His muscles ached. His head throbbed. Rising slowly to a sitting position he gazed at the spot Lara where had disappeared. Forever etched in his memory, the panic filling her face tore through his soul. He lifted his face to the cloudless morning sky.

Would she return as she promised? Was her love as deep as the well of feeling surging in his chest? Iain shook his head and then winced at the sharp pain shooting through his temples. A cool breeze lifted his hair to brush it back from his forehead as his mother had done when he was a boy. With a ruthlessness worthy of the Seanachai, he closed his mind to the soft voice. Why should he believe? What he believed in was taken from him.

Emptiness surrounded his heart as he struggled to his feet. Best to get on with life, follow the plans dictated by Castantin. Perhaps he should join the order. There would never be a woman to tempt him again; none could fill the jagged hole left by Lara's disappearance.

A soft whoosh of warm moist air blew past his ear. Turning, he faced the long nose of the carthorse that had drawn Lara to this ancient place. With a silent cry, he wrapped his arms around the security of the arched equine neck and let his tears fall unchecked. The horse stood patiently, snuffling in his ear and nibbling daintily on his tunic.

Drained, Iain forced himself away and patted the animal's shoulder. "There be work fer us. Work shall bring forgettin'." As the words grated from his tight throat, he knew the falseness of his statement. Even in death he would never forget.

Wrapping his fingers through the rough rope halter, he turned the horse toward the cairn. Although Edwin's lifeless eyes stared to the sky, there was still surprise evident on his coarse features. Knowing the old horse would not accept the weight of a bloody body, Iain searched for long branches to fashion a litter. He stretched the farmer's filthy shirt between the branches to make a place to lay the body and used the cart's harness to attach the litter to the horse. Rolling and heaving the farmer's weight onto the litter exhausted him, but he gave himself no rest.

Leading the horse around the cairn, he arranged the body of the anchorite next to the farmer. Unlike Edwin, the anchorite's face was full of peace; a look of bliss touched his aged lips. Iain sighed, cast a long look into the distance past the place where he had joined the battle against the Seanachai to the spot burning in his memory. "Lara. Sweet, return. Please."

The day was far into the afternoon before Iain reached Edwin's steading with his grisly burden. The farmer's woman stepped from the crude shelter, gave Edwin's body a single cold glance and then pointed to a stunted tree. Iain lay the body under the tree and turned to the woman with words of condolence.

She brushed the words away with a brusque wave of her hand. "I be well rid of the lazy fool. Me brothers will bury him, master Iain. Ye have done yer duty." Turning away, she returned to the shelter of her home.

Iain paused a few moments, then shrugged and moved on. He could not mourn the loss of the farmer, either, but had expected some response from the woman. Would Lara be so cold if he had died? He shuddered and let morbid thoughts flow through his mind to fill his soul with numbing doubt.

Standing in the middle of the narrow cart path, he could not force his muscles to function, could not take a step. How terrible the fate of the man whose death is unmourned. It was a fate none deserved.

Except the Seanachai. His death would have been celebrated, the tales told long over the winter fires. Anger warmed Iain's body. If the Seanachai were not dead, he would find a way to destroy him, if for nothing more than the unwelcome attentions he had visited upon Lara.

Thoughts of golden, shining Lara filled his mind. The memory of her frown, and knowing she would not condone his thoughts of revenge calmed him. Her sweetness encompassed him; the warmth of memories replaced the anger, finally chasing away most of the debilitating cold. She said she would return; he would wait for her.

Traveling more quickly with the lightened burden, Iain led the horse to the small stone kirk at the edge of the village. The priest, leaving the chapel, shook his head at Iain's request. Iain leaned closer to the man. "The anchorite was a man of God. Ye'll bury him in holy ground."

The priest shook his head again. "He was--"

"He gave life's blood fer his God. 'Tis enough. Ye'll bury him here." Iain laid the body on the chapel's single step and glanced back at the priest. The man hastily made the sign of the cross over the anchorite. "I will send ye coin fer the burial, and fer the generosity of yer kirk on the morrow."

The priest's face brightened at the mention of coin, and he nodded once before kneeling at the anchorite's side. Iain turned away, another duty done.

Weary beyond feeling, he returned to the manor, turned the tired horse over to the stableman and climbed the stone steps to his room. He paused outside Lara's door to press one hand against the heavy wood. The door moved, but he did not look into the place where he had found so much joy. So much love.

At the end of the hall, Stephen waited with the puppy settled comfortably on his lap. Spying Iain, he pushed the puppy to the floor and jumped to his feet. Iain held up one hand, and the boy skidded to stop his headlong rush to Iain's side.

"M'lady Lara is gone, Stephen. I dinna ken if she will return."

Unable to face the shock and sorrow that closely mirrored his own expression, Iain moved quickly past the boy and entered the stark loneliness of his room. Dropping into the chair before the cold fireplace, he rubbed his hands through his hair and leaned forward to brace his elbows against his knees. He hid his face behind his hands, and sorrow shook his shoulders as wracking sobs exploded from his chest.

Beitris entered the room and quietly moved to his side, his sorrow echoed in the lines of her face. She rubbed his back, waiting, until he turned with a cry and buried his face against her hip. When the tremors ceased, she took his hands and pulled him unresisting toward the bed. He lay back, eyes dull and lifeless. Beitris tucked a blanket around his trembling limbs.

Iain curled on his side, wrapped his arms about himself and closed his eyes. He knew Beitris remained standing by his bed, and he heard the sounds of her sorrow. But, he had no energy to comfort another when he found no comfort for himself.

L ara retreated into loneliness and depression. She refused to leave Faerie and forgot her responsibilities in the mortal world. She focused only on the tiny life within her and her eventual return to the past.

Sneaking away from the family that hovered around her, she tried to form a portal, but the sparking electricity would not grow beyond a pinpoint. Furious, she screamed at the magic, cursed the powers that kept her from Iain. When she turned and found the Queen waiting, she refocused the anger on her aunt.

The faerie Queen waited, calm and serene, until Lara's ranting slowed. Then she opened her arms. Lara rushed into the offered comfort and let the warmth of her family's concern sink into the emptiness.

"Mom used portals all the time when she was pregnant with me and Jayse."

"Those were not time portals. There is no danger in passing only between worlds."

Lara sighed. "But there's so little faerie heritage in this child." She laid one hand over her abdomen. "What possible harm could there be?"

"There has never before been one of the clans who both controlled the portals and carried a child. We do not know the dangers and will not allow you to take a chance with this precious life." The Queen's hand rested over Lara's.

"But--"

"I remember, darlin' niece, a time when young Bryce bemoaned the fact he had no faerie blood. There was naught Derrik or Tommy could do to comfort him. You and Jaysson prepared a ceremony. Do you remember?"

Lara shook her head. A ceremony?

The Queen patted Lara's hand gently, then lifted it and touched one of Lara's fingertips. "You three hid away and with a tiny knife cut your fingers. I was nearby and watched as you pressed the wounds together, three fingers bound by bright red ribbons. You told Bryce that now there was faerie blood within him, that even one single drop branded him faerie. He was exceedingly happy."

A sad smile touched Lara's lips. "I remember now. Jayse and I had just watched some old movie where a drop of blood gave a man a completely different heritage. And my child has more than one drop of faerie blood. Can't you bring Iain here, then?"

The Queen paused before shaking her head. "It is not possible. Time within the mortal world confuses me and we do not know what affect the actions of faerie in the past may have on a human future. Would you wish me to take this chance?"

"No," Lara sobbed, "but I need him."

"I do not understand human feelings, needs, but I do know of your love for this man of the past. Once your child is born, we shall determine if it is safe for you to return. Remain here in Faerie until then; the time may pass more swiftly for you here."

Lara nodded. "There's nothing for me in the mortal world of this time. Thank you, I will stay here. May I build my home here, in my glade?"

The Queen smiled. "Of course, it shall be done as you desire."

Each day Iain returned to the cairn; each day he brought a small gift. The pile of drying flowers, small sparkling stones, notes scratched on irregular pieces of hide grew as the weeks passed. After adding the daily offering to the pile, Iain would sit staring at the spot, willing the sparkling shape to form.

Beitris watched him with sad eyes and brought his favorite sweets. "Ye must eat, master Iain. Yer face be that o' a dead man."

Iain couldn't argue with that, for the joy of life had left him through a shining oval in the air. But, he suffered Beitris's caring touch and smiled his thanks. Then he would set the dish to one side, never to touch it again.

Iain chaffed at Castantin's concern, although he was thankful for the duties his cousin found to keep him occupied. Patiently explaining successful farming techniques brought him little joy. There was always something hovering in the distance, something that drew his attention from his lectures.

One morning Castan laid a hand on Iain's shoulder and stopped him from leaving the hall. "Ye've done well fer me holdin'."

Iain gave him a sad smile of acknowledgement. Castan cleared his throat, coughed and stared at a hanging on the far side of the hall.

"What is it ye wish, Castan?"

"Wish? Aye. I wish ye to remain. Dinna leave wi' the spring thaw. Ye've proven yerself an' yer home be here--as long as I be lairdin' o're it."

Startled, Iain studied his cousin, but saw nothing in his

expression save honest concern and hope. It would be tempting to stay and be honored for his accomplishments. To be here when Lara returned...

Iain sighed. It had been too long. Though he had pined for her these many weeks, she would not return.

If Lara didn't return, there was nothing for him there. He didn't know where his feel might lead, but it didn't matter. There was no place him now, no home, not without Lara. Shaking his head, Iain rose and held out his hand. He waited until Castan clasped his forearm firmly. "I am honored, m' lord...m' cousin... but I canna stay. I shall help ye through the winter, but be gone by spring." He held up his free hand to forestall Castantin's complaints. "Leave be, coz. Ye willna change m' mind."

Summer turned to fall, and Iain's visits to the cairn became less frequent--the small hope he had cherished for so long faded to a dim reflection of Lara's golden beauty.

After his long hours of toil in the fields, he spent the shortening evenings in the seclusion of the pleasuance. His mother's gardens brought small comfort, even though he often felt the cool touch of her presence.

Iain harvested the last tender medicinal herbs and left the rest untouched. As he spread the leaves on trays for drying, the low hum of his mother's voice intruded on his solitude.

Believe.

He tossed a handful of leaves to the ground, kicked at the small table and knocked the tray to the ground. "I dinna wish to hear that word."

My son...

"Nay. Yer words dinna help me, Maither. I believed she would return, an' she has no'. I believed her words." Iain fell to his knees and covered his face with his hands. "I believed she loved me." The words were wrenched from his soul--what little soul he had left without Lara at his side.

You must...

"Nay. Dinna speak to me again of this." He gasped. "Dinna speak to me again. I willna listen."

The voice fell silent. Inconceivable as it was to him, the emptiness inside grew. He had chased away both women who loved him. He was truly alone.

F all froze to winter. Iain stared often at the sea but never saw the long ships of the Norsemen. Messengers arrived weekly with tales of the destruction caused by the Viking raiders. Holdings along the coast suffered Viking attacks, yet Castan's holding remained untouched. Iain pushed Castan to continue training fighters and building defenses, for he did not wish to leave the holding defenseless. He did not know how long his tentative alliance with the Viking leader would remain.

Winter was long and hard, the snows deep; and the winds blasted in from the sea.

"But, coz, 'tis the Yule."

Midwinter. Soon the seasons would turn toward spring, and Iain's feet would carry him far from this land. He pulled a heavy tapestry away from a high window and peered out across the hills. From there he could see the last of the ribbon streamers attached to the maypole. The colorful bands whipped in the wind. The ribbons were as tattered as his heart.

Iain let the tapestry fall into place and turned to Castantin. Behind the red-haired man stood a small phalanx of servants. His gaze skittered over them, finally resting on Beitris. The old woman smiled timidly, but he recognized the worry deep in her eyes.

Passing a hand over his face and through the tangles of his hair, Iain suddenly realized how he must look to these people. He rubbed at the many days of stubble on his chin and forced facial muscles to form a long-unaccustomed smile.

"Aye. I shall read the tale of the birth of the Christ to ye at the gloamin'. Should ye wish it so."

Stephen whooped and rushed from behind Beitris's skirts. He

halted his headlong rush when Castantin cleared his throat. A flush covered the boy's face. "Thank ye, master Iain," he stammered.

Taking three steps forward, Iain reached out to ruffle the boy's hair. "Come, Stephen. We have neglected yer lessons. Ye must finish learning the ways of the letters. Then, perhaps, ye can read the tale next Yule."

Iain held a painful sigh in his chest as Stephen bounced with excitement. The child was quick and would easily learn the basics of reading. The rest--Iain was sure he would figure it out himself. It was the most he could do for the boy, the best he could leave the manor.

He silently reaffirmed his plan. He would leave shortly after the turning of the new year.

TWENTY-SEVEN

L eaving a bitter snowstorm Allyn passed through a portal into the eternal summer warmth of the Otherworld. Her daughter's small house stood to one side of the clearing. The glass in the open windows glinted merrily in the warm, dappled sunlight. She shook the snow from her jacket and slung the heavy garment over the porch rail.

The clearing was strangely quiet, waiting. A sense of unease traveled along Allyn's spine. Ready to knock loudly on the bright blue door, she was startled when it flew open. Lara leaned against the doorframe cradling her distended belly in her arms. Her features were strained, her face damp with sweat.

"Mom? It's time."

Lara allowed her mother to guide her to the bedroom and settle her on the bed. Soothing, Allyn's voice rambled on, softly talking of inconsequential things. Lara didn't care. The only thing that mattered was that finally their child would be born and soon she would take the child to its father.

"Your father will be here soon. I'll send him for the healers."

"Sure, Mom, whatever you want." A sharp pain ripped across Lara's belly and, twisting away from Allyn's hands, she cried out.

"You must help your child be born, Lara." Allyn grasped Lara's shoulders and shook her gently. "The ordeal will be over sooner if you help."

Lara nodded weakly. "I've had the pains for a long time now, Mom. They only get worse. I can't do this alone, I can't."

"Your family will be here, darlin'."

"Not Iain." Lara turned her face to the wall and shook off the comfort of her mother's hands.

Loud voices announced Jaye's arrival. Allyn hurried from the cabin and rushed into his arms. Jaye's brows drew together in concern. "What is it, Allyn?"

"Lara is in labor." She glanced between her husband and Derrik. "She needs help."

Jaye turned to Derrik. "Bring the Healer. Then gather the family."

Allyn laid one hand on Derrik's arm when he turned. "No. Jaye, you must bring the Healers. Derrik must return to the past and bring Iain here."

Jaye shook his head. "We can't chance a change of the present, you know that."

"I know." Allyn sighed deeply before pressing the issue. "But I don't think it will. Remember, Lara said he was to leave his cousin's holding anyway."

"What if he has already gone?"

Allyn glanced at Derrik and lifted her eyebrows. He nodded and grinned. "Aye, I can find him."

"Return quickly, please."

A sharp cry from the cabin sparked each into action. Derrik was the last to leave the clearing; concern filled his face as he gazed at the little house. "Aye, I will find him, darlin'. Forgive me."

After taking a tiny carved wooden piece from a pouch, Iain wrapped it carefully in one of his precious slips of silver paper. The shape of his carving was perfect, drawing to a soft point under the twist of the candy wrapper. He did not believe Lara would return; but if she did, this present, the representation of the chocolate she shared with him, would tell her of his love.

A deep breath filled his chest as he looked around the cairn. The small pile of gifts remained remarkably untouched by scavengers or weather. How long would it remain after he was gone? He shouldered his heavy pack. Late winter was hardly the time to begin a journey; but remaining true to his feelings, he could not stay at the holding when spring brightened the land.

Long ago having given up hope of ever seeing the shimmering portal again, he stared unseeing into the spot. With an automatic step forward, hand outstretched, he moved closer. Jerking, he shook his head. He could not believe.

You do, my son, else you would not be here this day. The calm voice returned after a long winter of quiet. Iain accepted the presence, but not the words.

A sparkle in the sunlight halted him. Slowly, reluctantly, his gaze was drawn back to the spot. The air shimmered. Iain held his breath until his chest burned with the effort.

The shimmer opened, showing a green, fragrant forest, and the tall, blond man stepped through. Iain slipped the pack from his shoulder and reached for the long sword at his side. The man stopped, smiled broadly and moved easily toward Iain, palms held up and open.

"What're ye doin' here? Come to hold me again? To what end?"

"I have come fer ye."

Iain lifted an eyebrow. "Aye? What torture do ye plan fer me, then? D'ye find joy in remindin' me of what is lost?"

The smile faded to seriousness. "I am Derrik, Alastriona for a faerie clan. Lara is a member of that clan. I did what I thought was right to protect her and m' people."

"And ye dinna let her return to me." Iain turned away in disgust.

"The Queen refused her passage through the portal. But the reason--"

"What care have I fer a reason? I only ken she is no' here wi' me. I only ken m' life is no' worth much."

Derrik took a deep breath. "I have come to bring ye to Faerie. To Lara."

Iain's shoulders slumped and he sheathed the sword. He spoke into the distance refusing to face Derrik. "If she dinna come herself..."

"She was unable."

Whirling to face Derrik, Iain lifted clenched fists. "What did ye do to her?"

Iain took a surprised step back when Derrik began to laugh heartily. The laughter continued until tears ran down the faerie's face and he bent over resting his palms against his knees. Iain inched closer. Confusion and the slight building of a strange hope warred within his chest.

Wiping his eyes, Derrik straightened and clasped Iain on one shoulder. "'Tis no' what I did, man, but what ye did."

Suspicion tinted Iain's features. "I did no' to harm her."

"I dinna say she was harmed. But ye are the cause fer her inability to pass a time portal. She carries yer child."

Believe, my son, your destiny waits.

Iain shook away the voice and stared. His child? Lara carried his child? Joy began warming his frozen heart and his mouth dropped open.

"Will ye come with me, then? Lara needs ye, the time of birthin' is now."

Iain nodded mutely but did not move until Derrik pushed the center of his back to force him forward. *Go, my son. Love awaits you.*

With Derrik's hand propelling him, they moved toward the portal. Derrik stopped just short of the shimmer. "Wait. I have but one other duty here."

Tense, Iain turned to watch the man's graceful hands make sweeping gestures over the land. Derrik cast an apologetic look at him as he stepped away to retrieve Iain's pack. "It would be no' such a good thing to leave the memories of Feidhlim and Lara fresh in the minds of those you leave behind. I have hidden those memories. Ye will be remembered as simply leaving on a journey."

"Aye. As I was."

"Then, let us journey to my world. I dinna think ye will find it unpleasant."

Side-by-side they stepped through the portal. The summer warmth and sunlight startled Iain, but not as much as the cluster of people before a fine, well-constructed cabin. Quickly noticed, he and Derrik were surrounded.

Chattering in a language Iain did not understand, the group pressed around him. He turned desperately one direction and then another searching for Lara. The frantic movements were stilled by a light touch on his forearm. Looking down, he gazed into eyes so similar to Lara's he took a swift step back.

The woman smiled at him and motioned to herself. He recognized the word mother. This was Lara's mother. He nodded understanding and spoke rapidly. The same quizzical look he was sure covered his face graced the expectant faces around him.

The small crowd silenced and parted as a regal woman advanced toward him. Derrik whispered in his ear, "Our Queen," before stepping away with a low bow.

Iain knelt and lowered his eyes before the royal presence. He gasped in surprise when she knelt in front of him. Her warm breath blew past his ear and then she leaned forward to kiss his lips softly.

"With my blessing, you may now understand and speak freely with us." She rested her hand over his heart; her mouth made a small circle of surprise. Looking up at those around her, she spoke softly, her clear voice awed. "He is of faerie blood."

A dark-haired man burst from the cabin and ran toward them, followed by a large black dog. Iain rose into a defensive posture, placing himself before the beautiful woman who had gifted him with understanding. The man skidded to a stop, his eyes widened and he fell to one knee.

"Master Iain."

The black dog advanced warily, hackles raised. Iain froze as the wet black nose sniffed at him. The dog sat back, tongue lolling and seemed to smile.

"I understand. I remember now. Master Iain disappeared one winter and was never heard from again. I understand now where he went." The man stood and patted his chest. "I am Stephen."

Iain stood and peered closely at the man. Yes, except for the coloring, he did look much like Castantin. But this was a man well-grown, not a young boy.

The dog drew a large wet tongue across the back of Iain's hand. Stephen laughed. "And this is Noid, the rascal you helped me name."

"I dinna believe..."

A sharp scream from the cabin stopped his speech and his breath. Lara. Pushing past Stephen, he leapt toward the cabin and burst through the door. A low moan led him to a side room, where an elderly woman hovered over a writhing figure on the bed.

"Lara, sweet." Iain collapsed at the side of the bed, took her cold fingers in his and chaffed them gently. Her hair lay in damp, dark-gold tendrils across a sweat-stained pillow. The fine veins in her eyelids were stark against her pale skin. Fear for her brought tears to sting his eyes.

Slowly, her eyelids lifted and her head turned toward him. "Iain?" Incredulous joy filled her face.

"Aye, sweet lowe. I am here wi' ye."

"How?"

"Derrik brought me."

One side of her mouth stretched to a tired smile. "Uncle Derrik? We're having a baby, Iain."

"Aye."

"It won't be so hard now that you're here."

"I will no' ever leave ye agin, sweet."

Lara nodded, her teeth clenched against another pain. Breathless, she spoke again. "I hope he looks like you."

"Och, such a thought." Iain brushed the hair back from her face and then let one of his fingers twist through a tangled curl. "She will be a golden child such as ye."

Lara tried another smile, but the pain that twisted through her abdomen stole her breath. The healer pushed at Iain's shoulder but he steadfastly refused to move. He let Lara squeeze his fingers tightly during the pain.

Moments later, the healer made a small sound of triumph and pointed at Iain. "The child comes. You...support her."

Iain nodded and shifted position so he could lift Lara's shoulders to hold her upright against the contractions. Together they brought their child into the shining world of Faerie.

The healer lifted the crying child. "It is a son." She laid the baby on Lara's stomach and handed Iain a soft, damp cloth.

Reverently, he wiped birthing fluids from his son's face and tiny body. Golden hair curled wetly over the small head.

Lara giggled weakly. "Looks like we both got our wish." She gasped and held her son steady as another sharp pain rippled across her belly.

"There is another." The healer cried. Triumphant a few moments later, she lifted another child into her arms and announced loudly. "A daughter as well."

The tiny girl joined her brother for her parent's inspection. Her lusty cries were full of life. Lara touched the damp, dark hair and smiled.

When the healer finished Lara's care, she wrapped the babies in warm cloths and lifted one in each arm. Iain reached toward them, but Lara stopped his hands. "The rest of the family is waiting to greet them, too. And I need time alone with you."

The door shut behind the healer and the muted sounds of joyous introductions filtered through the open window. Unable to look at him enough to satisfy her need, Lara lay back and stared at Iain. Her memories of him had been faulty; he was even more wonderful than she remembered. The depths of his eyes drew her in as he returned her avid stare.

Lara turned her face toward the wall. "I must look terrible."

Oh, gods. What was she doing? All these months she'd needed to see him, to be with him. She'd just given birth to twins. Twins. Their children. She'd lost count of the hours she spent in labor. Of course, she looked terrible. And now she was fishing for compliments.

Iain cupped the side of her face gently and returned her gaze to his. The emotion on his face filled her heart until she thought she would burst into flame.

"Ye are the most amazin', the most lovely...ah, sweet." Tears filled Iain's eyes before he clasped her to his chest. The tightness of his hold should have been painful, but all Lara found was joy, pure bliss at his touch.

Their searching lips met, tentatively at first, and then the repressed passions of long months apart took command of Lara's senses. Iain's kiss took her away, away from the pain of longing, away to where nothing existed but his lips upon hers.

A discrete cough sounded from the doorway. Forcing heavy-lidded eyes open but keeping her lips pressed to his, Lara peeked past Iain's ear. Her brother, Jaysson, stood just inside the door with his tiny nephew cradled protectively in his arms. Her father held his granddaughter just as lovingly while the rest of her family crowded behind them.

Tearing her lips from Iain's was one of the hardest things she'd ever done. At his groan of denial, she tapped his shoulder. His confused look made her smile gently. Lara used her fingers to wipe the tears from Iain's cheeks before turning him toward the relieved expressions of her gathered family.

Catching Derrik's eye, she nodded slowly, mouthing "Thank you, Uncle Derrik." Tension eased from the tight lines around his eyes. With a slight bow, he returned a relieved smile to her.

Lara wrapped her arms around Iain and rested her head against his shoulder. Mischief touched her eyes and she fought unsuccessfully to keep a silly grin from her face.

"Lookit what I found."

DEAR READER

Thank you for reading this tale. Bringing stories to life is one of my greatest delights and I hope you enjoyed your time in one of my worlds. Readers like you spark the energy needed to tell these tales. Again, thank you.

With today's world of vast reading choices, word of mouth is the best advertising. So please let others know about this book. Tell your friends, relatives, acquaintances, the dog next door (hey, you never know...). And please consider leaving a review at your favorite retailer or review site.

To keep up with new releases, sign up for *Starr Words*. Yes, it's a newsletter, but will appear in your email only occasionally. Your email is safe with me, will never be shared, and you can, of course, unsubscribe at any time. You can find the link on my website www.lizziestarr.com or go directly to the signup here.

Next, there's a bit about each of my books. Enjoy the love and discovery! Happy reading!

NEXT IN THE SERIES

Keltic Flight: *Double Keltic Triad 3*

To the Faerie Gentry of the Otherworld, the fairy wee folk are but a myth and legend. Until the fairy Korin falls in love with a half-Gentry maid. Forced to bargain with an evil king to woo her, he risks discovery, and his life, to fulfill the conditions

THE KELTIC MULTIVERSE: DOUBLE KELTIC TRIAD

By Keltic Design: *Double Keltic Triad 1*

It ain't easy to be fey when you don't believe in fairy tales.

In the fey Otherworld, a half-faerie child is born. To protect him from evil's crusade to ensure the purity of the faerie race, he is abandoned in the human world, never to know of his magical heritage.

Now Jaye Zeroun is a successful businessman, rooted in reality. Fantasy is only something from an undisciplined imagination. Until he meets Celtic artist and friend of Faerie, Allyn Keeley.

Allyn has found the man she can love but fears their age difference and the overwhelming task of helping him realize his destiny will tear them apart. But Allyn knots her way around Jaye's heart and fills his life with a fantasy he refuses to believe.

Until danger threatens their love, forcing him to either accept a deadly battle or lose the very things he never planned for in his life' a family and a love beyond his wildest imaginings.

Fires of a Keltic Moon: Double Keltic Triad 2
Can love find a way through time?

Lara Zeroun needs an adventure, so she opens a portal in time and travels to the ancient Scottish Highlands. She meets two mysterious men but dares not trust her heart with either.

Under a matriarchal line of succession, Iain is unable to claim his father's holdings--his home. With no lands or possessions, he fights the temptation of a golden-haired woman who came to the manor on the arm of a wandering storyteller.

The storyteller's deceptions bring danger in Iain's time and threaten the destruction of Lara's present. Will Lara and Iain defeat the power of this growing evil and find their ways through time to the love they both desire?

Keltic Flight: *Double Keltic Triad 3*
What does she need to believe in love?

Even as a mythical faerie, Nanceen doesn't believe in the legends of tiny winged fey. Until a soft voice compels her to search... for love. She doesn't know what she believes but what she discovers changes everything.

Korin Goodfellow has loved the gentry maid from afar. But showing himself to her is forbidden by the fairy king, until using deceptions hidden by dark plans, the king forces Korin into an agreement with seemingly impossible conditions. Fueled by his pure emotions, Korin appears to Nanceen as a wingless man. One she can see. Touch. Believe in.

The evil fairy king keeps Korin's heritage hidden, warping the conditions to force Korin into battle after battle until he discovers his true place in the fairy world. Will Nanceen stand at his side as he risks everything for love?

Wild Keltic Carouselle: *Double Keltic Triad 4*
Falling in love is easy, the possibilities endless.

After months of searching, Bryce accepts he'll never find the masked dancer who captured his heart. Time to get on with life. But when his darlin' daughter climbs onto the lap of a captivating woman in a coffee shop and calls her Mommy, he certainly wouldn't mind exploring the possibility.

After a lengthy vacation, Carrie dreads returning to the job she once loved. Especially when a blond-haired cherub insists on calling her Mommy. The tiny girl's father is intriguing, and Carrie believes she's ready for a real relationship. But memories of a horrific attack surface making her doubt and fear a happy future.

Although he's human, Bryce's family ties are to the Faerie Otherworld, so when one of his fathers is kidnapped, no one knows if the abduction was of human or fey origins.

Falling in love was easy. Telling Carrie about the Otherworld risks that love. But demons resurfacing from both their pasts and evil-doers intent of destroying the present are intent on tearing them from their newfound love. Will their love survive a world of deception, lies and revenge?

Keltic Dreams: *Double Keltic Triad 5*

Passion blazes hotter than the desert sun.

A spiritual quest throws Bard, naked and alone, from his world to the desert Sahara. In search of answers, each grueling step through the shifting sands only adds to his questions and confusion. What did the seven Guardians mean for him to learn in this strange place?

An ever-present evil continues to stalk her family, so Kaelea researches possible protections at the Fey Library of Alexandria. The appearance of a stranger at the oasis is an unwelcome interruption. Her instant fascination with the man, and the overly possessive actions of a fellow researcher are even more distracting.

Time alone might bring solutions to Bard's quest. But will unknown danger and the search for knowledge drive a wedge between him and Kaelea? Will they survive a passion that burns hotter than the desert sun?

*(**Author's note:** The action of the book *Prince of Dark Ness* takes place between Triad books 5 and 6. While it's not necessary to read *Prince of Dark Ness* here, it does give background into Lucidea's life prior to meeting Jaysson.)*

A Faire Keltic Renaissance: *Double Keltic Triad 6*

It ain't easy being fey... and the subject of prophecy

Lucidea had no idea her father wasn't human—until a chance assignment as a forensic artist leads her to Scotland and a family she never knew. With her uncle imprisoned in the World Between Worlds, she's forced to assume leadership of a parallel, underwater world as his half Alfar-Sindhu heir.

Then she meets Jaysson Zeroun who has Otherworldly issues of his own. Once again evil plagues his clan and protecting a newborn child takes priority over personal dreams. When Lucidea offers to hide the family at her uncle's manor, Jayse accompanies them to Scotland. He's falling for Lucidea, but he fears how she'll react to the fact he's part Faerie.

Three worlds are in peril. A pieced together ancient prophecy might defeat the separate evils, but will it also bring them love?

THE KELTIC MULTIVERSE: OTHER TALES

Prince of Dark Ness: Keltic Mulitverse

(Author's note: This story takes place between books 5 and 6 of the *Double Keltic Triad* and introduces the heroine of book 6.)

An ill-prepared Alfar-Sindhu prince struggles to protect two worlds from an ancient fire elemental.

Torn between duty and love, Morghan stands alone to protect both his Alfar-Sindhu underwater world and humanity from an ancient fire elemental bent on escaping the World Between Worlds. While he's loved Coralie long upon long, he never acted on his desire.

Raised in the royal household, Coralie has remained steadfast at Morghan's side through long human years. She's hidden her true feeling for him, even from herself.

A forensic artist from America, Lucidea Galvagin travels to Scotland to determine the identity of a skull found on Morghan's land. What she discovers changes her life and possibly the fate of two worlds.

Will Morghan's two worlds be lost if he chooses family and Coralie over battle? Or will his actions doom a multiverse of worlds to fiery destruction?

Blue Keltic Moon: Children of the Triad 1

Love and redemption? Only under the blue Keltic moon.

It's been twenty years since Morghan, leader of the Alfar-Sindhu, was trapped in the desolate World Between Worlds. Now blue moons are aligning in a multitude of worlds, signaling a magical opportunity.

Devoting his life to the Fey library hasn't saved Gowthaman from the agonies of his past, and the long moments he spent in the World Between Worlds. Now, the woman he loves stands ready to lead others into that cursed place. Only he holds the knowledge enabling them to enter. And with luck, safely return with the prince. The risk to his mind doesn't matter, as long as he keeps Breanna from harm.

A competent warrior, Breanna sets aside her personal desires to lead the rescue mission, facing the unknown to bring Morghan home. While she's loved Gowthaman forever, he claims their age difference is too great. But she's seen their soulfire and knows he loves her as well.

Together they must face the World Between Worlds. Can a place filled with despair and loss also be a discovery of love and redemption? Perhaps... only under the blue Keltic moon.

Candy Guy and the Chocolate Brownie: *Keltic Mulitverse*
A short story

*Who better to assist a struggling chocolatier
than a Brownie?*

Candy Guy is in trouble. Winning a design
contest will prove his abilities as a chocolatier, but creativity eludes him. An
enchanting intruder invades Trace's work-
space. She may be real, or she might be a
dream. It doesn't matter. Desire consumes
him at her lingering touch and the deep
chocolate flavor of her kiss.

Deleesi hopes to end the ancient fey curse haunting her
family, but the handsome wisher defies her sleep-inducing magic.
Something about this human calls to her soul, and, unbelievably,
to her heart. The sensual distraction proves impossible to ignore,
even while granting his unspoken wish.

By the end of the rainy afternoon, Trace has his inspiration.
But will he ever again see the tiny woman who captivated his
heart and became his muse?

ASPEN GOLD SERIES

The Aspen Gold Series is a multi-author series set in the small, but affluent tourist town of Spenser, Colorado. I'm delighted to join with these six fantastic authors to bring you these tales. Find out more about the entire series at www.aspengoldseries.com.

These are my contributions to the series... so far.

Ryder's Heart: *Aspen Gold Series Book 3*

Ryder discovers an intriguing woman in his bed...

Five celibate years in Hollywood didn't ease his guilt over his father's death, and now Ryder Barlow is coming home to Spencer with a new purpose—to create a camp specializing in equine therapy. When he discovers a beautiful woman in his bed, his plans aren't exactly derailed, but definitely knocked off kilter.

Escaping her past hasn't been easy for Vianna Harrison, but she thinks she's found a welcoming home in Spencer—as long as she can keep her ability as a psychic medium hidden. Not an easy task when spirits need to speak of forgiveness and joy to so many loved ones. Or when the owner of the exquisite cabin she's been allowed to live in comes home unexpectedly.

Neither can start a new chapter in their lives until they stop rereading the old ones. Will acceptance overcome their secrets and show them their Rocky Mountain path to love?

For Keeps: *Aspen Gold Series Book 4*
Hiding the truth is like denying the sun.

Widow Kate Michaels kept a secret from the man she loves, and from the entire community of Spencer, Colorado. She's content running her bookstore and life is good. But in order to pay for his medical care, she must sell the ranch that was her father's dream, and in doing so disappoint her 8-year-old, horse loving daughter. Madison makes an unlikely friend in someone Kate would rather forget.

Veterinarian Jackson Samuels is intrigued by the charming girl, and occasionally lets her shadow him in his nearby clinic. He's enamored with the child's mother, but her defenses are so sturdy, not even his charm or their shared past can make a dent. When Jack uncovers a family secret, the truth makes him question who he thought he was.

Will two people who once shared a heartfelt love, allow their lonely secrets to consume and define them? Or will they help each other, forgive each other, and build a future together—For Keeps?

Speechless: *Aspen Gold Series Book 8*

How many peonies does it take to get married?

It's a beautiful day in Spencer, Colorado, and the peonies are in bloom. A perfect day to gather for a wedding, filled with love, traditions, fun, and maybe even a prank or two.

Vianna Harrison and Ryder Barlow would love the honor of your presence as they celebrate their marriage.

Fortunate Cookie: *Aspen Gold Book 11*

This woman. Wearing Frosting. And nothing else...

Cookie Lamont owns a successful cupcake shop in Spencer's trendy tourist center. Life would be perfect if not for the escalating unwanted attention from a self-important town trustee. She has everything she needs—and a man is the last thing on her mind.

Until he walks into her shop.

Treehouse builder and TV personality Anthony Burnham returns to Spencer and finds focus building cabins for a new camp. His passion for treehouses is rekindled as a sweet, sexy new love blooms.

But the past haunts his steps and threatens his growing relationship with the alluring baker.

Some Days are Diamonds, a short story included in: **Yesterday's Promise:** *Aspen Gold Series Book 16*

A high-stakes poker game, first meets, a dog rescue, loves lost and rekindled, and life-altering choices fill the history of Spencer, Colorado. Discover the challenges faced in these heartwarming stories crafted by the multi-author group who brings you romantic fiction at its finest in The Aspen Gold Series.

This collection includes:
The Card Game~~ M.A.Jewell
Some Days Are Diamonds~~ *lizzie starr
Ah, Venice ~~ Debra Hines
First Chance ~~ Donna Kaye
Racing Hearts~~ Bernadette Jones
Rescue Me ~~ Cheryl St.John

FANTASY ROMANCE

Double Moon Destiny

On the night of the Double Moon a
child is born, and the destinies of an
acolyte and a rebel are changed forever.

Jermanah, acolyte of the religious
Compound, has never been given the
opportunity to make her own choices.
Although she accepts her way of life and
yearns to rise higher in the order, she
learns ancient, forbidden healing from the
Seer. On the night of the Double Moons, a
child is born and given into Jermanah's
care until the boy is taken to the king.

Kierigh was born moments before the rising of the Double
Moons, but his twin brother wasn't so lucky. Rumors flow from
the Stronghold—following an ancient prophecy, the king sacri-
fices the baby boys to increase his power. But Kierigh senses that
even after five cycles, his brother still lives.

When Kierigh's rebels attack the procession, he takes the
babe, and Jermanah, to his hidden camp. The captivating acolyte
disrupts Kierigh's ordered and simple life. He opposes her religion

and all the Compound claims to stand for. She's everything he doesn't need in his life. Yet she is everything he desires.

No longer considering herself one of the Compound, Jermanah discovers freedom, and truths she finds difficult to believe. But when the babe is taken from the forest, she will do anything to save the child, including face the leader of the Compound—and the king.

Can a rebel and an acolyte set aside pride and differences to find a lost brother, defeat evil, and discover their prophecy fulfilling destinies?

CONTEMPORARY
ROMANCE

Birds Do It!

A search for truth, switched babies, and a threat from the past

Macaws as lovebirds?

An avian expert, Birdie Simons is called to help control a cantankerous hyacinth macaw during a young girl's birthday party. Inexorably drawn to each other, she and single father Garr Logan share an afternoon of joy and bittersweet memories, for Garr's wife died the same day as Birdie's newborn child.

Something about Rachelle makes Birdie wonder if the golden-haired girl is her daughter, switched at birth. Then her child's father returns, dogging her search for understanding and throwing her deeper into fear and confusion.

Ready to move on after his wife's death, Garr wants the intriguing woman, but Birdie keeps the search, threats and hidden relationships to herself, driving a wedge between them.

Will discovering the truth from nine years ago bring them closer, or forever tear them apart?

SHORT STORIES

Written in Stone: '*Structs in the City 1*

Fantasy Romance

Undercover agent Stone Mason must find a data-link before a demonstration for underground bidders leads to mass destruction. His search of a posh hotel is risky, but time is up.

Monika Linberg returns to her hotel room after her boss dumps her and assumes the striking, robotic sex-struct is her consolation prize.

Stone is no construct, but a living, breathing man whose touch and need for information and assistance turn her world upside down. Will working with the sexy agent to keep the city safe be too dangerous for her heart?

Dead Lily Blooms: *At Death's Gates 1*

Fantasy Romance

For ages uncounted, Master Death has assisted souls in transition. But what happens when love gets in the way?

Someone wants vampyre Lily dead, and a bargain with Death has been struck. Death sends servant Agaar to bring Lily to him, but the task becomes more complicated than either Death or Agaar anticipated.

This short story originally appeared in the anthology Tales From The Mist.
This re-release has had minor corrections from the original edition.

Death and the Dryad: *At Death's Gates 2*

Fantasy Romance

For ages uncounted, Master Death has assisted souls in transition. But what happens when love gets in the way?

What's Death to do when a dryad appears at his gate without her soul? She can't move on, nor go back. Will Death find a place for her--at his side?

*This tale appeared originally in the **Martini Madness** anthology and this re-release has had minor corrections and additions from the original.*

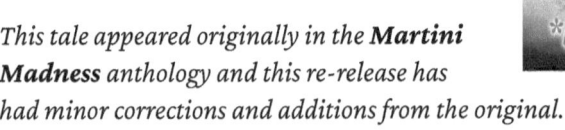

FUN STUFF

*lizzie also enjoys creating journals and guided workbooks for authors and other creatives. Look for them on Amazon.

About the Author

*lizzie always made up games and stories to keep her company. So, a cunning witch lived in Grampa's weather research station and was only held at bay by waving a certain weed. An ancient road grader morphed into a boat carrying wild adventurers to islands filled with fierce lions and dangerous cannibals, which really looked a lot like sheep.

Now filled with fantasy, love, and romance with a sparkling twist, the stories of her imagination swirl their way into the mundane world.

*lizzie recently retired from her more routine life of being *the Lunch Lady* at a private school. According to the kids, she was 'the best cooker!' Yes, she misses the students and teachers, but is delighted now to start her days by telling stories rather than opening cases of chicken nuggets and counting milk cartons.

Her tag line of
Author and lunch lady~~what a combination!
no longer holds true
(which makes her sad because she really liked that one)
Now you'll know *lizzie and her tales of...

~*Romance with a sparkling twist*~

Want to keep up to date with what's happening in all of *lizzie's worlds? Sign up for her newsletter here!

facebook.com/authorlizziestarr

twitter.com/lizziestarr

instagram.com/lizistarr

amazon.com/*lizzie-starr/e/B003F33Y0W

bookbub.com/profile/lizzie-starr

goodreads.com/lizziestarr

tiktok.com/@authorlizziestarr

pinterest.com/lizziestarr